THE BRASS OPERATIVE

KENNETH MARK HOOVER

Argo
NAVIS
PUBLISHING

THE
BRASS
OPERATIVE

KENNETH MARK HOOVER

NAVIS
PUBLISHING

PRAISE FOR KENNETH MARK HOOVER'S HAXAN SERIES

"After 2014's brilliantly brutal Haxan, [in *Quaternity*] Hoover revisits his nightmarish American West, a blood-soaked wasteland where 'land belongs to the man strong enough to take it, and keep it.'. . . Readers seeking a simple horse opera should look elsewhere; the depth of Hoover's narrative hews far closer to the moral complexities of Cormac McCarthy than it does the straightforward adventures of Louis L'Amour. A western of blood and violence with a marked lack of redemption tinged with hints of the fantastic, this is a pitch-black western that resonates."
   —Publishers Weekly

"Brilliantly brutal." *Haxan,* **—Publishers Weekly**

"A mixture of western and urban fantasy, with a cold, moody atmosphere." *Haxan,* **—Booklist**

"Mark Hoover's writing style and his dark fantasy Western series combine to create a magic that draws readers inside and keeps them there, allowing no escape until the thrilling conclusion." **–Matt Pizzolato**, editor of *The Western Online*

"It's the mid-1870s. The town of Haxan, in the New Mexico Territory, has a new marshal, John T. Marwood. But Haxan is no ordinary town; it's a focal point, a place where great historical events are poised to play out. And Marwood is no ordinary tough-guy lawman; he's a fighter of evil, a wanderer in time and place, who was summoned to Haxan by a dying man to protect the man's daughter but protect her from what? . . . [T]onally it's a mixture of western and urban fantasy, with a cold, moody atmosphere that makes us want to put on a sweater. The author leaves the door open for a sequel, but, given the kind of life Marwood lives, it could be set anywhere, or anytime." —**Booklist**

"The Old West wasn't all darkness and murder, unless your name is John Marwood, a man, by his own assessment, 'with a demon coiled like a watch spring in his marrow.' Simply put?He is a killer. Yet that isn't the half of him, and his true nature and his destiny alike remain a secret even to himself. Kenneth Mark Hoover tells the story of an immortal champion in an American West that never was, and so is all the truer for it."

　—**Richard Parks**, author of *Yamada Monogatari: To Break the Demon Gate*

"With Quaternity, Hoover paints a sparse and unflinching landscape, taking the reader down the dark trail his protagonist John Marwood rides while seeking what is lost and unremembered. As the gnawing hunger in his soul drives Marwood toward his ultimate destiny, the west as it was unfurls before the reader under Hoover's steady hand. If you love realistic westerns and dark fantasy, this is the book for you!"

　—**Michael Merriam**, author of *Last Car to Annwn Station* and *The Horror at Cold Springs*

"With a voice both sparse and poetic, Hoover takes on the hoary cliches of Western fiction and dismantles them one by one. In Quaternity, Hoover's unflinching look at evil will challenge everything you know about yourself and the world we live in."

　—Melissa **Lenhardt**, author of *Stillwater*

"Hoover does it again. Quaternity starts with a bang and doesn't quit until a satisfying conclusion. This is my kind of weird west. Love it!"

—**Jennifer Brozek**, author of *Apocalypse Girl Dreaming* and *Never Let Me Sleep*

"In Quaternity, his second outing in the richly evocative Haxan series, Kenneth Mark Hoover once again plunges us headlong into the bloody-minded fury of the Old West, mixing the raw violence of time and place with the eerie tenderness of a fantastical fever dream to gripping, visceral effect."

—**Melia McClure**, author of *The Delphi Room*

"Kenneth Mark Hoover's vivid prose delivers an unflinching look at the violent horrors and the stark beauty of the Old West."

—**Amy Raby**, author of *Assassin's Gambit* and *The Fire Seer*

"Twice as vicious as its predecessor, Quaternity is operatically mythological, a poetic, doom-laden Western soaked in blood and frenzy. This Cormac McCarthyesque terror fantasia of a prequel both frames and outstrips Hoover's Haxan, lending it the perfect amount of context, as Hoover's literally eternal protagonist Marshall John Marwood excavates his past in order to accept his future. Driven by philosophical musings both monstrous and humane, Marwood tracks an interlocking chain of massacres towards a lost city founded on 'the long blood of violence,' the same dark current underlying almost everything in Hoover's lawless, ultra-violent frontier . . . yet certain spots of brightness still occur here and there, inevitable collisions between fate and free will, love and justice. This is a hard book to read, but you'll savour its bitter aftertaste."

—**Gemma Files**, author of the *Hexslinger* series, *We Will All Go Down Together*, and *Experimental Film*

for Brantley

Three things cannot be long hidden:
The sun, the moon, and the truth.
—The Buddha

PART ONE
1949

ONE

DESPITE WHAT YOU SEE IN movies, guns are always more trouble than they're worth. People who don't know anything about them treat them like toys, and they're hard to ditch when you're on the run. I had kept my service revolver from my years as a policewoman in Santa Monica—not from any emotional ties. More habit, than anything else. Even so, you can do worse than carry a man-stopper like the Colt Detective. Those .38-caliber shells get the job done—if all you're looking for is to kill someone. The snub-nosed barrel doesn't hurt concealment opportunities, either.

Not that I expected to kill anyone, deserved or not, that hot, breezy morning in Los Angeles. I had a toothache and felt grouchy, true, but that's hardly legal justification for murder.

That aside, I felt good with the car top down and the wind tossing my hair while driving along Summit Drive. The winding road was lined with Italian cypress trees and old marble mansions lurking behind trimmed hedgerows and high stone walls crowned with broken glass.

I wondered what an aging silent film star in Beverly Hills wanted with a private firm like mine. A woman operative, too. We get all kinds, but this was the first time I had someone like Landers Shavin on the hook. I mean, despite his past, the guy was movie royalty. People said

Shavin was worth north of twenty million dollars. That kind of money can buy anyone respectability.

Oh, I should probably tell you about myself. My name is Pixie Parrish and I work—that is, I *worked*—for the Valkyrie Detective Agency. Our office is in Sacramento, and I have a small house in West Hollywood. My territory covers everything west of the Continental Divide so I'm not home often.

Landers Shavin was big news in Hollywoodland—they call it Hollywood now. He made the transition from silent movies to talkies as an actor/director and wielded money, power, and influence. That is, he did, until he was blackballed by the studios for having communist ties.

I motored past an empty stone gatehouse heavily overgrown with ivy. Ahead was Landers's estate—Summerchynne. I'd seen photographs of the place in old movie magazines, but nothing prepared me for the real thing.

As an estate, Summerchynne was no Pickfair. That's not a criticism. Few places were. But Shavin's mansion was Hollywood Byzantine: a head-on collision between a Mayan temple and the Taj Mahal. It exuded a palpable air of decayed opulence, indifferently occupied by restless ghosts: moldy memories hung around the place like ragged streamers of Spanish moss; the white marble was chipped, dirty; gray-blue rain streaks dripped from the cornices; the windows on the uppermost floors were shuttered. It was like the mansion had retreated from the modern world, content to sleep in a fitful cloud of faded memories of a brief golden past.

I followed an asphalt driveway lined with untrimmed linden trees and parked beneath a *porte-cochère*. I switched off the car engine.

I found myself looking at a big, empty courtyard. In the middle stood a dark-haired woman smartly dressed in tailored sharkskin, yellow and brown. She was addressing an Asian gardener. Rail-thin and spare, he wore khaki work clothes, boots, and wire-rimmed glasses with half-moon lenses.

I swallowed a couple Bayer aspirin for my toothache and watched them from my car while pretending not to eavesdrop.

"Quan, you must find the time." The woman pointed to a black and gold Cadillac in the garage. Beside it, another car was hidden under a paint-splattered tarpaulin. "That Caddie needs servicing. If you can't change the brake pads yourself then take it to a licensed mechanic."

The Asian man, Quan, was old. But he hadn't given up on life, or his pride.

"I am the gardener," he explained with infinite patience, "not a mechanic. Or a chauffeur." He removed his glasses and polished the lenses with a faded red handkerchief. "I can only do so much around here, madam."

"I can barely tell you're doing anything at all if you want the truth."

He pocketed the handkerchief and put his glasses back on. "This is a large estate, madam. It's too much for one person to handle."

"Well, I can't fault you for—" She noticed me parked under the shade of the *porte-cochère*. She touched Quan's arm with circumspection. "We will take this up later. I'm sorry if I was brusque. It's. . . There's a lot happening."

"As you have it, madam." Quan's demeanor was formal, but stiff. "I'll do what I can to help, of course." He walked toward the garage like he was approaching a gallows.

The woman turned to greet me. Her hair was brushed to a shine and done up in a neat pin curl. Her face and arms were deeply tanned. Outdoors type. Weathered, but not rawboned. Long graceful neck, black arching eyebrows, and that signature profile stamped from sheet metal I'd seen in *Life* magazine and bestseller book jackets.

I set the car brake and stepped out armed with purse, pencils, and notebook.

She came forward, her long, slim legs sheathed in nylons, her face sheathed in a smile. "Good morning. Are you from the detective agency?"

"Yes, ma'am. My name is Pixie Parrish. I came as soon as I got your message from my answering service."

She offered her hand. It was dry and firm with small callouses. "Pleased to meet you, Miss Parrish. I'm Pola Anne Goddard. I acquired the number of your agency from an acquaintance. You came highly recommended."

"Thank you."

She looked me up and down. "Engaging the services of a private detective isn't something one prepares for every day." Her gray eyes took me in like she was adding up the cost on a work bill and thinking she got overcharged. "It's quite out of the ordinary."

I was used to it. "There are more women in this job than people think. I can recommend a male colleague if it's going to be a problem."

"I wouldn't consider it," she covered smoothly. Her smile remained cool and cautious, but her eyes picked me apart. "I hope you'll forgive my impertinence, but may I see your private license? We get people who slip onto the property for one reason or another." She made a tiny, but defiant, gesture. "Tourists. That odd sort. Newspapers and magazines who pull dirty tricks. I'd rather Landers's final months be restful and without worry. The man deserves *some* peace."

"I'm sorry to hear Mr. Shavin is ill." I opened my wallet and handed her my credentials. "What sort of dirty tricks?"

She looked up from the printed face of the license. "Pardon?"

"You mentioned newspapers."

"Oh, *them.*" Her face registered disgust. "You can't possibly imagine."

"Try me."

"All they care about is selling their smelly newspapers. We've had reporters bribe people and make payoffs to spread lies and innuendo. We've caught them digging through our trash, if you can believe that." She handed my license back and we started towards a servants' entrance behind a cedar pergola. "They're awful. They give vultures a bad name."

She stopped with one hand cocked at her side, standing with casual, if not practiced, grace. A gold chain with a tiny jade heart dangled from her wrist. The sun in her face betrayed her age, but her gray eyes were clear and sharp. She was no pushover. You could sense her strength and iron determination even if you didn't know her background as an award-winning war correspondent.

"You know something about Landers? Or myself?" She was sounding me out.

"Only what I read in *Photoplay* and *Modern Screen* when I was a kid. My grandmother had a cardboard box of vintage Hollywood magazines packed in excelsior. I cut out paper dolls while she and my mother made Picon Punch for the ranch hands."

Pola smiled. "That sounds like a lovely memory."

I shrugged. "It reads better than it lived. I'll tell you what I know. Landers Shavin is a famous movie star and silent film director who transcended the leap into talkies. Good-looking man. Still is, from what I gather. Got his start on Broadway and moved to films at Crown Studio before they became Gold Panther Pictures. He signed with Matterhorn Pictures when talkies picked up. But no one wants to work with him today. Not even television, and that's the bottom of the entertainment barrel. You're a novelist, screenwriter, and war correspondent. You hobnobbed with Gertrude Stein in Paris and covered the Spanish Civil War alongside Hemingway. You won a Pulitzer Prize in 1937 and you and Mr. Shavin became romantically entangled much earlier than that. You've been inseparable ever since, though you've never married."

She laughed shortly, much impressed. "I doubt you learned all that from tawdry movie magazines. But I suspect someone in your line of work does her research on potential clients. Especially so-called famous ones with a dubious past." A fresh smile touched her lips. "It's common sense, I suppose."

We exchanged fruitful grins. "Guilty as charged."

She drew a deep breath. Something ineffable had changed between us.

"Landers was blacklisted after he was suspected of harboring communist sympathies," she said. "That was. . .two years ago. Years of absolute hell." She adopted a confessional and introspective tone. "Bottom line is, Miss Parrish, he was never a member of the communist party, or involved with any Red sympathies." She looked off in the distance with gauzy remembrance. "That was more my line, I'm afraid. I have the arrest record to prove it." She came back, much sobered and no longer grounded in the past.

I wondered if Summerchynne often had that effect on people.

"Landers has his faults like any man," she finished. "It doesn't mean I don't love him."

"I never said it did, Miss Goddard."

I let her talk because she was revealing a lot about herself, and in this line of work you learn to read people by listening. And, I like helping people. Despite it all, there was something oddly obscure about this dark-haired, handsome woman. A tentative wariness in her bearing which never ebbed or waned. As if she was constantly on edge against something barely hidden over the horizon.

"Miss Goddard, why am I here?"

"Straight and to the point. I like that. But please, call me Pola. Landers is dying, Miss Parrish. Tuberculosis. He is not expected to live out the year. Don't look surprised. We've done what we can to keep it from the papers, even though Walter Winchell alluded to it in his usual slimy fashion." She frowned, but again came back to herself. "Landers wants to assuage a personal sin. Make amends to someone he wronged. We daren't engage the police. Everything must be kept circumspect. Publicity, you see."

Part of her self-assurance slipped. She spoke deep in her throat. "I love Landers. I know he's going to die. I want to do everything I can to make his last days comfortable."

"Miss Goddard. Pola. I like to think I have many considerable talents, but I'm not a confessor. It sounds like you need a priest, and not a private detective."

Now I was the one dissembling. I knew a private investigator is frequently nothing more than a private confessor. It's often why we're hired. People want their problems solved, but more than anything they want them aired out. Have someone else carry the burden. So they look to us. I've seen it happen more times than I care to remember, and if truth be told, those jobs are often the most dangerous.

"What exactly do you want me to do?" I asked.

"We want you to find Landers's estranged daughter and bring her home. Her name is Tamar Bandesi." Telling me this cost her tremendous emotional effort.

"A child recovery case? I must warn you that can climb into a heap of money, and there's no guarantee my agency will be successful. There are legal and moral limits to what we can do. For instance, we won't kidnap a kid from his mother. That sort of thing."

"How much money?"

They always have time to talk money.

"Potentially thousands. Child recovery cases have a notoriously low success rate. You wind up fighting it out through the courts and that takes years. If you want my advice, hire yourself a crack lawyer."

"Well, Tamar is no child. She's nineteen. And we have a good lawyer in Elgin Tegel. Money is not an issue. We want this done right, you see. Which means no publicity. I can't stress that enough."

"Why is this girl important?"

"Tamar is Landers's daughter, and as such, when he passes away, she inherits the totality of his holdings and demesne."

"What's it worth? Ballpark it for me." Private dicks like to talk money, too.

"I'd say right around twenty-five million dollars."

"That's a big chunk of change for a silent film star."

"Exactly so. Landers is one of the richest movie men in the country. Few possess that much wealth. Mary Pickford. Chaplin, probably." She released a tight smile. "With that amount of money involved you won't be the only one looking for Tamar. Landers made a lot of enemies over the years. Perhaps you know what movie studios are like. They're venomous snake pits. Word will get out, it always does, and fortune hunters will stalk the high grass alongside you."

Her words adopted a darker tone. "The best thing will be to find Tamar and bring her under our protection as quickly as possible. Because, I'll be honest, considering the people involved and the sum of money at stake, failure could well mean someone's life." She stared at me. "Maybe even yours, Miss Parrish."

Two

I T WAS EERIE INSIDE THE silent mansion. I felt something was wrong here, and the deeper I went, the wronger it got.

It wasn't Goddard's bleak assessment of the assignment. A job, I might add, I had yet to accept. Movie people—and I suppose politicians fall into the same category—like to oversell the risk. When they slay a kitten, they claim it was a dragon. Plus, whenever someone says "I'll be honest" I automatically assume they're lying. A holdover from my days as a policewoman, but I've found it serves me in good stead.

Goddard was correct about one thing, though. Out here, Holly-wood is in everyone's veins. It's ubiquitous, like the air or sun or the open sky. It's a shining mountain towering above everything else. Given this, you don't attain the heights of stardom and wield financial power in Hollywood by being a saint. Landers Shavin was blackballed and labeled a Red by the House Un-American Activities Committee in 1947. But in Hollywood, like everywhere else in the world, twenty-five million dollars was twenty-five million dollars, and that made all the difference.

The foyer was paneled in bleached oak and rich mahogany. The parquet floor had cherry inlays. In room after room I saw elaborate *objets d'art* and Oriental carpets and silver candlesticks, but much of the furniture was dust-sheeted.

"Right this way."

Goddard brought me through an archway guarded by stone caryatids holding real medieval swords. The walls were enlivened by a pair of gleaming brass sconces and, between them, a neat row of oil paintings in gilded frames from dead Dutchmen. Above was a ceiling fresco of the Passion bordered in gold leaf. But the leaf was flaked, the floor covered in a patina of dust, and the closed doors we passed were perhaps locked, opening onto God knows how many other closed-off suites and galleries. Silent tombs, all. Distantly cold and forgotten.

Goddard picked up on what I was thinking. "It won't come again, that golden age," she said wistfully. "The world revealed a terrifying face to us all since those *années folles.*"

We climbed a grand staircase together. Goddard showed me into a glassed-in verandah that served as an ad hoc sunroom. An elderly man stood before the bay window with his back to us. I could make out his ghostly reflection in the bow glass. It was Landers Shavin, staring blankly at the world below.

The room was furnished in California Danish. Green plants with broad leaves swallowed up the sun. The walls were Mediterranean pink with indigo wainscoting. There was a chaise-lounge with Chinese silk pillows and a comforter where someone slept. From this height, I saw leaf-strewn tennis courts below us, and a heart-shaped swimming pool filled with brown rainwater. And far beyond, all the way to the horizon, the merest glimpse of the Pacific Ocean—or perhaps it was a *fata morgana*—like some azure memory floating through the California desert air.

I liked it here. This was an unexpected grotto of languid solace within the mummified constraints of the shuttered manse and its shadowed crypts.

Shavin stared out the window, unaware of our presence. He wore a matching bathrobe and slippers. The way Goddard talked I had half-expected to find him on his death bed, but he was tall and handsome, with that classic mane of silver hair, broad forehead, aquiline nose, and a jawline that could cut glass. There were pain lines in his waxen face, however, and his eyes were ringed dark from lack of sleep.

"Landers," Goddard said.

He turned with a wan smile. He held a brown Egyptian cigarette in an ivory holder. There was a bottle of pre-war gin close to hand, and an Art Deco drinks tray adorned with silver caster wheels.

"Oh, yes," he said, coming back to himself. "Sorry. I was wool-gathering."

"Landers," Goddard said again, "this is Miss Parrish from the Valkyrie Detective Agency."

I felt as if I should curtsy in his presence. Shavin's liquid smile widened a fraction. He drew on his cigarette before tapping the ash into a metal tray and offering his hand.

"Welcome, Miss Parrish. Please, make yourself comfortable. I hope you will find this chair adequate. It's Louis Quinze from the Régence, and a favorite of Jean Harlow's. Do you want anything to drink? I'm afraid we're rather roughing it at present. Pola can make anything you wish. Or if you prefer, we can send out for something. . .?"

"I'm perfectly fine, thank you." I settled in Harlow's favorite chair and flipped open my notebook. "I don't want to take up too much of your time."

"Not at all. I grow tired rather easily these days, but I've rested in expectation of our meeting. We have a lot to discuss, I think. Line our ducks in a row, as it were. How much did Pola tell you?"

"Only that you're searching for your estranged daughter."

Shavin refreshed his drink. I saw the red splotches on his sunken cheeks, the muddy eyes. Slight tremble in his hand. The subtle air of illness slipping inexorably towards death.

"Estranged?" he answered presently. "I suppose. Tamar was never the most forthcoming child. I cast no aspersions. I was hardly what you'd call a loving father. We were never close. I provided amply for her and her mother, Dolores, which was the sole extent of my familial inter-action. Even after Dolores died."

"When was that?"

"Dolores passed away February 22 of this year. I'd rather not delve into those personal details. I doubt they have bearing on what I require from you."

"I'll make that decision."

"Miss Parrish—"

"Humor me."

He sipped his drink in quiet contemplation and made up his mind. "Dolores suffered from debilitating hallucinations. She was not known to habituate drugs. Not even hard liquor." He lifted his glass. "I myself welcome the temptation of alcohol."

He continued. "She had no discernable addictions. But one night she was found wandering Sunset Boulevard dressed in her nightgown. There were several such incidents which we hushed up. Despite my current state of affairs, I retain a fair amount of political influence with the offices of the law. Dolores was hospitalized and diagnosed with paranoid schizophrenia. Following a brief illness, she succumbed. A funeral was held. Tamar disappeared shortly thereafter."

"Where was Dolores hospitalized?"

"A private sanitarium run by Arthur Hollack, a renowned European doctor of psychiatry. It's located in Old Hollywood. I wanted Dolores to have the best care available. No expense was spared, I assure you."

He approached me so I had to look up from my chair. I was reminded he was a consummate actor. Everything he did was for effect. Maybe he'd been in films so long he'd forgotten how to be a real person.

"It's been four months since Tamar's disappearance. The lawyer I've used to pass a monthly stipend to Tamar since her birth has had no contact with her, either. It's as if she vanished from the face of the earth. I'm quite concerned for her safety."

Shavin picked up a leather-bound album atop a credenza. He opened it and laid it in my lap. There were Kodachrome photographs under protective cellophane. All were of a young woman with black hair, dark eyes, long eyebrows, and a chin like Shavin's. She was definitely his child as far as I could tell. She also looked like millions of other young women in America: determined, uncertain, hopeful.

"These were taken last year at Christmas. The woman beside Tamar is Dolores Bandesi. The house in this photograph is one I purchased for their personal use. It's a two-bedroom Cape Cod on Olympia. They had a car. Dolores was a good person in her way, and extremely talented. She took up watercolors years after Tamar was born and sold a dozen paintings for a respectable price."

"How much of a respectable price?"

"One went for eight hundred dollars at auction in New York."

"Do you have any of her paintings here? I'd like to see one."

He was taken aback. "I. . . No. I do not, I'm sorry to say."

He retreated to light another cigarette which let me study the photographs and the album in full. Pola Goddard caught his attention with a discreet whisper.

"Landers, I've had another quarrel with Quan. I don't know how to handle the man. He won't do the work I assign."

"Quan is an old and dear friend, Pola. This place would never be the same without his presence. I can't simply dismiss him." I sensed a smile forming around his words. "He knows where all the skeletons are buried. More, I daresay, than I do myself."

"Everything is going to seed. It's too much for one person to handle. He's right about that."

"Let's get through this present difficulty before we discuss it further." They finished talking. A heavy silence suffused the sunroom.

"May I keep some of these photographs?" I asked.

"Of course. I have a copy of Tamar's birth certificate here, too. Anything that might help you find her is yours."

"How much did you pay Dolores each month? I presume there was a settlement and child support involved?"

"We never married but the living stipend was five hundred a month. That money went through a middleman. My personal lawyer, Elgin Tegel, handled it."

"Half a grand a month for twenty-odd years is close to $140,000. With a house and car on top of that. Plus, Dolores was selling her watercolors."

He shrugged. "Tamar had a good education and never wanted for anything material. I always saw to that."

"As long as you didn't have to spend personal time with her." I closed the album and laid it aside. "You're not anywhere in these photographs."

"Now wait a minute—" Goddard started hotly.

Shavin held up a forestalling hand. "Pola, no." He caught my eyes. "I am not offended, Miss Parrish. I am too selfish to be a good father or a caring husband. The motion picture business has no room for such a simple-minded creature. I have been called brutish and eccentric. My overriding mania was always for my work. I had no time for a wife and the burden of a family was the last thing I needed in 1930, or when I was fighting Senator McCarthy and the House Un-American Activities Committee. Of all things, I wanted to spare Tamar that familial stigma."

He crushed out his cigarette, put his drink down. "Few people are allowed to choose the nature of their destruction. I worked in Hollywood for thirty-five years. Silent films and talkies. I have been a director, producer, and mogul. It's not the money or fame that shapes one. It's the living. Or rather, I should say, the surviving. That's what few people outside our industry understand. Perhaps they don't want to. Because then they must face something grim. Something everyone carries deep inside. A hidden thing they themselves do not want to face. Even, I daresay, you, Miss Parrish."

It was a good speech. It had the right emotional ring and soulful flourishes, standing as he did with the light from the window falling across his face and his shadow angled across the room for dramatic effect.

Okay, I'm a cynic. Maybe he was being honest. But he was once the greatest actor in the world. Perhaps he still was.

"Miss Goddard said someone else might be searching for Tamar. Your enemies. Can you think of any reason that might be so?"

"I can name twenty-five million of them."

"Let's narrow that field. Anyone specific?"

"There are twenty or so such men, and not a few women. Someone with my reputation, both in business and politics, tows a lot of loose baggage in his wake. Given time it catches up to you." He reached for his drink and sipped contemplatively. "It always catches up."

"Say I find her, this Tamar. She's an adult. Okay, she's not twenty-one but she can do whatever she pleases. It's a free country. Well, for some people. Anyway, what do you expect me to do?"

"Inform her there is $50,000 free and clear if she is willing to see me one last time. No questions asked, no pre-conditions. If she does not agree, you are to give her the money anyway, along with the message that I pray she will one day find it in her heart to forgive me."

"Any idea where she might be?"

"No, but I've notified my lawyer. He will help you. Since he passed the money to Dolores and Tamar, he may have insight he isn't willing to share with me. It was a precondition he remains a cutout, representing Tamar, and Dolores while she was alive. His work for me has no other relevancy to this matter."

"Doesn't mean a thing. If he's your lawyer, he doesn't have to speak to me."

"Elgin and I have a. . .let's call it a convoluted history. He knows Tamar is missing. I'm sure he wants her back home safe as much as anyone else." He paused. "A man like Elgin, with his past life in the studios as a cleaner, knows how to keep his mouth shut."

Cleaners, sometimes called studio fixers, were heads of publicity, physicians, or security men who quashed scandals and provided illegal services to keep the talent happy. Blackmail, backroom abortions, and illegal drugs were par for the course, not to mention the occasional homicide or drug overdose swept under the rug.

What Shavin was saying was that Tegel was a gold-plated bastard. Cleaners earned every dime they made. They amassed tons of secrets on producers, directors, and movie stars who solicited their services. This made them dangerous in their own right. At best, they were double-edged swords.

Shavin produced an embossed business card with Tegel's office address and phone number. The address was West Hollywood.

"These cleaners rarely work alone," I mused aloud. "Who was Tegel's partner?"

Now we were at the heart of things. Shavin fixed another Egyptian cigarette to its ivory holder and lit it. His face was grim, and the pain lines pronounced. "Warden Krille. General manager and independent contractor. A man with his background would not be above using Tamar to get at me. I don't know if he's involved, but if he is, that frightens me, Miss Parrish. That frightens me very much."

I closed my notebook with a snap. I didn't like these people. I'd taken jobs from people I didn't like before, and refused jobs from people I did, but there was something about Tamar's photographs that clawed at me. Reminded me of another young woman who got into trouble while trying to find her way in the world. I'm no humanitarian. I've been in this racket long enough to know when a case can become too personal.

I stood up. Jean Harlow had better padding back there than I did, because that chair was lumpy as hell. "I'll meet with Tegel first. Then I'll decide whether to accept the case."

"Thank you, Miss Parrish." Shavin's bottom lip quivered with relief and his eyes turned moist. This was no act. He opened a drawer and passed me a thick manila envelope. "That's two thousand dollars. Consider it your retainer. The number on back is for the whole fifty thousand. Should you need more, I trust you will let me know."

He pressed my hand between both of his. "Good luck, Miss Parrish, and thank you for agreeing to meet me. Pola will see you out and give you an emergency number should you find the need to contact me again. Anytime, day or night. I am at your disposal."

He turned his back on me and stared out the window. "Good day."

Pola gestured and I followed her from the room.

THREE

W HEN WE WERE OUTSIDE UNDER the shade of the
pergola Pola Goddard spoke. "He was growing tired. You can
see it manifest in his eyes. It's the constant pain coupled with the
emotional distress of Tamar's disappearance."

"What does he take for it?"

"Morphine. He tried using cocaine, but he couldn't sleep, and was
wasting away faster. As it is, he's barely holding himself together."

"Christ. Where does he get the stuff?"

She ignored my question and looked at the paling sky. What clouds
there were shone with golden highlights. The courtyard was empty. I
wanted to have a few words with Quan before I left, but he was nowhere
around. The Cadillac was inside the garage, but the other car was gone.

Goddard flicked her eyes in my direction.

"Elgin. His lawyer procures it for him." Her voice was thick with
emotion. It was like dragging an anchor through mud. "Elgin has his
connections. We don't ask." Her tone took a new direction. Her lips
barely moved, as if in prayer. "He won't kill himself. He'll wait."

"You mean until he sees Tamar."

Pola Goddard's face lay stricken. I reminded myself I didn't like these people. Thinking that way made me not like myself very much, either. It's not easy being me. I don't recommend it.

"Miss Goddard—"

"Call me Pola," she insisted.

"All right, Pola. I have to be frank. I don't know how much I can help you. I'm not sure I'm being told the truth."

"How do you mean?"

"We're talking about a man who never cared for the woman he had an affair with or the illegitimate daughter she bore him. The only people he keeps around are you, an aged gardener, and some crooked lawyer named Elgin Tegel."

"If you don't trust us then I suppose you won't help us find Tamar."

"Trust has nothing to do with it. My job is to dig for the truth and go where the facts lead me." Now I was giving speeches. Emotion has no place in this line of work, but I couldn't get Tamar's face out of my mind. It burned deep.

I wanted to help them if I could. I thought it a fair bet Tamar was at least in trouble if not in danger.

"Ask your questions," Goddard prompted, "and I will answer them best I can."

"Do you know where Tamar is?"

"If I did, I'd tell Landers."

"That wasn't my question."

"No, Miss Parrish, I don't know where she is."

"What do you think of her?"

"I'm not sure I understand."

"Yes, you do." I waited.

She looked exasperated. "I don't like the girl, if you must know. I don't dislike her, either. Dolores was frightfully sick. Tamar is a little too. . .independent for my tastes."

"How so?"

"Running around with a loose crowd. Drinking. Staying out all night. Getting into bad company at school. Some trouble with the law. She's a bright girl, but I don't think that's how a young woman should comport herself when her mother was lying sick in a private hospital."

"What about Dolores? How did you feel about her?"

She crossed her arms, but it wasn't a defensive gesture. "I bore her no ill will. Landers met her shortly before he met me. I suppose he loved her, in his own way. As much as he allows himself to love anyone. Myself included. They were never together in a meaningful or loving way. I never viewed her as a rival. I rather liked her. She was extremely talented, and I respected her talent as an artist."

I found it interesting Goddard brought up the concept of a rivalry. "How did Mr. Sharvin feel about her pregnancy?"

"I don't think he felt one way or the other. It was something that needed handling, like a tax problem. That's Landers for you. He didn't push her for an abortion or adoption or anything like that. Dolores was devoutly Catholic. She wanted the child. Landers accepted that and made plans for their separate futures. He never spent time with Dolores during her pregnancy. I was in New York working on a Broadway play. When Tamar was born, he saw her, albeit infrequently, but when Tamar was twelve, she spent a whole summer with us. I think it's the one time she and Landers had a good, healthy relationship. As friends if nothing else."

"What did they do together?"

"He'd tell wild stories about the movie industry or take her onto the set when they were filming. When he was home, that is. This was 1942 when the war news was so bad. You remember. Landers was working hard, and it was before he got blackballed. We had servants who cooked and cleaned up after Tamar. Sometimes she and I would go for a walk around the grounds or play tennis or golf or go shopping. The swimming pool was open. There were Arabian horses in the stables. Any girl would have a fine vacation with all that going on."

"What did you two talk about?"

"Nothing remarkable. She mentioned she wanted to see Europe. She liked the idea of living in Paris. I think she wanted to be an artist like her mother. I'd catch her drawing sketches and things but she'd get embarrassed and tear them up with a sheepish grin. I don't know what else to tell you."

"Do you think she's in Europe now? Paris, maybe?"

"I couldn't say. I suppose it's possible."

"It'd be something concrete to work from. Where did she sleep when she was here?"

"In the sunroom. She liked it there. She played records on the gramophone and did a lot of reading."

"The place Mr. Shavin sleeps now."

"Yes. He has his own bedroom—our bedroom. He moved to the sunroom when he got sick."

"You think it's because Tamar used to live there?"

"I believe so. He wants some kind of connection with her."

I thought it time to switch gears. "Do you know Warden Krille?"

"No, I never met him. I have heard stories, though."

"What kind of stories?"

"You know Los Angeles. This city runs on gossip. It seems everyone knows everyone else's private business. But it's worse inside Hollywood. There's a hard center no one from the outside can infiltrate. It's where deals are made, and fortunes built. That's the real Hollywood, not the fake tinsel and cardboard glamour, and it's impossible for anyone on the outside to penetrate. God, why would you want to? People are used up and thrown away like meat scraps. Whole lives ruined. But from that pain and ugliness comes incredible art and sublime beauty and amazing talent that can change how we view ourselves as human beings. When you're talking about art and the innate power it possesses to change the world—nothing matters more than that."

She nervously chewed her thumbnail. "That's the real Hollywood, Pixie. That's the ugly secret everyone pretends doesn't exist. Warden Krille worked there, and so did a lot of other people like him."

"Including Mr. Shavin."

She gave me a sidelong glance. "Yes."

"Was there no one who took Mr. Shavin's side when he stood accused before the H.U.A.C.?"

"You mean friends and colleagues?" She raised the palms of her hands in dismay. "They saw an opening and took advantage. Landers might have done the same given the opportunity."

"I read the papers. People were scared. They still are."

"People see what they want to see. Before the war it was fascism—that was a real threat. Today it's communists. Tomorrow it will be something else. Or more likely someone else, because that's how these things always end up."

She jotted a phone number on the back of a card. "Here's the emergency number Landers referenced. It will connect you with a private phone where you can reach us day or night. Please, don't hesitate to call should you need our help." She saw me to my car. She closed the door and leaned forward. "I'm sure you are eager to begin your investigation. I'll phone Elgin to let him know you are on your way." She let me go with a wave.

I started the motor and drove away. Summerchynne retreated in my rearview mirror. I wasn't sorry to see it disappear.

~

I stopped at a gas station that gave out Green Stamps.

"It should take three," I told the attendant.

While he checked the oil and tire pressure and cleaned the windshield, I dug a nickel from my peplum jacket and closed myself in a wooden phone booth inside the station to call Tegel.

"Hello?" he answered.

"My name is Pixie Parrish with Valkyrie Detective Agency. I believe Miss Goddard was supposed to let you know I am coming for an interview."

"Yes, Miss Parrish. We're closed on Friday afternoons but I'm catching up on paperwork. Will you be long?"

"You're in the Continental Building, correct?"

"That's right. Spring Street and Fourth. Third floor. Southwest corner."

"I know the building. I'll be there shortly." I rang off, dug out another nickel, and dialed our main office in Sacramento. Artie Glass answered.

"Hey, Pix," his basso voice rumbled over the phone line. "What can I do for you today?"

"Got something to write with? Then here we go. Landers Shavin. Movie star and director for Gold Panther Pictures, fingered as a Red two years ago. Lost his clout when it hit the papers. He's been making monthly payments of half a grand to a girl who's his illegitimate daughter for years. Nineteen to be exact."

I heard the scrape of his pencil over the receiver. "Got it."

I opened my notebook to reference my notes on Tamar's birth. "Tamar Elizabeth Bandesi is her full name. Born May 15, 1930, Los Angeles County General Hospital. Her mother is Dolores Marie Bandesi, deceased February 22 this year."

"Payments for nineteen years," Artie interjected. "There must be a tax record if they were living off that money."

"Shavin purchased a house and car for them, too. They lived pretty well."

"There will definitely be records of that. But what has this got to do with the current state of the world, Pixie?"

"It's the new case I was assigned. Don't you ever look at the daily work sheet?"

"I believe in doing as little as possible around here."

"Tamar disappeared after her mother died. Foul play could be involved or maybe she decided she wanted to see the world. *Wanderjahr.* People are antsy because Miss Bandesi stands to inherit Shavin's twenty-five-million-dollar estate when he dies."

"How ill is Mr. Shavin?"

"One foot in the grave and the other on a banana peel."

"You think someone snatched this Bandesi? Maybe gonna use her to get at the money?"

I thought of Warden Krille. "It's possible someone either has her or is planning to grab her and she knows about it and is on the run."

"Pixie, it's going to be damned difficult getting this financial information on a weekend."

"Do what you can. Work your magic, Artie."

"I know some people who owe me favors. So, right, follow the money. What else?"

"I'm seeing the family lawyer next. Then I want to go through that house in Olympia once I've got the address and give it a toss. Might give me a lead on the girl."

"All right. You need anything else, you know where to find me. Oh. I almost forgot. Have you heard the news about Mrs. DeMoines?"

Agatha DeMoines was the founder and head of our agency.

I said I hadn't.

"She's decided to step down. Her son doesn't want the position and all her daughters live back East with their own families." Doubtful pause. "You sure you haven't heard this?"

I knew what Artie was hinting at. "I'm not the office type, Artie. I work the field."

"Mrs. DeMoines likes you, Pixie. What's more, she respects you. You're her top operative. I wouldn't be surprised if she offered you the chair."

I laughed shortly. "Like I said, I'm not the office type."

"Neither was Mrs. DeMoines before her gall bladder trouble. Okay, Pix. I'll get on this straight away."

"Thanks, Artie. You're a champ."

"That's what I keep telling people, but they never believe me. So long." The line clicked.

I paid for the gas. Traffic was a bore and the city was putting in a new sewer line so it took longer than expected to reach my destination. I parked my old Pontiac Torpedo two and a half blocks away from the Continental Building in a private lot—as close as I could get that time of day on a Friday.

A lot attendant in a starched uniform ambled up. He thumbed his blue cap back on his head. "Can't park here, sister. This here's the Sanderson-Kehoe building. You ain't got the right color tags on that jalopy."

I didn't want to park farther away and I was on an expense account. Shavin was footing the bill so I opened my wallet. "Five spot says I can."

The lot attendant rammed his thumbs in his Sam Browne and pursed his rubbery lips. "Sawbuck testifies I never saw you."

"Ten dollars? No way. Get lost."

He rocked back and forth on his heels. "It's a cinch bet. I'd take it if I were you. Where you headed, anyway?"

"Like it's your business. And you're not me. Dust off."

"They'll tow your car."

"Mark it on the day sheet as a temporary pass. Must I think of everything?"

"They catch me doing that I'll get fired."

"They catch you hustling they'll throw you in jail. Now make it easy on yourself and take the fin and let's forget we saw one another."

At twelve stories, the Continental wasn't the tallest building in Los Angeles—that would be City Hall. It was so blistering hot outside I was sweating like a race horse when I pushed open the doors and walked across the echoing foyer in my high heels. A Black elevator operator took me up to the third floor.

Tegel's office had double frosted doors, and they were open. The reception room had matching desks with two Electromatic IBM typewriters and Dictaphones with separate headphones.

On the other side of the room, a man with wavy blond hair and a narrow frame browsed a filing cabinet. "We're closed," he said, then glanced back at me. He took me in with a swift, approving glance. "Pola was right."

"Excuse me?"

"She said to look out for a Kay Francis–type with ice-blonde hair and emerald eyes. Christ, lady, you've got Kay's height dialed to the inch. I guess you're Pixie."

"I take it you're Elgin Tegel."

"The one and only." He slammed the drawer closed and locked it with a key that he then dropped in his pants pocket. "My girls have left for the weekend, but from what I gather you want this kept confidential."

"If you don't mind."

He drew out a silk handkerchief and blew his nose. "Excuse me. Allergies." He returned the handkerchief to his hip pocket. "No, I don't mind."

He wasn't a bad-looking man even if his smile was a little too practiced and oily. His moustache was thin, and his blue eyes piercing. He wore an expensive cream-colored silk suit, blue checkered tie, and brown Florsheim shoes. Gold Rolex wristwatch. Sapphire ring on his right pinky. He had money and didn't mind showing it off.

"Let us talk in my office, shall we? It has air conditioning. My secretaries have threatened to quit if I don't install a unit for them. I suppose I will have to acquiesce to their demands. They know too many secrets."

"Lead the way."

There was a polished wood railing behind the twin secretarial desks with a little gate he pushed open. Then he swung open one of the double oak doors with glass panels and rubber molding that led to his office.

The room was spacious and modern. Drop down ceiling, recessed lights, black leather divan with a glass coffee table and decorated with a few scattered magazines. Shelves of thick law books and bound legal papers. There was a half-open door leading to an attached washroom of Monel metal and yellow porcelain.

Tegel's desk was a single slab of black Lucite. Intercom, a phone with Hushaphone attachment, ink blotter, and an In/Out tray. Directly behind his high-backed patent leather chair were phone books, unopened correspondence, and a silver mantel clock with an old-fashioned winding key. A corner table held a water carafe and paper cups. High on the wall behind his desk were his law degree and a prominent slew of other honors suitably framed.

Tegel kicked back in his chair, crossed his legs. He selected a Cuban panatella with his left hand, snipped the foot with a small razor, and lit it. He placed the gold lighter on the desk, tilted his head, and directed a blue plume of smoke toward the ceiling. The air-conditioner rattled in the window. It was deliciously cool inside the room, and I felt perspiration drying on the back of my neck.

We sized one another up. I had him pegged as a vain man who knew a lot of terrible secrets. Maybe too many for his own good. A studio fixer had a short shelf life. That Tegel appeared to have beaten the odds was impressive.

He cleared his throat. "All right, Miss Parrish, how can I help you? I warn you I won't betray any private confidence I have with my clients. I will adhere to Mr. Shavin's guidelines concerning you as closely as possible, but I guarantee little else in the way of cooperation."

"That should be enough. I want any and all information you have on Tamar Bandesi."

Tegel spread his manicured hands. "Ask your questions. I'll determine if they're out of bounds." He puffed his cigar amiably.

I laid my photographs of Tamar on his desk. "This the girl we're talking about?"

He barely looked at them. "Yes. Her hair is shorter now. Her face more filled out."

"When was the last time you saw her?"

"Her mother's funeral. That was February 26." He answered questions like he was on a witness stand; this man played things close to the vest. Given his background, I wasn't surprised.

"You've had no contact with Tamar since? Phone call. Post card. Telegram."

"No. Nothing."

"What did the two of you talk about?"

"At the funeral? She said she felt badly for her mother." He was going to say more but clammed up.

"What else did she say?"

He ventured a noncommittal shrug. I was going to have to work hard to drag anything out of this man.

"Did she say she was going somewhere? Maybe a trip to clear her head?"

He blinked. "She asked what the weather was like in Nogales. I got the impression she was thinking of vacationing there."

"Mexico?"

"Excuse me? Oh. No. Nogales, Arizona."

"Did she know anyone in Nogales?"

"I couldn't say. I didn't press. It was none of my business." He puffed his cigar. "You understand."

"When did you realize she was missing? Four months is a long time before someone pulls the emergency stop."

"I don't know now that she's *missing*. She's an adult woman. Well, almost an adult. She will be when she's twenty-one. As it is I have no leash on her." He inspected the glowing end of his cigar. He was starting to let his hair down. Only to his shoulders, but it was a promising start. "Of course, I suspected something was amiss. It's not everyone who passes up a monthly stipend of half a grand." He showed a wolfish smile, his blue eyes glittering with avarice. "I wouldn't."

"How was the money transferred?"

"Dolores Bandesi came to my office every month and signed for it. There were times I went to their house to accommodate Dolores if she couldn't make the trip, but those were few and far between. Once when Tamar had the mumps, and then when she had chicken pox on the night of her First Communion. That sort of thing."

"Wouldn't it have been easier to deposit the money into a shared bank account on the first of every month?"

"Easier, but that's not what Landers Shavin wanted. He expected a monthly handwritten report regarding Dolores and Tamar. How were they getting along. Did they need anything of substance. Were they healthy. He was more than content to watch things from afar. He's not the kind of man to expose himself emotionally."

Tegel rolled the half-smoked cigar between his fingertips.

"I labored to get Mr. Shavin to come around regarding the latter. Tamar's behavior necessitated parental intervention. When she was small she was quiet, and withdrawn. Stubborn. Then she started coming out of her shell. As she got older, she fell into trouble. Small-time stuff. Stealing costume jewelry from a Five & Dime. She fell in with a bad group. I made discreet inquiries. There were drugs. Tea. Or sometimes glitter—cocaine. One morning Tamar told me she was no longer a virgin. I think she meant to shock me. She got pulled in by the police a time or two, and my legal connections helped get her sprung. She was a wild colt. Hated the harness. Precocious to a fault. Had her own mind about things and didn't mind letting people know what she thought. On the other hand, she was vivacious and charming when she wanted to be. You know how kids are."

"I was one once."

He smiled benignly. "Quite. Dolores couldn't do much with her. We sent Tamar to private schools and a couple of colleges. It didn't take. She hated being tied down."

"Maybe that's why she left."

"Could be. She took part-time work for the S.P.C.A. last year. She liked that. She may have seen something of herself in those abandoned animals, but I'm no psychologist. There's no pinning her down to a single description. She was her own person, and very much so."

"Most people are at that age. Was she jealous of her mother's success?"

He shook his head. "Not at all. When Dolores held her first exhibition, Tamar went through the crowd of buyers and critics with flutes of Dom Perignon on a silver salver. Bent the knee in supplication and blandishments. Tamar did these things because she *wanted* to, you see. If someone told her she had to do it, she'd buck. She's a lot like Pola Goddard. Same side of the counterfeit coin if you will."

That brought me up short. "Why do you say that?"

"Neither of them is what they pretend to be. I don't mean that in a disparaging way. It's just that some people prefer to keep their true selves to themselves." The inflection in his tone said he wasn't going to pursue the idea further.

"Did Tamar have no close friends?"

"There was one, name of Juanita Drexford. They met at the S.P.C.A. Tamar brought her by to visit one afternoon. Nice girl from what I remember. I couldn't tell you more than that."

"Was Dolores that fine a painter?"

Tegel blinked at the change of subject. He pointed over my shoulder. "That's one of her paintings there."

I got up to look. It was a portrait of Tegel. Surreal. The colors were vibrant. Elements of line and shape worked with the negative space to render something more than an ordinary portrait. I didn't know much about art, but I liked this.

"I never sat for that," Tegel said. "She painted it from memory. All her paintings have a biographical nature to them. She drew inspiration from the class disparity of southern California. She was compared to Frida Kahlo before she died. She took risks with her art, and it paid off handsomely."

"Did Dolores paint Tamar?"

He was taken aback. "I don't think so. Not that I'm aware. Funny. I never thought of it before."

I walked back and forth, tapping a pencil against my teeth. "I'm trying to get a three-dimensional picture here. This was a strange family. Patriarch who cut off all ties to mother and child yet demanded monthly reports. Wanted to know if mother and daughter got *along*. A talented mother who suffered from clinical schizophrenia. A seemingly uncaring stepmother, of sorts, in Pola Goddard. Hell, I'd take off like a bolt in the blue, too, if I was Tamar."

Tegel watched me.

I stopped moving. "When Dolores died who got the house?"

"It passed directly to Tamar. There's a housekeeper who keeps the place going for Tamar's return. Her name is Wanda Zipes. I suppose you want to speak with her?"

"I most definitely would."

Domestics knew where all the bodies were buried, like Shavin had said. She could be invaluable.

Tegel wrote the address on a slip of paper and slid it across the desk to me. He grabbed the phone and dialed a number from memory. "Mrs. Zipes? I have a young lady hired by Landers Shavin to help find Tamar. Yes, it's quite official. No, no police involvement as yet. Would you be so kind to speak with her if she dropped by? Tonight do? Her name is Pixie Parrish. Very well, goodbye." Tegel cradled the receiver. "She's expecting you presently."

We shook hands and he accompanied me to the door. I slowed. There was something Mr. Shavin said that I wanted to clear up. Now was the time to spring it.

"When is the last time you saw Warden Krille?"

The doors of his face slammed shut. "I don't talk to anyone about Warden Krille."

"You'll talk to me. I'll wait for you to call Mr. Shavin if that makes you feel better. You can talk to Pola Goddard, too. After she reams you out, you'll tell me everything I want to know."

His eyes searched mine. "What is this all about?"

"Mr. Shavin is afraid Krille might be after Tamar. Given Krille's background I don't need to go into reasons why that might not be to her benefit."

"I suppose you mean my background as well, Miss Parrish." He made a moue with his lips. "Here I was thinking we were getting along quite nicely, too. I assure you, I have not seen or heard from Warden Krille in five, no, make that six years. Truth is, Warden and I no longer occupy the same circles." His face was flushed and his ears bright red—he was discomfited at being caught out.

"I hope you appreciate what I'm confronting here," I told him. "A flighty girl destined to inherit twenty-five million is missing. She may be hiding or dead or held somewhere against her will. A man like Warden Krille is the kind of person who would engage in two of those three possibilities if what I heard about him is true."

"Warden is an unpleasant human being," Tegel allowed, "but he has no reason to harm Tamar. He never has."

"'He never has.' So he does know Tamar."

"I've heard stories about Warden I'd rather not believe. That's not the same man I worked with when we were under contract with the studios, and that's all I will say about that. Is there anything else I can do for you, Miss Parrish?"

His tone said there had better not be.

I rode the elevator down along with its operator. I hoped Artie could dig deep enough into the banking records to shed light on the enigmatic landscape I found myself in. I walked to my car, started it, and pulled away.

That's when I saw a tan coupe in my rearview mirror leave its parallel parking spot and start following me.

Four

I WAS HUNGRY. I STOPPED for a sandwich and coffee at a Harry Carpenter's drive-in. Tan Coupe rolled to a stop in the parking lot of a hardware store across the street, and he was smart enough to park so I couldn't read the license plate. I thought about walking over there to confront him—in another situation I might have done it—but instinct told me to let him tail me a while. Let this play out and see where it went.

A car hop took my order and roller-skated away. I read through my case notes while I waited, then put them aside. After a short wait the car hop returned with my tray of food.

I ate my ham-and-cheese sandwich and drank coffee while staring at the coupe in my mirror. Whoever this was got onto me fast. You get something like mission sense when you work a tough case, and this tan coupe did *not* add up. But if he made a threatening move, I had the .38 in the glove compartment. I wasn't too worried.

So, I tried to find a fit for the few pieces of the puzzle I had while chewing my sandwich. Everybody wanted Tamar found fast, but nobody had busted their tail for four months to make that a reality. Maybe they didn't want her found. Or maybe they knew where she was.

Either way, it was like they were ticking off boxes so anyone looking in from the outside—like the Los Angeles Police Department—would be satisfied. I found it impossible to believe a man worth millions couldn't find a runaway girl in four months if he *wanted* to. Unless there was something bigger shaping up in the background, something he had no control over.

I had a knot forming in my gut that wouldn't untangle. I felt I'd been hired to hare off on a cold trail so it could be said there was a legitimate attempt at finding Tamar. If that was true, I would be considered expendable by the people running the real show. They wouldn't be sloppy. They wouldn't leave any loose ends.

I took the steering wheel between my hands and drew a deep breath. *Calm down, Pix. You got spooked when you saw Tamar's photograph. Everything you've learned says she's a messy piece of work. Probably not worth the trouble.*

But once upon a time there was another girl very much like her. When someone came along to help me, I turned out all right. I thought about the gun in the glove compartment loaded with five hollow-point rounds—well, all right, considering.

I finished my lunch and handed the car hop my aluminum tray. She skated off, striped skirt swinging around her thighs.

I glanced in my mirror and cranked the Pontiac's engine.

"All right, Tan Coupe. Let's see what you're made of."

I took it easy through traffic. I didn't want him to lose me. By now he had to know I knew he was following me, so we both went out of our way to stay together with but a few cars between us.

Idling at a stop light I leaned over and popped open the glove compartment. I took the gun and slipped it under my seat. Believe it or not, we private investigators are averse to danger. We do a lot of running away from trouble whenever possible, but whoever was behind me wasn't going to take me without a fight.

～

Gold Panther Studios was one of the oldest movie lots in North Hollywood. It's on Sunset Boulevard and Gower Street, and it's where Landers Shavin got his start in silent films before moving on to talkies at Matterhorn Pictures. Gold Panther wasn't part of the "Big Five" movie studios like Matterhorn, though it had been one of the oldest and most influential in the early days of film making. I didn't know anyone who worked at Matterhorn, but I had a friend at Gold Panther. Her name was Irene Woolfe. She was a writer/producer which in the industry of motion pictures meant she was often out of work. But she had the background knowledge I'd need for this job, and I wanted to pick her brains.

I drove up to the main gate and stopped at the security checkpoint. A man in a blue and red uniform with gold braid on his shoulders and cap stepped forward. "Help you out, miss?"

"Pixie Parrish for Irene Woolfe."

He looked my car over with its old wartime blackout trim, before he gave me a once-over. Neither impressed him. "Got an appointment?"

"She's expecting me."

"That so." He probably heard this twenty times a day from ingenues looking to break into the business.

"Call her up if you don't believe me."

He stepped back. "Back lot, section C. Room 203-A."

"She moved her office?"

"They closed the east-side lot for sound-stage renovation. Moved a lot of people into the old rundown section. Want a map?"

"I know where it is."

"That's good, because I don't have a map." He registered the license plate and stamped time of entry for my car on his sheet. He handed me a time-stamped pass initialed with his illegible scrawl and raised the security bar.

I drove through a faux-medieval street with a group of cowboys and white men dressed as Apache Indians standing on the corner shooting craps and smoking rolled cigarettes. One of the horses had a blanket thrown across its back, and beneath the blanket was the outline of an English riding saddle. Ah, the subtle magic of Hollywood.

I found the row of offices, parked my car, and climbed a flight of steep wooden steps that needed a fresh coat of paint. The place looked like a two-story motel of cheap rooms rented out by the hour. I walked past offices and heard the blended clack of typewriters, a radio tuned to the afternoon horse races, a soprano singing off key. The door to 203-A was open. I walked into a cracker box with stacks of newspapers and galleys and scattered boxes of Chinese takeout meals. A rickety rattan fan fluttered strips of crumpled flypaper in the open window. A red-headed woman with thick eyeglasses was on the horn. She pounded her fist on a desk covered with unread movie scripts, film treatments, and inter-office memos.

"Bullshit. I know Hancock needs that second unit director, but he's three weeks behind on his shoot, and his main star got herself arrested on a cocaine charge. Fuck if I know where she got the glitter. Yeah, she's fucked. No shit, she's fucked. What? They found it in the spare tire, that's how stupid she is. First place they look. How should I know? She ran three red lights at two o'clock in the morning. The motor cop figured something was up seeing how this drunk bitch side-swiped a Borden's milk truck, which then crashed into a florist shop. He pulls her over and she comes at him with a clawhammer. He takes out his night-stick and breaks her jaw. Oh, it's a gold-plated goat fuck, all right. The picture is over budget. If Hancock can't get his act together, I'll hire a new director. No, I'm not kidding. Yeah, you tell him that. Tonight? Can you make it nine-thirty, hon? Okay, see you for dinner. Bye, love. Kisses." She cradled the receiver and reclined back in her white leather chair, lit a filtered cigarette, and blew out the match.

"Well, well. Look what the proverbial cat dragged in," she said. "You slumming, Pixie? I've been wanting to see you. Got a proposition—hear me out before you say no." She puffed her cigarette airily. "I've got this director on another picture who needs a stand-in for his leading lady. She's a tall drink of water like yourself. It's easy work. You'll get paid scale. Two weeks max. It's that new Roman Colosseum picture they're shooting in Death Valley. Could be the start of something big. I always said you have what it takes to make it in this business. Make a lot of money. I'll be your agent. Ten percent. I'm not greedy. I can book you into hair and makeup this afternoon for a test shoot."

"I'm not interested in the movies."

"Don't be ridiculous. This is America. The most capitalistic country in the history of the entire goddamn world. Everybody's interested in the movies. The goddamn commies are interested in the movies. My dog is interested in the movies and he's a cat."

"I'm not."

Irene's face fell. "Same Pixie, working the Sherlock gag. You'll never change. Never make any money, either. Not real money. Not fuck-you money. All right, what brings you to my inner sanctum? Can you believe they moved me out of my patented leather office? Say, hand me one of those Frescas from the fridge, and grab one for yourself. That's a girl."

I handed her the soft drink. "I want information, Irene."

"Now that's something I know all about, kid. Information is the glue that holds this industry together. You think it's money? Sex?" She shook her head violently. "Information, baby. Knowledge. Who knows what, and who are they screwing over when and why and by how much. Desperation is the oil that keeps this industry running smoothly. You can sleep your way to the middle, but not the top. Remember that."

She tapped the side of her head. "This here is my own encyclopedia. I remember what the elephant forgets. You knew that so you came to old Irene to dish out all the lovely dirt. Okay, shoot. What can I help you with this time?"

We had worked together in the past, when I'd been on vice, and become friends. Irene was someone I liked and trusted, even though she was always trying to shoehorn me into the movies.

"I want everything you know about Warden Krille. Soup to nuts."

She puffed out her cheeks and blew air between pursed lips. "Well, that's a topic and a half right there." She opened her bottle of Fresca, flipped the metal cap into a wastebasket, and sipped thoughtfully. "What do you need to know other than he's a certified shitheel?"

"He could be involved in a case I'm working. On the fringe, maybe."

"Honey," she broke in, "if Krille is involved, he's at the dead center of things. That man doesn't work fringes."

I told her as much as I could, leaving out everything between Landers Shavin and Tamar.

Irene grunted. "Hm. So you spoke with Elgin Tegel. He was Krille's partner, once upon a dim time. It was before the Deluge. Practically an antediluvian partnership. People called them Sturm und Drang and they weren't far off from that description. They were a hell of a team. They solved problems—expensive, nasty problems. They cost a lot because they always got results. They didn't farm their work out to any one studio, either. They were independent, which itself is a rarity for this town. Over the years they amassed trade secrets other studios were willing to pay gold bullion for. But they never capitalized on it. They never shopped their secrets to other studios and we're talking easy *millions*. That's why everyone trusted them and that's why everyone used them and why everyone feared and hated them. Until they had a falling out. Honey, it was a regular *cleaving*. Only after they split up did studios get nervous and back away. One of their wiser decisions, I must say." She sipped her Fresca.

"What caused the split?"

"Krille had a daughter. Came by some woman in Orlando he got in the family way. She was Roman Catholic so options, shall we say, were limited."

"She gave the girl up for adoption?"

"I don't think so. Years passed and the kid, now a young woman, came out to California to stay with her loving father. Elgin took a liking to her and she to him, but Daddy Krille didn't like that at all. He packed her off to Switzerland. Word has it Elgin learned this finishing school was a very expensive and very private home for wayward girls in trouble. Elgin was going to be a father. He wanted to do right, so he arranged to bring them back to the States. Krille blocked every move Elgin tried to make, but somehow Krille's daughter made it back to Orlando. Not much else is known because, despite their falling out, Warden and Elgin kept the lid clamped down tight on all personal events like that."

"What happened to the baby?"

"There were medical complications and mother and baby died in childbirth. They're buried in Orlando. Krille never forgave Elgin for it, they say."

I considered this. "From what I know about these men, I rather doubt that's enough to cause a rift."

"Never underestimate the power of male fragility, my dear. Elgin and Warden were immensely powerful in their former line of work, and it was a balancing act to keep not only their business intact but their private lives inviolate from any blowback their business might bring them. Mother and child were the two things neither could agree on, and as a result their partnership dissolved."

"I wish I knew this when I spoke to Tegel. What's the timeline on all this?"

"Generalities are all we have. The Great Rift started in the late twenties. Around the time Al Jolson opened his big mouth and ruined films forever. Ward and Elgin don't permit any more to be known—upon that much they do agree."

She saw me out of her office. "Hollywood is built on secrets, and this is one of the biggest. Be careful how you go forward, Pixie. You're entering a world of land mines and Warden and Elgin aren't the only nasty sons-of-bitches in this town. You go disturbing long-buried secrets and people might take a disliking to you. I'd hate to see you wind up in a hole in the desert because you stepped on too many toes."

She gave me a chaste peck on the cheek and waved goodbye. "Be very careful, love."

~

I drove to the Bandesi address on Olympia. I had some trouble finding it, as many of the suburban tract houses didn't have visible numbers. I finally found the eight-hundred-square-foot Cape-Cod house on a cul-de-sac off the main street.

The front windows were dark and curtained. But for the car in the driveway under the carport, I would have thought the place abandoned. I parked on the street. My tail, Tan Coupe, settled in a lot at the end of the block, the late sun glaring off his windshield.

I gave the coupe no further thought as I walked up the gravel driveway to the house.

Randomly, I realized I'd been so busy on cases that I hadn't called my dad in weeks. There's not much of a private life in this profession. Time slips away. You find yourself so involved in other people's problems and lives that yours take a back seat by necessity. I didn't regret my choices, but I made a mental note to call Dad soon.

The driver's side window of the parked Ford was rolled down. I stooped to read the registration on the steering wheel: Wanda Zipes, home address on 41st and Central Avenue. Since I was under the carport, I rapped my knuckles on the back door. A tall brunette with olive complexion opened the door. Her dress was yellow cotton with blue trim, and she wore sturdy white shoes. Her eyes were autumnal brown behind tortoiseshell frames. Her nose was long and straight, her mouth wide. She had strong-looking shoulders and gripped a straw broom in one hand.

"Yes, may I help you?" she asked with practiced politeness.

I introduced myself. "I'm Pixie Parrish. I'm here at the behest of Mr. Tegel."

She stepped aside to let me in. "I'm finishing up. No one lives here but I can't let a nice place like this sit unoccupied without the occasional mop and sweep. Please, come inside."

I followed her into a kitchen with painted cabinets and wooden shelves stocked with canned goods, flour, sugar, and crockery. Modern appliances sat on the countertop; the floor was that yellow-green Linoleum you find in a lot of houses because it wears so well.

"I'm Wanda Zipes," she said, "but I guess you knew that." She looked around the bright kitchen with an air of distress. "Maybe it's not right I kept my house key after Miss Tamar left, but the property isn't up for sale. Not yet, anyway. I do what I can. These were good people living here." She shot me a challenging look. "I want you to understand that."

"Yes, ma'am."

She parked the broom in a corner. "I keep hoping Miss Tamar will return. Not for me, you understand. I found new work. I keep a house on Sugar Hill and it's good money. Well, it should be. It's Sugar Hill."

"You haven't heard from Tamar?"

"No, nothing." She watched me, cautious.

"You can call me Pixie." In the Reid technique of interrogation, you make the other person comfortable by building trust. I pegged Zipes as old-school European, a domestic who honored the people she worked for, and I wasn't going to pull much out of her if I didn't get her to trust me. "Did Tamar do any packing before she dipped?"

"She threw a handful of clothes into an overnight case. Then made a couple phone calls."

"Is that so?"

"One was long distance." Wanda paused, deliberating if she'd revealed too much. "I'm telling you these things because Mr. Tegel wants me to cooperate, but I'm not the sort of person who spills family secrets. I'm just the cleaning lady. If it gets out I can't keep a confidence I might have a difficult time finding future employment. I hope you appreciate my predicament."

"I do. It's rather the same with me and my job. What kind of woman was Dolores Bandesi?"

"I'm not sure I know what you mean."

"To work for. Was she a good employer?"

It was like a floodlight switched on. Her whole attitude changed. "Would you like to sit down somewhere and be more at ease, Miss Pixie?"

"Only if you'll join me."

She opened the door to a Frigidaire. "I have Coca-Cola. Or I can brew tea. We don't have much else to drink, I'm afraid."

"Nothing for me, thank you."

She snapped the cap off a Coca-Cola with a bottle opener and poured it into a glass filled with crushed ice. "Come with me," she said.

We walked down a short hallway with two bedrooms at the far end. In the middle of the hall was a black Bakelite telephone on a rosewood *escritoire*. There were stacks of letters, paid envelopes, stamps, a checkbook, and a calendar with the last four months dutifully crossed off on the desktop. Someone was paying the bills, someone well organized.

Wanda Zipes pawed through paid receipts and took out a Western Electric phone bill.

"This way," she said. A Spanish arch gave way to the living room. The furniture had handsewn slipcovers and white antimacassars. Wanda switched on a table lamp and motioned me to a comfortable chair facing a walnut music cabinet. She took a wooden rocker for herself.

She sipped her soda. "I like a cold drink at the end of my workday," she confessed. "I find simple pleasures most enduring."

I dared not move. She was building up to something and the air in the room had turned electric.

"I am not in the habit of airing dirty laundry." Her manner was grave. "I respect the families I work for. I'm doing this because I want Miss Tamar found and brought home."

"Found. Do you think she's in danger?"

"I don't think there would be this hustle and bustle otherwise. Cops and detectives and I don't know what else."

"When were the cops here?"

"February. After Dolores died. They said the same thing everybody else did, that Tamar was old enough to do what she wanted and if she wanted to leave after her mother's funeral that was her business."

"I see." I didn't, but I wanted to keep her going.

Wanda Zipes shrugged. "Dolores wasn't real wealthy, but she did all right with Mr. Shavin's help. If she'd had more money maybe the police would've thought differently about pursuing this case."

"From my personal experience I can guarantee they would have. But Dolores was affiliated with Landers Shavin. He has plenty of money. Do you think the police were paid off?"

She didn't answer.

Then it came to me clear as day. "You miss them," I said in a low and confidential voice. "Tamar and Dolores. You don't care about the housework. You miss them. You're paying the bills and cleaning up. You're doing all that because you miss them."

She rocked back and forth a few times. "Dolores always treated me right. Friendly, always respectful. Never a cross word. Tamar, well, you couldn't put salt on that bird's tail. But she wasn't bad. Not like people say."

"What people?"

"People who don't know any better. Like that awful Goddard woman. She and Tamar had the most fearsome brawls. Goddard wanted Tamar to act like more of a daughter to Mr. Shavin, and Tamar would shout back he should have been more of a father."

"*Act like* or *be* more of a daughter."

I had given her something to think about. "If you put it that way, I'm not sure."

"Did Tamar have a friend named Juanita Drexford?"

Wanda looked somewhat uncomfortable. "She knew Juanita."

"Were they friends?"

"I'd say they were friends. They met at the S.P.C.A. I don't know if they were close friends."

"Any idea where I can find Juanita?"

"I heard she got married and moved to Pasadena." She was hedging and I wondered why Juanita was such a sensitive topic.

"Did Pola Goddard visit here often?"

"Not so you'd notice, but enough to remember it when she left. That woman leaves human wreckage in her wake." Wanda amended quickly, "I don't mean she's a home-wrecker. She tells everyone how much she loves Mr. Shavin. Obsessed is more like it. She was young when they met, and her initial infatuation turned into a deeper mania. Maybe there's not a decent English word to describe what it is, but whatever it is, she has it."

"Are you telling me she's involved with Tamar's disappearance?"

"I wouldn't go that far. Don't put words in my mouth, Miss Parrish. But deep currents run through her, that's certain. Maybe it's not all her fault. You do know she was captured and held prisoner by the Fascists in Spain?"

"No, I did not."

"It was 1935. They did something awful to her."

"I was never told when I visited Summerchynne."

"Pola wrote about her time in Spain and won a Pulitzer for it, but she didn't write about this. She phoned one day demanding to speak to Tamar. They were shouting at one another and Tamar was near tears when she slammed the receiver down. She said those Spanish Fascists should have shot Pola when they had the chance. Every morning they took her from her holding cell and tied her to a wooden post. They'd line up and point their guns, then lower them and lead her back to her cell."

"My God."

"She was rescued by republican partisans. The sort that blow up bridges. They shot up a motorcade and liberated her. She lived with them in the hills and forests for months. That's when she became a hardened communist. They were the only ones willing to help her and she never forgot it." Wanda Zipes took another drink of her Coca-Cola. She frowned. "I'm an old woman. I talk too much."

"Mrs. Zipes, you're the first person today who has been straightforward with me, I think."

She returned a faint smile. "Then you haven't talked to many people, I guess. Yes, Pixie, I want Tamar back home. I liked this family. Dolores was an accomplished artist; she had a God-given talent and that's rare." Wanda looked away then back. "When she got sick, she lost something of that talent and her energy to create. She would say, 'If only I had more time.' She deteriorated fast. It burned through her like fire and, before you knew it, she was dead and our world was a little smaller for it." Her voice was thick with emotion. "I pay the bills out of the monthly house money, and I clean up because I believe something good and decent should come out of all that sadness. Otherwise, what's the point of life? It's just senseless and I can't. . .I can't believe that God would do that."

"Mr. Tegel said Tamar asked about Nogales after her mother died."

She watched me. "Died." Her voice had no emotion. "That's what they told you?"

"Yes. Why?"

"Yes, she died, but they didn't say Dolores took her own life?"

It was like being hit between the eyes with a brick. "Wait. . .what?"

"Dolores was a patient at the private hospital when it happened. I guess the pain or whatever she was experiencing got to be too much for her."

"No one said anything like that to me."

"Summerchynne guards its secrets well. So does Elgin. Dolores was taken to the Hollack Sanitarium after she was found wandering the streets half-naked, and it was there that she died."

Wanda Zipes got up and dropped the folded phone bill on a cobbler's bench.

"There's a spare house key inside the pantry. Leave it under the back door mat. I respect the families I work for, Pixie, but I don't have to stay and watch you do it."

Without saying another word, she disappeared into the kitchen. I heard running water and the closing of the back door. A car engine fired. Through the front window I watched Wanda Zipes's sedan back away down the driveway. My loyal Tan Coupe remained at its post, and I was left alone in a house filled with many restless ghosts, silent but for the ever-present thunder of the past.

PART TWO
NOIR

FIVE

I UNFOLDED THE TELEPHONE BILL. It was from February of this year. On the 26th, the day of Dolores Bandesi's funeral, three phone calls were made from this address, I assumed by Tamar, but it can be dangerous when you guess. I kept it as a working supposition.

One call was an international connection to Tijuana. The second was to someone named Emil Staaken. The third and final call was to a taxi service in the city. The taxi was easy. I could put Artie or someone local on that one. They could trace the waybills and see what turned up, but four months was a long time to keep those records. I picked up the phone in the hallway and dialed the operator. I asked her to connect me to the Mexico number. She said it would take a minute or two, and I waited on the line.

A woman with a pleasant lilting accent answered. We didn't have a great connection. The line buzzed and clicked and I had to repeat myself several times.

"Hola. Hotel Nelson, Senora Amalie Gonzales speaking. *Buenos dias*. How may I help you?"

"Hello? Hello. I'm in Los Angeles and I would like to make a reservation at your hotel. I had your address in my Rolodex, but I lost it."

"The Nelson is on *Avenida Revolucion 721*. You will need a passport, or you can apply for a Mexican tourist card, if you wish to stay with us."

I told her I had my passport and booked myself a single room.

"Before I let you go," I said, "I was wondering if my friends are already there. Miss Tamar Bandesi and Mr. Emil Staaken. They would have arrived in late February."

"*Uno momento*," Papers rattled. "No, we have no current guests under that name. Did they leave a forwarding address?"

"I'm not sure. I'll check with the home office."

She said the hotel looked forward to my arrival and I cradled the receiver.

There was a phone book for greater Los Angeles inside the *escritoire*; Emil Philip Staaken lived on Grand Central avenue at the Commerce Apartments, No. 18. If I remembered correctly, that was three or four blocks off the Strip. His number listed in the phone book matched the one on the phone bill. I dialed and let it ring a dozen times. Either he wasn't home, or he wasn't answering.

Bedrooms were next. First Tamar's, where I searched the chest of drawers and her clothes hanging in the closet. Stack of board games sat on the floor: Monopoly, Life, an old Ouija board. I turned up a receipt pinned to a blue jean skirt. It was from a dress shop in Tucson, The Lucky Clover Dress Shop, dated last year. I tucked it in my notebook. There was nothing under the bed, pillows, or mattress. I overturned a red and gold throw rug expecting to find nothing underneath and wasn't disappointed. Usual complement of beauty products beside a vanity mirror and a chiffonier. Tray of loose hair pins. A couple of stray black hairs caught in a brush. Jar of cold cream. I poked my finger in the jar and wiped it clean with a Kleenex tissue. Nothing.

I was striking out big time. Or maybe I was learning something. There was no diary or locked journal around. This girl kept all her secrets in her head. She was smart, calculating, and very, very cautious. I could phone Sacramento and get permission to have the room, nay, the entire house, dismantled plank by plank if that's what I wanted. I did it on the Puckett-Smith job, but then I was looking for counterfeit Treasury bonds worth a quarter million dollars, not the secrets of a troubled runaway.

I stood in the center of the room. Think, Pixie. I used to be her age. I knew the usual hiding spots, but what about the unusual? There was a framed studio photograph of Landers Shavin atop a walnut dresser. Odd, that, considering Tamar's supposed enmity towards him.

I picked at the cardboard backing with a fingernail. It loosened. Between it and the sepia photograph was a folded handwritten letter in blue gall ink. The notepaper was deckle-edged and fragile with age. The folds were uneven, as if it had been opened and read many times. Dated August, 1929, it was written on Crown Studio stationary with the legendary eagle logo before they renamed the studio Gold Panther Pictures. The writing looked masculine, but you can never be certain, and I'm no expert when it comes to handwriting analysis anyway. It read:

L*ottie My Darling,*
    I will have everything prepared by next week. When Pola and I leave Milan, I look forward to seeing you at the place and time arranged. Pola will be there, too. Lottie, I will give you everything I have, and everything you ever lost will be yours again after the baby is born. I can't tell you how much I appreciate your help in this. Fate has given us all a new lease on life. When this trouble is over, and your charge complete, I swear, you will never want for anything ever again. I will see to that.
    Love, L.

I carefully folded the letter and slipped it inside my notebook alongside the clothes receipt.

I walked into Dolores's bedroom next. She had a leather-bound photograph album and a heavy cedar keepsake box, locked. I took my penknife and worked the simple brass lock until it popped open. Inside the velvet-lined cavity was Tamar's original birth certificate and the deed to the house in the name of Dolores Estrella Bandesi. I compared the original birth certificate with my copy. There was no discernable difference.

Digging through the keepsake box, I found a handful of crinkle-edged black and white snapshots. One was of Dolores and Landers Shavin in a tuxedo at the Cafe Trocadero, 1929. Another of a svelte Dolores standing alone on a beach wearing a straw hat and a one-piece jersey swimsuit in 1930. A snapshot of her and Landers holding hands in a white gazebo, spring azaleas in the background. The last was a Kodachrome of Pola Goddard sitting cross-legged on a green lawn holding a three-month old Tamar. That's what was written in red pencil on the back: *Tamar 3 mos.* I put that one in my notebook.

At the bottom of the cedar box was a sheaf of old city bonds worth about a thousand dollars, along with a Browning .32-caliber automatic. I pulled the breech back and jacked the Remington shells one by one onto the chenille bedspread. Eight rounds. I reloaded the magazine and put everything back inside the keepsake box the way I'd found it and locked it.

I sat on the edge of the bed and flipped through the family album. Birthdays, vacations, school outings, holidays. Dolores and Tamar having a pretty happy and comfortable life from the looks of things. But an idea was forming—call it a working hypothesis. I tried coming up with another, but it was no use. My hypothesis clung to the back of my neck and wriggled feelers deep into my brain. It was simple and fit the facts—Occam's Razor, and all that—and I liked it.

I closed the album, stared at the floor, and frowned.

It was the pictures in the album that bothered me. That is to say, the lack of photos of Dolores and Shavin. It's an unusual woman who doesn't keep any personal photographs around, and though they never married, there was no hostility between them. But all I'd found of consequence was Tamar's birth certificate and that letter from "L" to "Lottie" dated ten months before Tamar was born. "L" could be Landers, Lottie, a diminutive of Dolores. But it was the photographs that had me going. And the dates involved. *Ten months.*

Even I could do the math.

Dolores had been hired as a beard by Shavin to care for Goddard's illegitimate child. That explained the $500 a month stipend from Shavin. Pola had gone out of her way to tell me she was in New York when Dolores was pregnant with Tamar when I hadn't even asked. Dolores did her job well but was ready to move on with her burgeoning art career once Tamar had grown up. Tamar knew about the setup or learned the truth around the time Dolores died. That's why she had no reason to stay in this house. Everything she knew had been a lie, so why stay?

I scrounged a flashlight from the kitchen, climbed a ladder in the walk-in pantry, and crawled into the attic. I got a face full of spider web for my trouble and dropped the flashlight. When it hit the floor, the batteries dislodged, plunging me in darkness.

I don't like spiders. I fought off the web, flailing wildly, and picked up the flashlight, shaking it until I got it working again. There were boxes of house junk piled up around the attic, one of Christmas ornaments and one with old, musty linen. Nothing else. I climbed back down.

I'd been through the house with a fine-tooth comb and no matter how hard I looked I hadn't found a single canvas. Not one paint brush or used tube of paint. That was beyond strange given what I knew about Dolores Bandesi.

Or what I was *supposed* to *believe*.

I gave the single bathroom a thorough going over. Inside the medicine cabinet was a prescription bottle for Seconal from Dr. Hollack. The same Hollack who treated Dolores for schizophrenia. I copied the address into my notebook. Another glass pill bottle didn't have a label. I shook the yellow tablets into my palm. Nembutal, called yellow jackets on the street.

I put them back where they belonged and dialed Tegel. He answered, sounding snappish and harried. "Yes, what do you want now? I told you—"

"Pixie here. I thought you might have left your office by now."

His foul mood evaporated. "I got. . . sidetracked. Where are you? I want to lock up and go home. It's been a long day."

"I'm at the Bandesi place." I traced the zig-zag pattern on the wallpaper with my finger. "I spoke with Wanda Zipes."

His pregnant pause saw birth and graduated college. "What do you want to know?" he asked cautiously.

"Is Tamar Pola Goddard's illegitimate child?"

"*Jesus,*" Tegel whispered fiercely. "Where did you hear that?" I heard his pencil tapping against an ashtray over the line. "Look. We'd better talk."

"You didn't answer my question. I might have a lead on Tamar. She left Los Angeles in the company of a man named Emil Philip Staaken. Ever hear of him?"

"I do not know any Emil Staaken. Why would I know him? I don't know him." His tone was brittle and three denials in a row told me he knew Staaken like the back of his hand. "I'd rather not discuss this over the telephone," he insisted. "Can you come back here? I. . . I have something of a sensitive nature to tell you." He amended: "It's not what you think. Tamar isn't Pola's child." He swallowed audibly. "God in heaven. From what you've told me it's not what I believed, either."

"Why didn't you tell me Dolores killed herself?"

"Well, I. . . I thought you knew. Or Shavin told you. It's public record. That's not important. When can you drop by?"

"I'll be along directly. But I want straight answers or I walk off this case."

"Of course."

"I'm going to make a couple stops." He started to bluster. "You're going to wait for me. Do you understand, Tegel? You're going to wait until I get there."

"What? Yes, yes. Just hurry. God what a mess," he moaned. "Hold up. Where else are you going?"

"The Hollack Sanitarium for one."

"What for? Oh, never *mind*. Just hurry."

"I'll see you shortly." I hung up.

The last place I looked was the kitchen. I snooped around but didn't find anything important until I opened a cabinet beneath the sink. Way in back behind all the cleaning products was a Mason jar. I opened the lid and sniffed. Alcohol with an underlying pungent odor. Chloral hydrate. I put the jar back where I found it, thinking hard.

Afterwards, I locked the house and kicked the key under the rubber mat. When I unlocked my car, I saw my Tan Coupe was no longer around. That worried me. He may have followed Wanda Zipes home after all, or maybe he got bored because I'm such a dull and uninteresting person. I didn't believe that, but I had a sneaking idea where he might be found.

The Commerce Apartments were a quick detour on my way to the sanitarium. I turned off Central and parked in front of a row of single-story bungalows clustered around a common court. Concrete benches, wooden flower boxes. I walked up the steps of No. 18. There were no lights on inside or out. Empty milk bottles sat on the stoop. The mailbox was jammed with political flyers, junk mail, and grocery ads from the local A&P. I knocked on the front door.

No answer.

I bent down to examine the lock. It didn't look too formidable, but there was daylight left and cars driving up and down the street, so I thought twice about breaking and entering. Instead, I knocked on the door of an adjacent bungalow. They weren't home, either. Nobody was home. The world wasn't home. I walked around back and barked my shin on a garbage pail, knocking it over with a loud bang. I rubbed my shin ruefully. The yard was vacant except for a child's Radio Flyer wagon stacked with bricks. Someone had built an old fashioned flat-based barbeque pit here. These were leftovers.

There was no rubber mat outside Staaken's door, but an oblong rock set at an unnatural angle between the walk and a plumbago bush. I kicked over the rock. A clutch of slimy nightcrawlers greeted me as well as a shiny key. I used a stick to scrape the nightcrawlers aside and tried the key on the back door. It opened with a long creak. I stepped inside and swiftly closed the door behind me. It was quiet. What little daylight remained painted the walls in striated shadows. Fusty, too. The bungalow hadn't been aired out in months.

It was a cheap apartment at first glance. The furniture was service-able, and that's all you could say about it. Film of dust everywhere; Wanda Zipes would have lots to do here. I thumbed a wall switch and light washed across the brown kitchen tiles. Beyond was a single bedroom. Rumpled clothes scattered on the floor, a man's shirt and pants pulled from a dresser, hastily discarded. Unmade bed, blanket half on the floor. White brassiere draped on the headboard. A single black nylon stocking curled on the floor and a pair of black pumps tucked under the bed. Bit of a mess in the bathroom's medicine cabinet, too, as if someone in an awful hurry threw what they needed into a medicine case before bolting. There were feminine products and contraceptives in the medicine cabinet, things any sensible woman might keep for an emergency when visiting her lover. In the closet was a black dress with black hat and veil on wooden hangers. There were a few stray dark hairs inside the hat.

The room told its story clearly enough. Two people in a hurry packed their things and took off. Staaken and a woman, presumably Tamar given she'd phoned him before leaving the house on Olympia.

I checked my wristwatch. Tegel was waiting. I slipped out back, returned the key to its hiding place, and headed for my car feeling I'd done a good half hour's work.

"Who are you and what are you doing here?" An older woman shone a flashlight in my face, blinding me. "Who are you?" she demanded again.

I shielded my eyes. "My name is Pixie Parrish. I'm a private investigator and I'm looking for someone. If you douse that flashlight I'll show you my license."

"What do you want here?" she insisted.

"I told you, I'm looking for someone. Perhaps you know her. Tamar Bandesi."

"Oh, yes, I know her right enough." The beam from the flashlight dipped. The woman holding it was dressed in dark blue and her hair was marcelled. She wore bifocals. Her blue-gray eyes remained accusatory. "How do I know you're a private investigator and not one of them?" she asked.

"Them? Them who? May I ask who you are first?"

"I'm Rhea Sheldon, not that it's any business of yours. My husband and I own these rental units. I saw the light in number 18 and thought Mr. Staaken had returned." She paused briefly. "He's been gone four months."

"Is he often away so long?"

"I wouldn't say it's usual or unusual, seeing how I still don't know who you are." She fired questions like shots: "Why should I tell you anything? How did you get inside the house? Who did you say you are again?"

I gave her my card. She inspected it and handed it back with a sniff of disapproval. "I suppose it's official," she relented. "Though I dare say anyone can get one of those from a Woolworth's five and dime. However, I don't know about peeking through bedroom windows if such is what you do for a living."

"That's not what I do."

"You say you're looking for that girl. Here now, you better not have broken the lock to get inside. I'll call the police if you have."

"There was a rock with a spare key underneath. This is who I'm looking for." I showed her Tamar's photograph.

"That's her." Rhea Sheldon's lips pinched together. "I'm not somebody who tells renters how to live their private lives, but a young lady should think twice before spending weekends with an older, unmarried man."

"It takes two to tango. The man could take responsibility, too. But I'm not here to discuss sexual mores. You know Emil Staaken and Tamar?" I took out my notebook and pencil.

This simple action impressed her. It promised semi-official overtones and she wanted to be part of it. They always do. She stepped close and held the flashlight so I could write legibly. I smelled gin on her breath which she had tried to mask by chewing cardamom seeds.

"I wouldn't say I *know* them," she corrected. "Well, know her, I mean. I saw her around. Never saw Mr. Staaken much except when he paid his rent. Then one day, he pays three months in advance. Says he has to go on a business trip and could I keep an eye on the place. When the three months ended, I received a letter with a cashier's check for another three months. That's why when I saw the lights on I became suspicious. I almost called the police, but figured maybe I should check it out myself." She waited for me to compliment her detective work.

"Did this letter from Staaken have a return address?"

"I didn't say the letter came from Mr. Staaken. I said I received one in the mail. There was no return address; it was mailed from within the city. That's how it was stamped." She looked smug. She liked showing me she was smarter than any private investigator; given some of the private detectives I knew, that wasn't a high bar.

"Don't you find it odd he would mail his rent check for another three months from Los Angeles?" I asked.

"I don't see anything odd about it. I don't know what personal business Mr. Staaken has ongoing. Perhaps he is busy and it's the best arrangement he could make."

"Or maybe someone else mailed that rent check for him. Did Staaken say where he was headed?"

"Only that he had business of some import. I didn't press. It wasn't my concern." Her face fell. She realized she had made a mistake. "I didn't want to pry into his personal affairs."

"Rhea?" a man called from the darkened end of another set of bungalows. I made out a thick shadow framed in the doorway, the red glow of a pipe. "Who're you talking to?"

"It's no one, Reuben," she answered. "Someone asking about our Mr. Staaken. Go back to your supper before it gets cold, dear."

"The garbage disposal is on the fritz."

"Then I expect you will have to phone the plumber tomorrow," Rhea Sheldon explained patiently. "I'll be at my sister's all day. I told you that."

Reuben puffed his pipe. "Warm night," he observed, then disappeared inside the house.

Rhea turned around. "My husband," she explained. "He worries about me. He's a bit lost since he was forced into retirement. It's his health. Things were never the same after we lost our son—you can see his military star in the front window there. Sometimes I come out here to stand under the night sky and think. I think about a lot of things, I guess."

She started as if waking from an unpleasant dream. "You were saying?"

"No, I understand." Our shared silence grew. "I lost someone dear to me in the Pacific. My brother and my uncle died in Europe."

Rhea drew a ragged breath. Her eyes were vulnerable. Her voice came out soft. "It was a bad time. Reuben says we were forced to grow up during the war, become things we never thought we would, or should, become. Things God didn't intend people to be. I expect he's right. Though it doesn't seem worth the cost."

"I don't think it ever is," I said.

Turning back to me, her demeanor was sedate. "What else would you like to know, Miss Parrish?"

"What did Mr. Staaken do for a living?"

"Well, I wouldn't know exactly," she demurred.

"You asked for references before renting the bungalow?"

"My dear woman, I have two good eyes and my God-given conscience to guide me. Mr. Staaken was a nice man. He paid his deposit in cash. I saw no reason to give him the third degree."

"As long as his checks cleared."

She ventured a hard smile. "I'll tell you what I wasn't right with, and that was his keeping that girl around. Not that I saw much of her. Except the time they built the barbeque pit. Reuben watched them from our bedroom window. They were at it all night. Mr. Staaken said he wanted anyone in the complex to use it this summer, that it was for everyone. I thought it very gentlemanly of him," she reflected. "I thought he was a nice man. From the tenor of your questions, I guess I was fooled."

"I can't say for certain. When was this barbeque business?"

"Oh, late February sometime."

"And after that he left with Tamar?"

"You'll think I'm an old busybody." Rhea worried her bottom lip. "A taxi dropped her off. She was dressed in black. At first, I thought she was in widow's weeds. It wasn't long before a second taxi drew up to collect them and their luggage."

"You keep a close eye on things, Mrs. Sheldon."

"I have to," she answered presently. "You wouldn't believe what renters get up to. We have children on this block, families living here. Reuben and I maintain a clean, safe place, and we don't discriminate, either. We've had difficulties with renters, but I'd be lying if I said Mr. Staaken was anything but cordial."

"What does Mr. Staaken look like?"

"He's ordinary. Medium-sized with dark hair and dark eyes. Mid-forties, keeps himself in shape. Good looking in a rugged way. Keeps to himself, but who doesn't these days? I suppose some women might find him attractive."

"Did Tamar?"

Rhea Sheldon shrugged defensively. "She was that kind of girl."

~

Before leaving, I stopped to look at the barbeque pit. I shone a penlight I got from my car into the square chimney and down the iron grate. It was a brick barbeque pit, all right. In detective fiction, the inspector is always faced with a paucity of clues, but in the real world we find way too many which clutter up the truth we're seeking.

I unwrapped a stick of gum and popped it in my mouth. I balled the wrapper between thumb and forefinger and flicked it into the black maw of the barbeque pit. I wanted this barbeque pit to mean something. I argued with myself that building a barbeque pit in the dead of night was no more strange than other things I'd come across in my career, but, to paraphrase Freud, maybe sometimes a barbeque is just a barbeque.

I chewed my gum and waited for divine inspiration. That happens in the detective magazines, too, the ones with the lady tied to a chair in her underwear while a crook threatens her with a hot poker. The embattled inspector pauses in the midst of the action and has a brainwave. Case solved. Lady rescued. Except my brain wasn't cooperating—it rarely does.

Rhea's husband was right about one thing, though: we are often forced to become things we never foresaw. In college I double-majored in mathematics and philosophy. I liked the idea of a strict numerical structure to things, cold and infinite, where truth could always be established, but things didn't work out that way. I became a policewoman and lost several people dear to me during the war. When my position on the police force became untenable, I resigned and became a private investigator, something I'd never expected.

Which is why I now found myself nursing a toothache and sitting on a barbeque pit on a hot, dry California evening looking for another woman who was out there, somewhere, running through the night. But when you run away, you are, by default, also searching for something. I'd done the same in my life, and too often the results were less than stellar. This time, I was looking for someone who clearly didn't want to be found, and I likely wasn't the only one. I only hoped I would find her first.

A good detective uses the weaknesses of others to her advantage. My feelings about Tamar shouldn't matter. The case superseded everything, especially my own personal feelings. Emotions don't solve cases. They never have, and they never will.

But people aren't soulless machines, either. I was already emotionally caught up in this case. I saw too much of my younger self in Tamar. It was the most dangerous thing I could do, feeling this way, letting myself relate to Tamar. If I had any sense, I'd phone Artie and have him assign this job to someone else.

I hopped off the brick shelf and walked quickly to my car. I no longer had any doubt. To find Tamar it would take someone who thought like her.

I was officially taking the case.

SIX

THE HOLLACK SANITARIUM WAS IN an affluent neighborhood of over-priced baronial houses and manicured lawns the size of baseball fields. The sanitarium was tucked away in a secluded lot, surrounded by a thick band of trees, and a wide-open steel gate gave way to the property from the main road. Strange security, I mused, for a place like that.

I parked in front of a two-story house with Greek columns and a row of flowering bougainvillea. Attached to the house proper was a garden path that snaked away to a couple of small buildings which I put down as gardening sheds or machine-tool shops. Beyond those was a large complex, three stories high. Many of the windows had iron security bars, but not all of them.

There was a man stepping off the porch of the main house, headed for a 1939 LaSalle in the parking lot. He had red-brown hair, black-framed eyeglasses, and was dressed in a gray business suit with a hat and tie. A silver watch chain draped from his waistcoat. He carried a cordovan briefcase. He looked like a banker heading home to a whiskey sour.

I got out of my car to intercept him. "Excuse me, sir, are you Dr. Hollack?"

His polished shoes crunched gravel when he ambled to a stop. He studied me shortly before speaking, and when he did, his teeth were white and straight; he looked put together from perfect pieces of disparate people. "I am Arthur Hollack, and I happen to practice medical psychiatry." His voice was soft, mellifluous. "How can I help you, young lady? I hope this won't take long. I want to get home to my wife and dinner."

I went through the canned spiel introducing myself, explaining I was hired to find Tamar Bandesi.

He thought for a long while before he answered. "What concern is that of mine, or my practice?"

"Well, Tamar was the daughter of a patient of yours who committed suicide on your watch. Dolores Bandesi."

"Guest," he interjected.

"Pardon?"

"We prefer the term guest. The other carries what I consider harmful connotations. It precludes there is something fundamentally wrong with the individual which must be corrected before they are deemed normal. That's another word which has too much baggage: *normal*. Who is to say what is and is not normal? These societal definitions always change over time. I have found such labels put a person on the defensive when they come seeking my help. I prefer them to feel comfortable and at ease. It's more empowering and they respond quicker to treatment."

"Does that really matter when you're zapping them with electricity?"

The corners of his mouth turned downward. "We don't do that. Our treatments are normative and much less invasive to the human psyche. The human mind is a delicate instrument, would you not agree? You wouldn't use a blowtorch to repair a Swiss watch. Likewise, we take precautions when handling our guests."

"That's fascinating."

He saw I wasn't going away and sighed. "I shall have to phone Mr. Shavin and get verbal permission to speak to you about Dolores Bandesi's medical record. I hope you understand I'm not being recalcitrant."

"Of course not."

"It might take some time. Tomorrow would serve better."

"I can wait."

He gave a tiny frown. I wasn't leaving. "All right, come along, then. Although I don't know why revisiting that unpleasantness will help you find Tamar. I should think the two incidents are mutually exclusive."

"That's where we differ, doctor. I don't think they are exclusive at all."

His step faltered on the marble stairs leading up to the primary residence. "Indeed?"

"I don't believe in coincidence," I said.

"Coincidences do happen," he demurred. "That's statistics." He fished a key ring from his pants pocket to unlock the front door and bowed me through.

The house was decorated in tasteful furniture and wine-red carpet. Hollack's office was in the back. He beckoned me to a seat as he settled himself behind it and then folded his hands on top of his desk.

"What do you want to know?" he asked.

"You're not going to call Mr. Shavin?"

"No. I believe you are here on official business and such a phone call would be redundant. I prefer to get this over with as soon as possible so I can go home."

I looked around the room. "This place looks nice enough to be a home."

"This place?" A fleeting smile. "No. It serves as offices and a halfway house for some of our guests who transition out of their medical contracts once they are cured. Little else."

"You make your patients sign a contract?"

"Guests, please. I implore you to apply the correct term. The contract—we prefer to name it a private medical statement—is another safety measure we employ. It protects them and myself. It's not as legally binding as you may think. They are free to leave anytime they wish. The —" he made a face "—contract, as you call it, is but another instrument that gives them personal authority to see the treatment plan fulfilled as they wish."

"Did Dolores sign such a document? I'd love to see it, please."

"I assure you that will have to wait until tomorrow morning," he insisted. "My receptionist, Miss Paige, has those documents filed and locked away. I could look for it myself, but it would take all night and I'm not going to do that."

I was growing tired of his beatific smile. He hadn't answered my question and, in fact had gone out of his way not to answer.

"Can you tell me what happened the night Dolores died?"

"She was diagnosed with paranoid schizophrenia when she first came to us. We were doing everything we possibly could, but she wasn't responding to standard treatment. She loosened her restraints and went up to the third floor of the sanitarium. One of the nurses tried to stop her but Dolores hit her with a bed spring. She then forced open a window and jumped to her death."

"Did the fall kill her right away?"

"I should think so. We called for an ambulance and police, but she was pronounced dead at the scene."

"What was the injury, specifically?"

"A basilar skull fracture. There was other trauma engendered by the fall, but that's the specific injury the coroner believes killed her and I concur. It's quite lethal."

"How many patients. . .I'm sorry, guests. . .have you lost in this manner?"

"Dolores is the first guest I have ever lost. I've operated this facility for more than twenty years and never had such an accident and I pray to God I never lose another one like that."

"You said Dolores was restrained."

He nodded. "And sedated, albeit lightly only to help her sleep. It was for her benefit. As you might suppose, we eschew such barbaric practices as restraints, but in more extreme cases we must bow to practicality. We wanted to ensure her safety."

"What did you sedate her with?"

"I prescribed secobarbital."

"I know. I saw the bottle of Seconal in her medicine cabinet. You prescribed it a month before she was admitted to your sanitarium."

"That's right," he said carefully. "She was having difficulty sleeping. She came to me for help at the behest of Mr. Shavin."

"You increased the dosage when she arrived here for her mental treatment?"

"I did, but only by a slight amount."

"Did you give her Nembutal?"

"No."

"Did you prescribe or give Dolores chloral hydrate for any reason?"

"Good god, no. Why would I ever do such a thing?"

"Had she tried to harm herself in your care before she died?"

"She expressed signs of it and mentioned an interest about it in therapy. Yes, I think suicide was always in back of her mind."

"Are you sure she didn't want to get away from here when she jumped? Maybe she didn't like being locked up."

"I told you our guests are free to leave whenever they wish. In Dolores's case, that would not have been practicable given her deteriorating mental state. If she had private care waiting on the outside, yes, I would have felt more at ease releasing her from my custody, but she did not. Landers Shavin put her here because he thought I could help her most. I am aggrieved that we failed so utterly in that regard."

"I'm almost done here, doctor. Something you said sticks out to me, though. You said you would have felt more at ease releasing Dolores if she had somewhere to go. Did someone try to get her released? Someone other than Landers Shavin who put her here initially?"

That erased his damnable smile. I was wondering when he would lose it. I'd been pushing him hard and everybody has a limit.

He saw the mistake he'd made, knew there was no way out. I hadn't boxed him in—he'd done it to himself.

"Yes," he admitted regretfully. More regretful that he had been tripped up than anything else. "But there is no way I can betray that confidence unless I have permission from the individual in question."

"Was it Pola Goddard?"

He became adamant. "I will answer no further questions along these lines. It is private information. If you insist, I shall have to ask you to leave."

I backed off. "I don't mean to bully you, Doctor Hollack. I'm only doing my job. I've taken up a lot of your time and I want you to know how much I appreciate the help you've given me." I was laying it on thick, but it assuaged him. "If I may ask one last favor: May I see Dolores's hospital room and where she killed herself? Things like that go a long way into giving perspective when I'm trying to tie these loose ends together."

"It's a most unusual request," he allowed, "but I see no discernable harm. Then you will have to leave. The sanitarium is closed to the public at nine o'clock every night. No exceptions. Security, you understand."

"I do understand and thank you for your patience."

He made a quick call, spoke to someone on the other end, and we waited. A few minutes later an athletic man dressed in white with a black collar and gray tennis shoes came into Hollack's office. I knew muscle when I saw it, and this guy had it.

"Yes, sir?" he asked.

"Louis, this is Miss Pixie Parrish. She is here at the behest of Landers Shavin. She wants to visit the room Dolores Bandesi occupied. You are to give her all the assistance she requires within the constraints of facility protocols and nothing more."

"Absolutely, Doctor Hollack." Louis beamed at me. "Pleased to meet you, Miss Pixie."

I looked at Hollack. "May I use your phone?" He was nonplused but pushed it forward. I dialed. "Hi, Artie. Pixie. I'm at the Hollack Sanitarium in Old Hollywood." I gave the address and read aloud the phone number on the rotary dial. "I've spoken to the principals involved, and I'll write up the case notes later tonight. Doctor Hollack is showing me where Dolores died then I'm headed back to the office. Yes. He's right here. All right, sport, see you then. 'Bye."

I cradled the receiver. I hadn't called Artie. It was getting late and that man had a family. I had phoned my automatic answering service.

"There was no need for that," Hollack said defensively.

"How's that?"

"That phone call to your office. We have no intention of causing you harm, Miss Parrish."

I rose from my seat. "Now I'm certain of it. Ready, Louis? Or do you prefer Lou?"

The man beseeched Hollack. "Doctor?"

"Show her what she wants and then escort her off the premises," Hollack said, barely containing his anger. "See no harm comes to her. God help us if she twists her ankle or breaks a nail opening a door."

"As you will, sir. This way, Miss Parrish. And I prefer Lou."

"I'll be around tomorrow to see that contract Dolores signed," I reminded Hollack. "Probably best if it doesn't go mysteriously missing overnight. Oh, and the treatment plan you authorized. You can leave it with your receptionist. I think you said her name was Miss Paige. Mr. Shavin will be in touch with her in the morning to clear all the paperwork."

"Good *night*, Miss Parrish."

"Night night."

Lou had a little battery-operated lamp attached to his belt. He switched it on and we followed the trail down to the sanitarium. Halfway there he burst out laughing.

"I haven't seen Doctor Hollack so perturbed in years." He wiped his eyes with the back of his broad hand. Then he sobered. "But you got the wrong idea about us, Miss Pixie. We don't do things like that here. Doctor Hollack is a good, honest man. He has the best of intentions towards our guests. You can be assured of that."

He was doing his darndest to make me believe it, but I'd been around the block a time or two and I knew when someone was snowing me.

"Did you know Dolores?"

"I was here the night she was admitted. She was a sorry sight. Emaciated, run down. Anemic, too. She was far gone. I'm no noodle doctor but I could see that."

"Do you get many patients like Dolores?"

He shrugged his heavily muscled shoulders. "Sometimes. Most people come of their own free will. Alcoholism, depression. Delirium tremens. Shell shock from the war. It's a rare case like Dolores when she's committed on the personal authority of a private family member."

"Who was the family member?" Landers wasn't family, not in that regard, and he hadn't said he'd personally committed Dolores into Hollack's care.

"I can't speak to that, ma'am." His teeth flashed behind his smile. "Guess I said too much already. But nice try."

"It doesn't matter. I already know it was Landers Shavin." He didn't take the bait. "Was Dolores violent?"

He lifted his arm to show me two white crescent scars. He rubbed his thick, hairy forearm. "Took a bite out of me when I tried to fasten the restraining straps. Fought like a wildcat." He shook his head. "She was gone, like I said. I don't think there was anything Doctor Hollack could do to help that lady. Shame. I heard she was a real good artist. Well, they come in all shapes and sizes around here. You'd be surprised who I've seen come through that gate."

The inside of the sanitarium was about what I expected. Clean floors, air that smelled faintly of disinfectant, walls painted white, molding and door jambs painted that uninspiring industrial green seen all over the world. It wasn't that large a building, but it was sure as hell a mental hospital. I could only guess what Hollack was charging patients to stay here.

"How many rooms?" I asked Lou.

"Twelve. This first floor has an admitting office, game room, central meeting room, cafeteria, and a reading lounge. On this floor—" we had taken stairs to the upper landing "—are medical facilities including an examination room and five rooms for single-guest occupancy."

We climbed another flight of stairs. Before us was a long hallway with closed doors on either side. A security desk with a goose-neck lamp, phone, and scattered papers and clipboards stood unoccupied in the middle. I looked at Lou.

"No one up here now," he said, "so we don't need active floor security."

"Who was on duty the night Dolores died?"

"Me and the admitting nurse. That would be Hester Paige. She's a registered nurse. Everyone here has the medical experience needed to take care of the guests." He flashed another brilliant smile. "Except the floorwalkers like me."

"How many floorwalkers are there?"

"Three. We work shifts. I was the only one on duty that night."

"What do the floorwalkers like yourself do?"

"We're not hired for our brains. Not that there's much call for muscle, either. But sometimes a guest gets violent or they have the DTs and we have to restrain them so they don't injure themselves."

He unlocked a door. "Here's the room Dolores was assigned. See those canvas straps? She cut through them with the pointed end of a bedspring she worked loose." He lifted the corner of a thin cotton mattress. "The springs are big and heavy. When she got free, she used it to break the window in another room and jumped to her death. This is the room here across the hall." We crossed into another room with chairs lined against the wall. "The door to this conference room wasn't locked. She came in, smashed the window, and you know the rest."

I unlocked the window and looked down. It was a long drop.

"Where's the table?"

"Huh?"

"This is a conference room. Those are chairs. Where's the table?"

He shrugged. "I guess it got moved into the storage shed. They mostly use the meeting room downstairs anyway for that stuff."

"Lou, what goes on here?"

"I don't know what you're angling at, Miss Pixie."

"What do Hollack and his medical staff really do around here?"

He reached past me to close and firmly lock the window. "I don't know what you mean." He glanced at the open doorway. We were alone on the top floor, but he lowered his voice. "I have a good job here," he explained resolutely. "I'm not going to jeopardize it. What *I* do here," he emphasized the pronoun, "I already said. What other people do when they're on the clock is their business. It's not my department."

"But you've heard things."

He shrugged and kept tight-lipped.

"I could use your help, Lou."

He leaned close until we were face-to-face. "You're not going to get it, Miss Pixie. You go asking anybody else, they're not as liable to be as accommodating as your old friend Lou here." He took half a step back. "I'm not saying I haven't seen things, but what I've seen I've seen, and that's the end of it. Get me?"

I slipped him my card. "You can reach me at that number if you remember anything important. Or if by some miracle you grow a conscience one day."

"First chance I get I'm going to tear this up and throw it in the trash."

"I don't think you will, but that's a chance I'll take. I'm ready to go now."

When we reached the ground floor I asked, "Is there a daily record of visitors?"

"What? Well, sure. It's in the Document Room yonder."

"May I look at it?"

He balked. "I don't know if that's permissible."

"I only want to see if anyone visited Dolores on the day she died. Nothing else. I don't even have to see the name. Just tell me if anybody saw her."

He fixed his lips in a thin line. "I guess it's copacetic. The visitor book isn't restricted as far as I know. Okay, one look then you have to leave like Dr. Hollack ordered."

He unlocked a door with his keys and flipped on an overhead light. The tiny room was an adjunct to another security station on the floor. Lou pulled a leather-bound book from the top shelf and laid it on the desk. I flipped to the date in question. It wasn't there—the calendar page for that day was missing. When I bent to look closer, I discovered it had been excised with a razor or a sharp knife.

Lou didn't say anything, but his face was troubled. He closed the volume and replaced it on the shelf and switched off the lights. He closed the door after me.

We didn't speak until we reached my car. He was big and powerful and maybe not that smart, but I knew I had found an ally in the enemy camp. He had not turned on his belt lamp when we left the sanitarium. We had walked back to my car in the pitch dark.

"Watch the stone column post when you pull out," he said. "It's hard to see when you make the turn onto the main road."

"Lou."

"Like I said, I was on duty. I counter-signed her admittance. Look here. I've said enough and maybe too much. I hope I don't lose my goddamn job over this." There was conflict in his voice. "Maybe I'll call you. Maybe I won't. Now get out of here. Go on."

I started the car and drove away, his large shadowy frame filling my rearview mirror and the glow from a local security light reflected in his eyes.

~

The doors to Tegel's office were shut. A cleaning lady mopped the floor at the end of the long hallway. I opened the double frosted doors.

You always know when something's off. Maybe it's instinctive from when cave bears wanted to eat us, an animal sense of danger we never lost. Maybe it's from years on the job as a policewoman. But I knew something was wrong as soon as I stepped into the office.

The reception office was hushed, the filing cabinet open, files stacked on top with a handful spilled across the floor haphazardly.

"Mr. Tegel." My voice echoed in the empty room.

I pushed open the door to his private office with the back of my hand. Which was foolish because my fingerprints were all over the place from my earlier visit. Tegel lay face down behind his desk, his head in a pool of blood soaking the carpet. There was a gun lying in his right hand and an ugly hole in the occipital bone behind his ear. His eyes were open and blank and dead.

The air-conditioner in the window hummed and rattled. It was the only sound in the city of Los Angeles and it brought gooseflesh to my arms.

I straddled the body to avoid the blood stains and frisked him. The keys I'd watched him drop into his pocket were missing. The gun was a Luger P08, the kind the *Wehrmacht* used during the war. I found the spent casing under the desk. A floor safe was open and empty. Taped to the underside of the desk was a recording wire. I followed the line to a tape recorder in the bottom left-hand drawer which could be activated with a foot pedal. The tape recorder was at the end of its run, which meant it had been activated a final time but never turned off.

I could see Tegel's wan face straight-on from this angle. We looked at one another. It was a sloppily staged murder scene. People shoot themselves behind the ear, but it's uncommon. The primary targets for suicide are the temple, the mouth, or the heart. Also, the ejected shell was in the wrong place for Tegel to have shot himself while sitting in his chair, but not if someone had killed him while standing behind him. Neither did the blood spray on the wall match the angle of the spent shell casing thrown from the Luger. And, from what I remembered, Tegel was definitely left-handed.

But it was the recorder I wanted to test out. If Tegel hadn't changed the reel after I left, then I was on it and his killer might be too—if Tegel had activated the machine when that person arrived. There was but one way to find out.

It was awkward working around the body. I used the eraser end of a pencil from the desk to rewind the reel.

Did Dolores paint Tamar?

I don't think she did. Not that I'm aware. Funny. I never thought of it before.

This was me and Tegel. Too far back. *Go forward a bit more,* I told myself. The recorder clicked and played.

Warden is an unpleasant human being, but he has no reason to harm Tamar. He never has.

A little more. The sound of the solenoid turning on the recorder told me where it started.

Got here when I (muffled). Man's voice, gruff, muted. Not Tegel. It sounded like he spoke from several feet away. Perhaps standing just inside the office doorway.

You can't stay. Tegel.

(Indistinct) Man.

You know I can't do that. Tegel.

. . .Arctic expects loyalty. It sounded like he said "Arctic." The sound of his voice improved as he came farther into the office.

There was a scuffle and the hollow thump of something hitting Tegel's desk and then the sound of a shot. After a while, the sound of running water. The murderer in the washroom tidying up.

I put everything back the way I'd found it and stood, thinking I should call the police right about now. Tegel's bloody brains drip-splattered the wall behind his chair like a grisly Rorschach. You could smell the blood. It's never a good smell. But this man wasn't dead twenty minutes, and his body was warm. I'd missed his killer by that much.

The question was: Why was Tegel killed and what was the killer thinking by staging such an absurd tableau? It was almost as if the murder had been random, or impulsive. Or maybe they were trying too hard to be clever. Or, just maybe, they didn't know Tegel was left-handed. Which meant the murderer had been a stranger and someone else was known by both men as Arctic.

I gave the office a once over and that's when I saw the painting by Dolores was missing. Tegel's killer had cut it out from the frame. I didn't know what that meant, but I knew it meant a lot.

I also knew I was running out of time. I was now convinced Tamar was in danger and every second counted. I went to the main entrance and peered out. The cleaning lady and her mop bucket were nowhere to be seen. I used a phone in the outer reception to call the police. They arrived in fifteen minutes. After taking a quick look around, they peppered me with questions. A police photographer snapped a picture of the blood splatter, his magnesium flash bulb popping and smoking. While he changed it out, one of the detectives gave a startled cry. They had found the spent casing and the tape recorder.

That's when I was handcuffed and taken downtown.

SEVEN

I WAS ALLOWED ONE PHONE CALL. I didn't call my lawyer. Goddard picked up on the third ring.

"Hello?"

"Parrish. Don't speak, just listen. Tegel is dead. Murdered."

She gasped. "Elgin?"

"That's right," I said. "It's supposed to look like suicide. I have a lead on Tamar. Do you know a guy named Emil Staaken?"

"No. Is he with Tamar?"

"They left for Tijuana together. Do I have access to those fifty thousand dollars?"

"Of course you do, Miss Parrish. If you need more let us know." An optimistic note crept through her voice. "Does this mean you're taking the case?"

"Yes, I am. I may need the money to secure Tamar's release." I stared at scribbled phone numbers and pornographic doodles on the concrete wall. A hard-faced matron watched me from the concrete entrance housing the temporary holding cells. She made a motion for me to hurry up. I turned away. Some of them can read lips.

"I think there's more to this than a missing girl. I don't want to alarm you, but Tamar is in danger. If she's still alive."

"Oh, God, do you think that's a possibility?"

"You have to prepare Mr. Shavin for the worst. I don't know where it will end but I don't think it's going to be good."

I heard her rapid, heavy breathing as she moved her mouth closer to the receiver. "I. . .I don't want to tell Landers now. He had a bad turn. He got drunk and broke down. Blamed himself for a lot of things. This is taking its toll on him. I know you don't think he's a good man, but he is. I'd rather wait and see what you can turn up definitively. He will be glad to hear you're working on our side, however."

"I didn't say I was on your side, Goddard. I said I'd take the case. Those are mutually exclusive things."

"Of course," she flustered. "I only meant—"

"Skip it. Did Tamar have a friend named Juanita Drexford?"

"Why, yes. They were quite good friends as I remember. Juanita married a man named Thomas Neff and moved to Pasadena. Tamar was at her wedding."

"Do you have that address?"

"No, I'm afraid I don't. Maybe I can find it. Why?"

The matron at the end of the corridor came for me. I'd had my three minutes. "I've got to go. I'll be in touch."

"Thank you, Miss Parrish."

"Sure." I hung up.

The Matron jerked her thumb sideways. "You know the drill, sister. I'll have a go at you and you'll cool your heels somewhere nice and cozy until the detectives send for you."

First, they threw me into the night tank thinking that might soften me up. The bored women there watched me from their concrete benches.

"What'd they nip you for, sugar?" one asked.

"Murder."

A lady on the edge of the bench turned to her companion. "This one's graduated."

Someone offered me a cigarette, but I said I didn't smoke so we shared my pack of gum instead.

Later, I was taken to the interrogation room. The detective on the night desk grilled me. I yawned. Hours dragged by but he kept hammering. Around 4:00 a.m. a lieutenant backed into the interrogation room carrying a manila file. He kicked the door closed. I sat up in the chair. I recognized him— Erik Nagel. We had worked burglary together in Santa Monica. I hadn't expected to see him here. I didn't know he'd transferred over to Los Angeles.

Nagel was lanky with wiry hair and wolf-like yellow-brown eyes. His black tie was crooked, and his sweaty shirt stuck to his body in several places. The interrogation room wasn't air-conditioned, but a metal fan did its best to kick the stale air around. A red-faced sergeant with a cauliflower ear occupied a wooden chair in the corner of the room. He was sitting with the chair ass-backwards, arms across the top. He chain-smoked Lucky Strike cigarettes and stared without expression at the pile of butts building between his feet.

"Hello, Pixie," Nagel said.

"Hello, Lieutenant Nagel."

He and the night detective shared a whispered conference. When the night detective left, Nagel sat down opposite me. He opened the file and spread out three single-spaced typewritten pages.

"Is this your statement?"

He let me read it over. I handed it back. "Yes, that's all of it."

His wolf eyes remained unblinking. "You're going to stick with that stupid story?"

"I saw Tegel earlier on behalf of a client. He got hold of me later and said there was something urgent he wanted to tell me."

"Tegel or the client?"

"Tegel. He was dead when I arrived."

"If you didn't kill him, who did?"

"Tegel knew a lot of dangerous secrets. In the past he paid doctors so movie stars could get illegal abortions and buy marijuana and cocaine. Had his grimy fingers in a lot of pies. Man with a past like that—it's no surprise when it catches up to him."

"I knew he was a cleaner," Nagel said, "but people like that don't walk away from easy money on principle." He resumed reading. "He also dealt with Hollywood skins." He raised his eyes from the open folder. "You know what I'm talking about?"

"Cutters. Men and women who get plastic surgery to resemble

movie stars. They sell themselves so men can pretend they're making love to Veronica Lake or Greer Garson. Or Cary Grant if their predilections run that way. Extortion and blackmail go hand-in-hand with that lousy racket. I hear it's good work if you can measure up."

"We've known about Elgin Tegel a long time," Nagel said with finality. He sat back, fingers laced across his stomach while his thumbs played with the end of his rumpled tie. "No one in this city will mourn his passing. He was a piece of shit the day he was born. The nurse should have slapped him twice and then smothered him."

Nagel bolted forward, thrusting his face at me like the prow of a ship. "Pixie, I'm not asking as a cop. I'm asking you as a friend. Off the record. Okay?"

"I'll think about it." I was wary. I hadn't expected this.

"This client, he have anything to do with the side business Tegel was running?"

"You mean drugs? Hell. This is Los Angeles. You can get drugs on every street corner and in every bar."

"You know what I'm talking about. The drugs, the skins, child sex rings, all of it."

"I didn't know about the children, but I'm not surprised. Sickened, but not surprised. No, lieutenant, I can say categorically my client knows nothing about that."

Nagel ran his eyes down the last page in the file. He scribbled a note in the margin. "Tegel's death tossed a giant stink bomb in my lap. He got what he deserved but I have to go through the lawful motions of pretending I give a shit."

His eyes leapt to mine. "You're not going to tell me your client's name?"

"You know better."

"You have a good rating in this city, Pixie. I'm willing to bet you'd like to maintain that rating. Along with your investigative license. A couple phone calls, I can have it pulled."

I rolled my eyes. I was tired and my body ached and I was hungry. "Climb down, lieutenant. You're not where you think you are."

"I can hold you twenty-four hours without cause. Longer if I wake up a judge. If I wake up a judge, he'll be mad that I woke him up. So it will be longer. A lot longer."

I gave a thin smile. "But you won't."

He frowned. "Why the hell not?"

"Because you want to take me to breakfast instead."

"Haw," the big cop sitting in the corner barked laughter. He rose, stretched his arms over his head until his bones cracked. He took a final drag and crushed the cigarette under the toe of his polished shoe. "That all, lieutenant?"

"That's all, Sergeant Breton. Thank you for staying."

Leaving the room, Breton shook his head at me in admiration. "Lady, you are one brass op. Beats the world and she asks if it wants some more. Haw."

Lieutenant Nagel closed the file with a slap. "Let's go get something to eat," he agreed.

~

I wasn't arrested because of course they knew who my employer was; they would have listened to the tape. They wanted to throw their weight around, show me who was in charge. It's a thing cops do when the heat's on and they're flailing for answers.

Nagel and I walked to an all-night diner. I was hit in the face with the delicious smell of frying bacon and fresh coffee and hot steam. The waitress poured us coffee and we ordered. It was five o'clock in the morning.

"How is Jeremy?" I asked. Jeremy was Nagel's oldest boy.

"Got his first tooth. Jenny had her solo concert last week."

"Nice." I was godmother to both children but hadn't been around to visit in a long, long time. I sipped my coffee and let the invigorating warmth work its magic. "And Nancy?" That was Nagel's wife.

"She's great. Got a big promotion at work." He spooned sugar into his cup. "How've you been?"

"Busy." I shrugged. "You know how it is."

"How's your father?"

"Doing better after his surgery." Mentioning my dad made me

remember I should call him. We hadn't spoken in months. Just the occasional postcard from different cities while I worked for Valkyrie.

"When did you transfer out of Santa Monica?" I asked.

"It was about a year ago. I wasn't going down with that ship." He lifted the coffee cup to his lips. "I have my family to protect."

Nagel was there for moral support when I quit the force. While it's true crooked cops never last, neither do honest ones who refuse the monthly take. Not to mention I was working vice at the time. Unforeseen accidents can and do happen all the time in vice. The precinct captain made it clear what I should expect if I didn't sleep with him. That's when I quit, hiding out at Nagel's home with his wife and kids until the heat died off.

"Mrs. DeMoines is stepping down."

Nagel eyed me critically over the expanding silence. "You don't look pleased."

"Grapevine has it I'm her number one pick. I've only been with the agency since the war ended. Four years. That's nothing."

"Four years without a break," Nagel countered as the waitress brought our food. "When is the last time you had a proper vacation?"

"That's scarcely the point. When the war ended, well, the goals I set for myself were taken from me on Tarawa."

"It could be the right move, Pixie. I'd think about it if I were you."

The waitress sailed by to refill our coffee cups. "The agency is in arrears. It needs to be modernized. I'm not up to the task and I'm not sure I want to take on that responsibility."

"You're making excuses. I've never heard you do that before. What will you do if you leave Valkyrie?"

I wiped my mouth with a napkin and threw it onto my empty plate. "I don't know. Maybe start my own agency. Nothing says I can't. Lots of businesses retooled after the war." I put on a brave face that felt more like a mask. "It's a brave new world."

"Not the best world, though."

"Yeah, I read the papers." I realized I was nervously tapping the table with my lacquered fingernails and stopped. "I'm not very good company. I apologize. I'm on a nasty case, Erik. It has emotional overtones I can't shake."

Nagel's hair blew in wisps across his forehead in the breeze from an oscillating metal fan. "You don't have to excuse yourself to me. When did you first meet Elgin Tegel?"

We were back to business. "You found the recording, of course."

"Hard to miss. We listened to your conversation with Tegel. Don't worry, it's not going to get out."

"Landers Shavin has nothing to do with Tegel's side practices. He's searching for his missing daughter. What did Tegel have in that floor safe?"

"We found traces of brown heroin. The F.B.I. thinks it's coming in from Marseilles. Are you positive Shavin had nothing to do with Tegel's death?"

"I wasn't there to see him killed, but if Landers Shavin wanted Tegel dead he'd hire someone to do it. He wouldn't kill Tegel himself."

"He's a communist, isn't he? Shavin."

"Everybody is a Red if you ask Senator McCarthy. The man's a lunatic. He sees Reds in his soup. What were Tegel's politics, anyway?"

"He was pink, but I don't think he was a full-blown communist. Still, you never know. Maybe they had a falling out and Moscow ordered Tegel's assassination. It happened to Trotsky. I don't believe that, either, but I'm forced to explore all possibilities."

He didn't say anything else for a while. Then, "What's your gut tell you, Pixie?"

"I think it's the heroin. Hell, I'd put money on it. I didn't know about it, but now that I do, I'd say it's a given. I mean, it's gone missing, hasn't it?"

"There's nothing to say *when* it was taken, but yeah. Now it's gone along with one of Dolores Bandesi's paintings that was hanging in Tegel's office. What do you think that means?"

I shook my head. "I don't see any connection there. A professional killer isn't going to take something like that for his own purpose. He was told to do it. I'd like to know why. It might be the key I'm looking for."

From what I knew about Krille, he was the sort to ice Tegel and make it look like a suicide, except he wouldn't bungle the job, and whoever staged that scene didn't know Tegel was left-handed. Tegel was defensive when I asked him about Krille. Maybe they were not on the best of terms, but someone as cautious as Elgin Tegel doesn't lose touch with someone like Krille. It wasn't good business sense, and it wasn't safe.

"You saw what I saw," I told Erik. "Tegel didn't kill himself. He was shot from behind. Whoever did it took the heroin and the painting."

"We have a working theory about that."

It rushed at me like a storm blowing over the ocean. Nagel must know. It wasn't like Tegel's partnership with Krille was sibylline. All Hollywood knew.

"Let me guess. This working theory is named Warden Krille."

"Is that what you and Tegel talked about in the front room? We couldn't make it out on the tape. He only had one directional pickup under his desk and hadn't wired the outer office. You've heard of Krille, then?"

"Oh, yeah. I've heard of him."

"I can keep this unofficial only so long. I won't lie to you, Pixie. We could use some help. When the papers hit the street, this is going to erupt into the biggest goddamn mess you ever saw. A homicide in the middle of West Hollywood always makes good copy. Especially when you consider the people and the politics involved."

"What does the District Attorney say in his infinite wisdom?"

"I heard the hammer dropped hard last night in Sacramento. He fielded a call from the governor. He wants it off his desk, one way or another."

"Solved or covered up."

"Whichever is more expedient. He doesn't care which."

I drew a shaky breath. "The last time I spoke to Tegel was over the phone. He sounded out of sorts. He thought I was someone else when he picked up, and I got the impression it was someone he'd been arguing with. I can't prove that someone was Krille. I can't prove it was anyone. But he made an odd statement. He said he wanted to get out of his office in one piece. That struck me as strange. He might have been expecting company—company he didn't want to meet."

Nagel paid for our breakfast, and we walked down a sun-drenched sidewalk together.

"It's not much to go on," Erik acknowledged, "but maybe I'll get lucky. You want a lift?"

I said I did. Nagel drove me to my car. Before I stepped out, he took hold of my arm. "Watch yourself, Pixie. You dodged a bullet last night. Next time you may not be as lucky."

"You needn't worry yourself over me."

"But I do."

It got quiet in the car. We could hear the morning traffic outside.

"I know," I said softly. "You take care of yourself, too, Erik." We hugged. He wasn't the kind of man to make a pass, but the hug between friends felt damn good and I needed it. It had been a nasty night.

"I'll tell Nancy I saw you," he promised. "Drop by anytime. The kids would love to have you over."

"I promise that I will."

I unlocked my car and drove to my home in West Hollywood. When I turned down my street, I saw the Tan Coupe parked on the corner. I quickly turned left on a side street and kept making left turns until I worked my way back around. I parked on a residential street perpendicular to where he was parked. I remembered the gun in my car but didn't think I'd need it. I got out and approached the car.

I saw his face in the side mirror. He was an amateur; he was watching my house and not his mirrors. I touched the fender of his car with my forefinger. Old police habits die hard. Then I walked up to his window and knocked.

"Quan."

He started, eyes wide. Sheepishness came over him. He rolled the window down. "May I get out?" he asked.

I stepped back in case he wanted to get crazy with the door, trying to hit me with it or use it as a shield to allow him to hurt me.

He closed the door and leaned against it. The morning sun was bright and cheerful on his weary face. If anyone looked out their kitchen window, they might think we were discussing the latest water tax proposal for the city.

"What are you doing here?" I demanded. "Why are you following me?"

He looked away then back at me; he was caught and knew he might as well come clean. I thought he might have been the one following me when I saw that the garage at Summerchynne was missing another car that was not the Cadillac and he was nowhere to be seen.

"I was told to keep abreast of your actions in case you got into any trouble you couldn't handle. If you did, I was. . .to help. I have a baseball bat in the trunk," he finished lamely.

"You tell Pola Goddard I'm a grown person. I don't need anyone to tuck me in at night. Got that?"

Quan's face twitched. "Yes, I. . . Sure."

That's when I saw it. "Wait a sec. It wasn't Pola Goddard who put you up to this. It was Mr. Shavin. Am I right?"

He looked relieved he didn't have to lie any further. "Yes, ma'am. It was."

"Call me Pixie. We both work for Mr. Shavin so we might as well be friends, right? Why did he want you to babysit me? Does he not trust me?"

"No, ma'am—Pixie—he does. But he feels there's something off about Tamar's disappearance. She's always been headstrong, but her sudden disappearance weighs heavily on his conscience. Not only that, but everything else."

"Like what?"

"His illness. His ongoing trouble with the House Un-American Activities Committee. He sees the past slipping away from him, and the past is all he ever had. He never had a future. He never wanted one. Not like that, not like you and I might. The only thing that mattered was his work and Pola. Now he sees the mistake of thinking that way and he's afraid he won't have time to set things right with Tamar."

"Was he in love with Dolores?"

"They were together briefly. He's always been something of a wolf. But when Dolores got pregnant, he wanted to do right by her and see the baby taken care of. That's all I know."

"Did he ever call Dolores Lottie?"

"I've never heard him say that."

"Why did you leave the Bandesi house?"

"You were in there so long I didn't know if you were staying overnight. I figured I had time to call a quick report in, but when I came back you were gone."

"Shavin certainly likes his secret reports on people, doesn't he?"

"He does at that, Pixie. The only place I knew I might be able to pick you up again was here. I waited most of the night for you to show up."

"Did you know Tamar?"

He nodded. "A little. She was a good kid, I thought. We spoke in passing, but no more than that. Do you think you will be able to find her?"

"I hope so. I'm trying." I took a deep breath, counting to ten. This wasn't Quan's fault. The poor man had sat here all night long at the request of Shavin. I was done questioning Quan, but I wanted to keep him as a contact. "Do you want to come inside for coffee? I can make breakfast if you're hungry."

Quan shook his head. "Thank you, but no. I am driving back to Summerchynne. I have a lot of work to do *there*." He emphasized the word.

I asked him to tell Shavin or Pola to call the Hollack Sanitarium and give me access to Dolores's medical records. We said goodbye and I went to retrieve my car. Inside my house I threw off my clothes and jumped under the shower, then I crawled into a pair of clean pajamas, set my alarm, and went to sleep.

When I awoke, I checked my answering service. Crickets. I phoned Western Union and sent off a batch of telegrams to the Valkyrie agency's branch offices west of the Continental Divide and got someone to work on those waybills. Nibbling an apple, I phoned the main office in Sacramento. Vera Smalls picked up. She was one of our day operatives, and a fifty-five-year-old Italian grandmother with the jab of a prizefighter and the mouth of a longshoreman.

"Valkyrie Investigations. Yeah, what d'you want?"

"Pixie here, Vera. Is Mrs. DeMoines in today?"

Her attitude immediately softened. "She's not coming in today, Pixie. I can take a message for you."

"Don't bother. Say, you looking for work?"

"I'm always up for a job."

"I've got something I think is in your wheelhouse. I should warn you, there could be trouble."

Vera chuckled drily. "And if frogs had wings they wouldn't bump their asses when they hop. What's the job?" Vera was always game for a tough assignment.

"I want you to tap your underground movie contacts and see what you can dig up on Warden Krille. He was a Hollywood cleaner. Ran with a partner called Elgin Tegel who set up back-alley abortions and procured underage boys and girls for said movie stars. Real Tinseltown stuff."

Vera grunted. "A humanitarian, this guy."

"Tegel got snuffed last night. Warden Krille might be on the hunt." I told her everything about Tegel, Tamar, and Landers Shavin. I could always confide in anyone working for Valkyrie. "So you'd better watch your back, Grandma."

I heard her pencil scratching furiously. "Yeah, I saw the morning papers over my bowl of Corn Flakes. Busy doings in your part of the country. Where can I reach you?"

"I'm off to Tijuana. You can always try my answering service. Oh, if you run into Artie tell him to expedite any information he has for me. If he can't reach me by normal means, try carrier pigeon."

"Sure you don't want to leave a message for Mrs. DeMoines?" There was a subtle hint in her voice. The whole network knew of Mrs. DeMoines's plans for my future.

"I'll bring her up to speed later regarding this case."

"Understood. *Ciao*, baby."

"*Ciao.*"

I called Mexicana Airlines and booked a DC-3 to Tijuana. My flight wasn't scheduled until later that afternoon, so I threw on fresh clothes and got in my car and drove to the Hollack Sanitarium. It looked different in the bald light of day. There was an uncanny sterility to the house and grounds, and I couldn't shake a sense of artificiality about the place.

To be honest, it looked spookier than it had last night.

The main house was unlocked. In a room made up to be an auxiliary office attached to Hollack's examination room I found the receptionist, Hester Paige. At least that's what the gold nameplate on her desk read.

"Good morning," I said. "I'm Pixie Parrish. I'm here at the request of Landers Shavin to pick up Dolores Bandesi's medical records. Do you have them for me?"

The young lady at the desk was auburn-haired and willowy, with penetrating eyes the color of witch hazel. "Indeed, I do," she smiled. "I fielded Mr. Shavin's phone call this morning and was told I should expect you."

I'll give Shavin this: he was on the ball.

Hester unlocked an old-fashioned safe. She picked out a green file and kicked the safe door closed with her heel. "Here you are," she said, smiling. "I hope you find everything in order. Should you have any questions I will relay them to Dr. Hollack."

"He's not in this morning?"

She was about to pass the file to me and drew it back. "No, not this morning. Maybe later."

"Can I ask you a question? Were you present the night Dolores died?"

"Oh, no," she said. "I finished work early and was driving home. I'm not licensed to be in the sanitarium. I'm a registered nurse but Dr. Hollack provides a special license to be in the sanitarium for security reasons. Do you have any further questions?"

Hester Paige was good at her job, I reflected. She knew how to deflect questions with smooth efficiency, but she was an awful, awful liar. She didn't know I'd talked to Lou who said she was on duty that night. He had seen no reason to hide the truth about that. But she did, and I wondered why.

"Is Lou around?"

"Lou Calloway? He's on night shift this week."

"How long have you known Dr. Hollack?"

She laughed self-consciously. "I knew Arthur when he was doing residency under my father. He's a very great man. I was glad to accept the position as his receptionist. It's good money if nothing else."

"Then you've known him quite a while. I mean, you know him well."

"You might say that."

"He's a very good-looking man."

A pink flush crept over her face. "Yes," she said shortly. "I suppose he is."

"Hester, I know you were here the night Dolores died. Lou told me. If you were here, but not in the sanitarium, then why were you here? You see what I'm saying? It doesn't make sense. Unless you were doing something you weren't supposed to be doing, but wanted to be doing. Like seeing Dr. Hollack."

"Those are some pretty large assumptions on your behalf, Miss Parrish."

"Yeah, but I'm right, aren't I?" When interviewing a reluctant person it's a smart idea to change your demeanor to keep them off balance. But, if you want the truth, I felt like I was coming on too strong to someone who probably wasn't guilty of a whole lot other than maybe having an affair with a married man, which was her concern.

I softened my tone. "Hester, I'm not trying to hurt or embarrass you. I'm not going to tell anyone. How long have you been seeing him?"

"I. . .I don't have to answer that."

"No, you don't, but that's an answer, too, isn't it? I don't care if you're seeing Hollack on the sly. That's not my business. I want to know what happened the night Dolores Bandesi died. I think you know something you're not saying. I used to be a policewoman. I can see it in your face."

The public puts a lot more store in the authority of the law than you might think, and you can always use it to your benefit if you play your cards right.

Hester looked at me with trapped eyes. Her mouth clamped shut. She shook her head forcefully. "You should probably leave."

"Is Dr. Hollack coming in this morning?"

"I. . .I don't know. He didn't say." She stopped to pick nervously at papers on her desk. Her voice was distant. "He doesn't tell me everything."

"What happened in the sanitarium the night Dolores died?"

"I don't know anything."

"Let me spell it out for you. No, look at me. If Dolores was murdered, that makes you an accessory. You were in the building and on the third floor. You won't go to the gas chamber, but you'll go to Tehachapi. You won't get out for a long, long time. When you do, Hollack will have found someone else young because you'll be old and gray and not worth his attention."

She licked her lips. She didn't like me. *I* didn't like me.

"I wasn't at the sanitarium that night. Not. . .not at first."

"But you were on the grounds."

"Lou phoned me here from the sanitarium. He said Dolores got free and locked herself inside the conference room. I called Dr. Hollack who was at home and ran over to the sanitarium. Dr. Hollack arrived shortly thereafter, and he and Lou spoke to Dolores through the door. We heard breaking glass. That's when Lou smashed the door in. Dolores was climbing through the window before Lou grabbed her. I screamed when she fell. We heard her hit the ground. It was. . . She made kind of a crying whimper when she landed. We ran downstairs but I could tell right away she was dead."

"What happened then?"

"Dr. Hollack made a phone call from this office. I was with him. He had to look through my Rolodex for the number."

"He came all the way back here to call the police?"

She didn't speak.

"An ambulance?"

Nothing.

"He called someone else first," I said. "Someone whose number he had to look up. Who was it?"

"I don't know. He told the other person there was an accident and asked them to come right away. Then he said yes, he would take care of it if that's what this person wanted. 'Just make sure you get the stuff out of the house.' I don't know what he meant by that. When he hung up he looked at me and said, 'You didn't hear anything, Hester.' I said I understood. That's when he finally called the police. He told me to wait outside for them and he went back to the sanitarium, but before the police arrived, a taxi dropped by and someone ran out of the sanitarium and jumped inside. It was too dark to see, and I couldn't make out who it was."

"Someone who was inside the sanitarium when Dolores died? Someone other than yourself, Hollack, or Lou Calloway?"

"Yes. Like I said, they got in the cab and left. I thought the person was a woman, but I can't be positive. Anyway, the police arrived, and the death was ruled an accident. I'm sure it was an accident. Dr. Hollack would never intentionally harm anyone. I know him. I. . . Well, he wouldn't do something like that."

"Do you know who he called that night?"

"No, I don't."

"You saw him look through the Rolodex."

"I can't remember."

"You do realize I can have the phone records pulled."

She was defeated. "It was Elgin Tegel."

"Can I have that file now?"

"Yes, here it is." She handed it to me, glum.

"Thanks. If I need you again, I'll be in touch."

"Can't say I'm looking forward to it."

"Tell Lou you spoke to me. I think he's an okay guy and he will want to know what you know. Maybe the two of you can get together and finally do the right thing. Goodbye, Hester."

I carried the file to my car and checked the clock in the dash. I had plenty of time to drop by the Bandesi home before my flight.

When I got there, I looked under the rubber doormat for the key, unlocked the house, and made a beeline to the bathroom. I opened the medicine cabinet. It was cleaned out. I closed it and stared at my reflection in the mirror. *Idiot.* Maybe that bottle was filled with Nembutal sleeping tablets, maybe something else. Now I'd never know. I knew what I'd find, or wouldn't find, before I searched under the sink too: the Mason jar of chloral hydrate was gone.

Loose ends happen all the time in this job, but it's worse when they're a result of your own clumsiness. Worse, I couldn't shake the feeling I had missed something else vitally important.

It was obvious another call had been made last night between unknown parties. Something along the lines of, *"Hey, you sure that stuff was got out of the house the night Dolores died?"* A call to someone who had come here and finish what Tegel should have done four months ago.

Maybe Hollack himself. Maybe that's why he wasn't at the sanitarium this morning.

I stashed the key under the rubber mat and drove to Pasadena. There was a Thomas Neff listed in the phone book on 1268 Sycamore. I unfolded a map of Pasadena I kept in the glove box and looked the street up. When I got there, I saw a warm beige two-story home with a spectacular view of the San Gabriel Mountains. It wasn't *nouveau riche* but it had enough dollar signs behind it to keep it prestigious.

I rang the doorbell and shortly thereafter heard quick footsteps. A Black domestic dressed in starched uniform answered the door. "Yes," she said pleasantly, "may we help you?"

"Hello. My name is Pixie Parrish. I'm a private detective looking for Tamar Bandesi. I believe Mrs. Neff knew her at one time. Is she home? It's vital that I speak with her."

"Wait here, please," the housekeeper said and left me cooling my heels on the front porch; she wasn't about to let some oddball stranger into the house.

After a few minutes, a very pregnant young woman came to the door. She had dark hair done up in a curl, long eyebrows, and bright, quick eyes. "Marion said you wanted to see me?"

I told her who I was and who I was looking for. In ten minutes we were sitting in the parlor drinking coffee while I let her spill her guts.

"Of course, I knew Tamar," Juanita said. "Missing you say? Good god, that's unnerving. I'm afraid I don't know anything about that. I hope she's all right, of course. I'm willing to help all I can. What would you like to know?"

"When did you meet Tamar?"

"It was at the S.P.C.A. in Los Angeles. I was doing volunteer work. It was funny. We got to talking one day and became quite good friends. We found out we'd been born within a week of each other. I guess friendships have been built on flimsier excuses. Her mom was an artist, you know. Her death was such a tragedy. That was the last time I saw Tamar, at her mother's funeral."

"Did the two of you talk at the funeral?"

"Only a little bit. Did some catching up. Nothing more."

"Did she say where she might be going?"

"She mentioned Tijuana or maybe Orlando. She had relatives in Orlando."

"Orlando, Florida?"

"On her mother's side." Juanita watched me jot that down in my notebook. They're always impressed when you write something down. It makes them feel connected to the investigation.

"You haven't heard anything from Tamar since the funeral?"

"To be honest, we kind of lost track with one another after I got married. When I left the S.P.C.A. I thought about becoming a candy striper, but I got myself hitched instead." She grinned as if to say *Life, what can you do except live it?* "Thomas has this great job with a lot of opportunity for business growth and now we have a baby on the way." She smiled happily. "I'm due in August. It's a lot to juggle, but I'm doing my best."

"Congratulations on the baby, by the way." We talked about that and her husband for a while, since I wanted to keep building rapport. Later, I asked, "Did Tamar mention anyone named Emil Staaken?"

"No, I never heard that name."

"What about Elgin Tegel?"

"No. I mean, I met him once is all. Wait. Didn't I see something about that in the morning paper?"

"You might have. Tegel was murdered last night. Did you meet Tamar's father, Landers Shavin?"

"Isn't he that old film star? No, but I got a signed copy of Pola Goddard's novel. Tamar never talked much about those two. To be honest, she never opened up about her personal life at all. I guess you could say we're opposites. I like being around people and talking to them. Tamar prefers keeping to herself. Maybe that's why we became such good friends."

"What kind of things did you do when you visited Tamar?"

"Oh, play board games or grab a float down at the drugstore. Listen to Frank Sinatra on the radio. You know, the usual things." She sipped her coffee from a china cup.

I didn't know. I'd never done the usual things. I was shoeing horses or repairing tack or kissing boys in a hayloft when I was her age. For me those were the usual things.

"But you met her mother, Dolores."

"She was such a sweet person," Juanita said, sadly. "It was a shame about her illness. I always had a pleasant visit to their house. Her grandmother was friendly, too."

I kept my face and voice neutral. "What can you tell me about her grandmother?"

"I don't know there's a lot to tell. She was from Orlando. I think. At least that's what I gathered. Maybe you shouldn't write that down, though. I'm not certain about that."

"What kind of—" I started.

"There was something—" she began.

We exchanged awkward smiles.

"I'm sorry," I said, "please, go ahead. You were saying?"

"Oh, I was only going to mention there was a big spat between Tamar's mother and her grandmother the last time I was there. We heard them from Tamar's bedroom. Dolores said she wanted out, said she'd done her part and more than her part, whatever that meant, and she didn't have to do what Tamar's grandmother said any longer or spin any more lies. Dolores's mother scolded her and said they'd discuss it later, but things weren't finished, and Dolores had promised to see it through to the end. Then it got eerily quiet, but I could hear them murmuring. You know how people do when they're fighting and don't want others to hear, but you can tell they're arguing? Tamar took it in stride like it was a common occurrence. Later, when I asked her about it, she sort of smiled and said her life had a lot of secrets that weren't worth keeping." Juanita shrugged. "I didn't know what she meant by that. I let it drop. It wasn't my business, and I didn't see any reason to further embarrass my friend."

"When was this?"

"Oh, I can't remember for certain. Before Thomas and I got married, anyway. Sometime last year."

"Did Dolores have any paintings and art supplies in the house?"

"Are you kidding? They were everywhere."

"Did you go to the house with Tamar after the funeral?"

"No, Thomas and I drove home after the graveyard."

We talked a while longer, but she couldn't recall anything else helpful. I thanked her and told her to call my answering service or the main office if she thought of anything, and she promised to do so.

Before leaving I asked Juanita the name of Tamar's grandmother. I had an idea, but I wanted it confirmed.

"Her name was Wanda Zipes," Juanita answered.

~

I drove home and dressed for my flight. I made a late lunch, called to stop the milk and paper deliveries, and threw an overnight case together. I put the .38 in a drawer. It's not difficult getting a handgun through Mexican customs, but I didn't want the hassle. I called for a cab to take me to the airport.

A plane to Tijuana was faster than driving and gave me time to think—and I had a lot to think about. However, soon as we took off, we hit turbulence. My tea spilled in my lap. The windows were pitch black, and we were tossed this way and that while lightning flashed and the plane's metal fuselage groaned, popped, and shrieked. A woman two rows back was sick to her stomach. A baby up ahead of me screamed. I felt my stomach drop when we lost lift, until the wings caught air once more and we were back to being buffeted and slammed around.

I was on my forty-fifth Hail Mary when we broke into a clear blue sky.

When we touched down, we deplaned and walked—unsteadily after the rough flight—across hot tarmac towards the customs shed. I had my passport ready and breezed on through. At a rental lot I picked up a gray 1938 Chevrolet truck with rusted springs popping through the seats. There was a piece of carpet for the seat cover. The inside of the cab smelled of old wool, rubber, and rusted metal. I got directions to the Hotel Nelson from a stoop-shouldered man with greasy hair selling sweet ices and pornographic Tijuana Bibles on the street corner.

"You want to buy?" he asked, offering me the dirty comic.

"Not today."

I fueled the truck at a Pemex station.

"Check the oil and brakes, *por favor*," I told the attendant, which was about the limit of my Spanish. But Mexican roads were notoriously bad, and I didn't want to be stranded.

I drank an RC Cola while the truck was serviced. I slipped on a pair of green sunglasses I'd purchased at a kiosk. The sun was fierce. I was sweating. My Parisian beret didn't do much to cover my head, so I bought a wide-brimmed straw hat with a colorful ribbon.

I hadn't been to Mexico since before the war. Mexico reminded me of growing up in Soledad. I could do without the unwanted sexual advances, but a woman endures that to some degree no matter where she goes. I felt safe as long as I kept my wits about me, but, again, that's anywhere for a woman.

Which is why when I parked my truck and strolled over to the hotel entrance, I became uneasy. Two men dressed in black suits, hats pulled low, left a taxi stand and started following me.

They didn't look like locals. They were white and stood out from the locals like sore thumbs, and though night is when most white people descend on T.J., these men didn't belong here any time of day.

One fellow had a wide face with razor burn, coal-black hair, and a determined stare. Handsome, if a little too intense. The other was fair-haired with white-walls around his ears. I put them down as East Coast torpedoes. New York or Miami, maybe.

"Pardon, *senorita*," the fair-haired man said in pidgin Spanish, "may we ask your assistance?"

That put me on guard. There was no reason to affect a bad Spanish accent. Americans recognize one another all over the world, so do French and Germans and everyone else. People recognize their own kind; it's a human trait. He was trying to get close to me with this pathetic pantomime, and I wasn't going to play.

I had a fat roll of nickels from my pocket clasped in my left hand. My right dipped into my purse to fit a brass knuckle duster. They might be lost tourists, and everything was jake, but when Razor Burn slipped his hand under his coat I caught him flush on the chin with the duster. I drove my shoulder into it. I'm no prizefighter, but I can sucker punch with the best of them. He dropped the leather sap and stumbled back, arms windmilling as he lost balance. Blood spilled from the corner of his mouth. He collapsed heavily in the dust, legs splayed in a comedic way, mouth and eyes wide open with shock.

The other man was on my right. I couldn't punch across my body so I drove my shoe heel as hard as I could into the arch of his foot. He screamed like a rabbit. That gave me the time to spin around, grinding my heel deeper, and whip my left fist with the roll of nickels across his temple. His eyes rolled back in his head and he collapsed. The paper roll split open and bright silver spilled clinking into the street.

Around me people ran and yelled while car horns honked and a police whistle shrilled. I bent to pick up the sap Razor Burn dropped. It wasn't a sap, but a leather wallet. I flipped it open to read a card behind the plastic window:

ARCADIA INVESTIGATIONS, INC.

Aiden P. Weatherwax, III

New York, New York

I tossed the wallet in his lap. "Sorry, fellas."

"Stupid bitch," Razor Burn snarled. "We jus' wanted to talk." He wiped blood from his mouth. "You made me bite my lip. Hey, Eddie, I bit my lip clean through." He eyed me appreciatively. "You got a stellar right hook, sister."

Eddie held his foot, squeezing tears of pain from his eyes. "To hell with your lip, Aiden. I'll be lucky if I ever walk again." Nevertheless, he got up unsteadily, favoring his injured foot while I helped pull Aiden to his feet.

"You Valkyrie lot are plenty damn touchy." Grimacing, Eddie brushed himself clean.

I picked my hat off the street, knocked the dust off, and stuck it back on my head. "I'm going to check into that hotel across the street. If you boys want to talk you can find me in the bar. Deal?"

They looked at one another then back at me, squinting in the bright sunlight.

Aiden removed his hat and threaded his fingers through his thick hair. "Deal," he muttered. Then he bent to gather the bright silver scattered around his feet.

Eight

AFTER CHECKING INTO MY ROOM I freshened up and strolled downstairs. The doors and windows of the bar were open to admit a stray breeze or two. The outside glare was so bright it was hard to see in the dim interior. Aiden sat hunched at the bar. No sign of Eddie.

I slipped onto the barstool next door. "Hey, sailor. Buy me a drink?"

He sipped his Mexican beer deliberately. "Go to hell."

"Come on, let's be friends. I said I was sorry."

"Lady, I don't wan'ta be friends with the likes of you." He condescended to glare at me. "Poor Eddie is upstairs, his foot swathed in bandages the size of a football."

"I thought you boys were pulling a sap on me."

"In the middle of the street in broad daylight with a cop standing on the corner and in front of the Hotel Nelson we gonna pull a sap. Jesus." He put the beer on the counter. "*Jesus*," he repeated in disbelief.

"Like you said, I guess I'm a little touchy." I nudged his arm. "Look, I really am sorry. I had other things on my mind and I overreacted. I apologize. My agency will pay for any medical bills. Submit them to our office in Sacramento."

"Lady, you aren't touchy, you're downright disputatious." The ice between us thawed. I smiled and he allowed a touch of liquid humor to lighten his eyes. Up close they were the color of rain clouds ready to burst.

"Buy me that drink now?"

He signaled the bartender. I ordered a whiskey sour. A three-piece combo in the corner played music. We carried our drinks to the patio and sat under a thatch of palm fronds. I had changed out of my travel suit into a blue and white shirtwaist dress and open-toed sandals. I stretched my legs out to catch some sun. Aiden parked across from me so we could share a table. The bottom of his chin had sticking plaster and was heavily bruised beneath a fat bottom lip where I'd caught him flush. For all that, he was a decent-looking man who came across as honest, if a bit rough around the edges.

"Why are you evil men in Tijuana trying to waylay innocent American girls?"

"I tol' you we weren't. . ." He wound down. "I see now," he mumbled. "I catch your drift."

"You see more than I do," I confided. "Okay, I'm teasing. You're right, Aiden. I'm a no-good bitch who checks payphones for loose change. I always call collect and I make change in the collection plate during Mass. But other than that I'm an all-right girl." I held out my hand. "Truce?"

He considered the offer. We shook. "Truce," he agreed grudgingly. He shook a cigarette from the pack and lit it. Smoke dribbled from his nose. "You aren't what me and Eddie expected."

"I hear that a lot from people. But what were you expecting? Why *are* you here? Our agencies have worked together in the past when short of manpower, but I've never met anyone from Arcadia before."

"Eddie and me got a long-distance call from a gent in Sacramento. He said be on the spy for a blonde drink of water who wears Parisian berets. Make contact with her since we were already here delivering a summons to a San Diego deadbeat who skipped out on his gambling debts."

"Let me guess. This Sacramento gentleman is Artie Glass."

"You know Artie?"

"He's a thorn in my. . .in my side."

"You win a Kewpie Doll. Artie knows us from when we three worked the Detroit train yards during the Depression. We was night bulls running off hobos and runaways and bums. Oh, we never hurt nobody too much, even though the yard bosses gave us wooden truncheons and hand lanterns. We knew cops looked the other way so long as we didn't kill nobody too bad. Mostly we made sure people who wanted on the trains, and those getting off, didn't hurt themselves. Kids rode those trains, too. Anyway, the yard bosses, they didn't care if a 'bo hitched a ride, so long as the train left on time and the freight was secure. It was theft they were concerned about. But most of the stealing was done on the loading docks by the mob. Nothing we could do about that. The terminal boys were paid to look the other way."

"Did Artie put you onto anything while you waited for my arrival? It'd be like him to squeeze work out of you if he could."

Aiden reached under his sport coat and drew forth a folded sheet of hotel stationary. He snapped it open with a flourish. "I got everything written down. Took a bit of doing, but a little money spread here and there helps people remember. Eddie snuck a look at the hotel book while I canvassed the car rentals and taxi services. On February 26, fifteen people checked into the Hotel Nelson and seven checked out. Of those fifteen, four were couples. One of those four had their belongings shipped ahead from Los Angeles. The Nelson keeps records of that, and when luggage arrives, so they can avoid an insurance hit."

He stabbed his cigarette out. "You hungry?"

"Maybe later. What did you find?"

"The couple in question registered under Mr. and Mrs. Brown. Yeah, a real competent duo." He laughed. "They arrived by taxi. They might have rented a car in Los Angeles and drove across the border before renting a taxi. Or took different taxis to lay false trails. No telling. But I doubt they were that cautious given they couldn't think of a better name to register under."

"I know they left the man's house in a taxi. His name is Emil Staaken and hers is Tamar Bandesi. I've got an operative checking the waybills, but four months is a long time for those records to be kept."

"I got lucky myself." He was bragging. "There's a rental place here in T.J. and they have everything from bicycles to donkey carts. It was there the Browns, or I guess your Staaken and this Bandesi broad, rented a 1946 Ford sedan. Dark green two-door with a white front fender. Claimed they wanted to drive to Mexicali and enjoy the scenery. Like there's anything to see except cactus scrub and sand piles down there. Crazy duo."

Aiden drained his beer and ordered another. He shot me a look. "Want a refill?"

"I'm fine here." I lifted my glass. "Could use more ice."

He waited for the bartender to return with his drink and my ice before continuing his story. "Now here's the good part. I got smart. Yeah, you wouldn't think it looking at me but I have my moments. I got to talking with the concierge. Those people notice everything and are always good for scraping up dirt."

"That's true," I said.

"Well, she says Mr. and Mrs. Brown asked how to reach the Immaculate Rose Convent in Playas de Rosarito. You know where that is?"

"Not the convent. Rosarito Beach is southwest of here somewhere down on the coast. Maybe fifteen miles?"

Aiden nodded approval. "On a very rough road. Most Mexican roads are lousy unless you're in a big city or frequenting the better touristy spots." He tapped my knee. "Here's the kicker. Staaken and Bandesi leave for Rosarito early one morning and return twenty-four hours later."

"Okay, I'll bite. Where did they go?"

He lifted his chin as if he was summing up a case before a jury. "Not so fast, doll. So far nothing to write home about, right? But I know what you're thinking. Why would a concierge remember something that dull? People leave Tijuana for Rosarito all the time. Maybe this concierge, she's spinning yarns so I'll think I'm getting my money's worth, but it just so happens a month after this, our concierge runs slap into a nun from the convent who relates she saw something on that beach the night of March 5. That's the night Staaken and Bandesi were in Rosarito before they left for Mexicali. The nun reported what she saw to the Federales. They investigated, and everything went sort of strangely quiet."

I was intrigued. "What did she see?"

"That's what you and me are going to find out," he said pointedly. "We're driving to Rosarito to dig up this here nun who sees things. If that fails, we pry what we can from the Federales. Those boys are eager to talk if your wallet is fat."

"You and Eddie did all this in the course of a single morning?"

"We're Arcadia," he said, as if that explained everything. Perhaps it did. They had access to a larger workforce and more international contacts than Valkyrie. We were regional in scope. They were worldwide.

"I hope Artie paid you boys for this work." I could see my fifty thousand from Landers Shavin dwindling fast.

"We get paid what we get paid." Aiden tilted his beer bottle and drained it. He wiped his mouth with the back of hand. "Don't worry yourself none about that."

Before we left for Rosarito I stopped by the concierge desk. Not that I thought Aiden had done an inadequate job. Quite the contrary. I wanted to pump the concierge for information Aiden might have overlooked. I knew more about the case than he did.

"What was the name of the sister you spoke to on March 5?" I asked.

The concierge was an elderly local in a dark rebozo with a tortoise-shell *peineta* and black Spanish lace mantilla. She consulted her logbook. When she spoke her voice conveyed a pleasant Spanish lilt. "I went back and made a note after speaking to your gentleman." I didn't know Aiden was my gentleman, but I saw no reason to correct her. "Her name is Sister Paul. She was coming from a country mission station where she attends the sick and poor. Mexican farmers and *indios* who require medical attention. She doesn't go all the time to the station. Maybe once a week. The people are destitute and have trouble finding a ride into Rosarito. Sister Paul rode a *carreta*. You know this thing?"

"A cart with big wooden wheels."

"*Sí.*" She nodded. "A cart drawn by a horse. Sister Paul was following the coast road and stopped to water the animal at a stone well. This is near the *playa*, the beach. It was after sundown. Sister Paul saw something on the water." The concierge crossed herself. "The way Sister Paul spoke, it was something of great portent and evil bearing. I thought nothing more of it until I spoke to the gentleman and put two and two together." She touched her forefingers together.

"This Sister Paul, can we find her at the convent?"

She shrugged. "Either there or the mission station where she works as *medico*. Not many people are willing to do much to help the poor like Sister Paul. She has a saintly soul."

"Where is the mission church?"

"Misión El Descanso is twenty kilometers south of Rosarito. But you must know this place lies in ruins. Nothing remains but an adobe wall and scattered stones. There is a *rancho* nearby where Sister Paul has her *medico* station. It's part of an oil field where the workers went on strike in 1938."

"It seems strange anyone would bother going there. Rosarito is so small and desolate."

"Not so small and not so desolate, *senorita*. It is very picturesque. The beaches are gorgeous. During Prohibition people drove from California and the movies to the Rosarito Beach Hotel where drinking was legal."

"From Hollywood?"

"And why not? Rosarito Beach Hotel welcomed the Hollywood elite. They were its main clientele. Orson Wells and Ava Gardner stayed there. Many Hollywood stars lived at the Rosarito Beach Hotel during Prohibition. So many I cannot remember them all. Wait. I have an old pamphlet somewhere. Let me find it. . ."

She dug through her desk and handed me a colorful tourist pamphlet from September 1929. I flipped through it, reading the names of film history printed inside. Landers Shavin was one of the film stars, and there was a photograph of him standing beside Pola Goddard.

~

Rosarito was a fly smudge on the map. Aiden traced our route in pencil. He was the type of person who liked to plan his steps ahead one at a time, leaving nothing to chance. I liked that.

"We'll take this here road," he explained. "It ain't more than a goat trail, and part corduroy road, but your Chevy truck can make it." He folded the map. "Long as we don't bottom out in a dry wash or bust open the oil pan, we'll do all right."

I tossed Aiden the keys since he had a better idea of where we were going. It took the better part of an hour to drive the fifteen miles to Rosarito. We got stuck behind a public bus overloaded with people and their baggage. There was no place to go off-road so we followed them into Rosarito.

We agreed our first stop should be the hotel. We poked around and generally made nuisances of ourselves but could not pick up the four-month-old trail of Tamar and Staaken. To save time, Aiden and I split the remainder of the duties. He took the police station and I went to visit the convent. I had little hope of gaining useful information from the nuns immured there, and I was right. Perhaps due of my Catholic upbringing, or because I donated twenty American dollars to the church registry, the Reverend Mother granted me an audience. While she sympathized with my problem of trying to find a runaway nineteen-year-old, she wasn't about to disgrace her vows by turning into a tattletale.

"Can I speak to Sister Paul?" I inquired politely.

She smiled demurely at my naivete. Her face was long and narrow with dark eyes. "I'm afraid not, *senorita*. Sister Paul is engaged in essential medical work. Her life is dedicated to helping farmers in the outlying region. She is not available for impromptu conferences. Perhaps if you come back another time, daughter. I cannot promise more. *Lo siento.*"

I was sorry, too, but I left with a good idea where Sister Paul *could* be found.

I met Aiden in the hotel lobby at a prearranged hour.

"I didn't get much," he relayed first. "There was some sort of accident on the water that night. A fishing boat named *Ten Penney* out of Seattle went missing. Before you know it, the Mexican officials clamped down hard and the incident was hushed up. The officers I spoke with were circumspect. I couldn't pry much out of them. Money wouldn't make them talk, which says something right there when you think about it."

I wondered aloud, "What's a fishing boat from Seattle doing way down here? What does that have to do with Tamar?"

"That's a question that deserves an answer, I think. How did you fare?"

I told him about my meeting with the Reverend Mother.

Aiden glanced at his watch. "We've got time. You up for another trip on bumpy roads?"

"It's what I live for."

We grabbed sandwiches and ate in the truck while Aiden drove. Neither of us had any idea where Sister Paul had witnessed the boat accident, but we possessed solid information about where we might find her. One step at a time, I reminded myself. A case is a marathon, never a sprint.

When we were in the general area, we stopped by a *rancho* to ask where we could find the medical office. In half an hour, Aiden parked the truck in the open dirt yard of a wooden shed with sleepy chickens out front and white crosses painted on the windows. There was no wagon, no *carreta*, but there was a moped parked under a mesquite tree. From *carreta* to moped. Sister Paul was moving up in the world.

Sister Paul was old, frail, and dressed in black. Her face was long with deep lines carved on either side of her nose and at the corners of her mouth. Her eyes were black and empathetic. Her English was better than my school Spanish, and, more importantly, she wanted to talk to us.

"I am glad someone wants to listen," she said. "I witnessed an evil I cannot forget. I have prayed many times someone might believe me."

"You went to the police?"

"*Si*," she told me. "Official men in suits and sunglasses told me not to worry. They knew what happened and it wasn't important. I was to forget everything I saw. They warned if I did not do this, I would be interfering in a federal investigation which involved Mexico and the United States. I cannot imagine what such an investigation contains, but I found it most discouraging."

"We aren't sure, either," Aiden interjected, "but might be the *Ten Penney* was smuggling drugs into Mexico."

Sister Paul rocked back as if struck. "I had no idea. That would explain much of what I saw."

"Can you please tell us what you witnessed that night?" I asked.

"I can do more than that. I will show you where it happened. It's not far."

She locked up the medical center and kicked started her moped. The sun was sinking fast. We followed her bouncing taillight until we reached a secluded cove with a crescent beach of intermixed sand drifts, tufts of dry salt grass, and tiny sand crabs. There were cliffs and heaps of boulders that extended out from either side of the beach, funneling the seawater landward. The waves crashed with recurring booms. It was night, and a wide canopy of crystalline stars arched over our heads.

I used to work with a revenue agent who dealt with interdicted shipments of molasses during Prohibition. He told me boat runners preferred a landing where the boat could slip in fast, deposit its cargo—usually by throwing it over the side in reinforced barrels—and slip out. A place like this was perfect for smuggling, I thought.

Sister Paul showed us the stone well. From here we had a clear view of the beach, the open sea, and a rising hill to the north topped with scattered patches of scrub brush. A copse of trees grew thick around the well, which would obscure the silhouette of anyone standing there. It was an excellent observation post.

"I was on my way to the convent when I stopped to water Anselmo. That's my donkey. It was a tranquil night. Moonless, with few stars. No sound save the beach combers and insects singing in the tall grass. Like tonight. I was preparing to leave when a light flashed on top of that hill. Out on the black water another light responded. I believe it was a code because the outline of a wide, low fishing boat approached the beach. It was blacked out like during the war, its motor barely turning over."

"Where did it beach?"

Sister Paul shook her head. "There was a current and the tide was running out. The pilot had difficulty navigating past the rocks. He threw out an anchor and climbed down, trailing fishnets into the breaking seawater. The water was waist deep. He carried a container the size of a coffee can—perhaps it was so. It was at this time another man quit the high scrub and came down to wait on the beach to receive him. I could not hear what they said, but everything about this rendezvous was a bad omen." She touched her breast with her palm. "I felt it here. I cannot explain, but the man waiting on the beach was an evil man. In my heart I was sure of this. My suspicions were proven correct. He took something from his jacket and there was a spark of gunfire. The fisherman fell backwards, dead. The waves rolled his lifeless body back and forth." She crossed herself.

Aiden descended to the saltwater's edge and played his flashlight along the incoming combers. I watched him and turned back to Sister Paul.

"What happened after that?"

"A most unexpected event. A third figure crept down the hill. It was a young girl. I clearly saw her face and dark hair. She accepted the coffee can while her accomplice fastened a rope around the dead man and hauled him aboard the fishing vessel. Then he started the motor and backed the boat out of the cove while the girl watched."

Sister Paul's voice shook with her next words. "I saw a flare of red and yellow and heard a crack of thunder. It rolled across the water. A bloom of fire climbed high into the night. After many minutes the killer returned. He had swum to safety with a life preserver after destroying the boat. He and the girl walked to a hidden car. They drove away, and I was left shaken to my bones."

Aiden continued to poke around the beach and boulders using his flashlight and a piece of driftwood he'd found.

"You told the police all this?"

"On my soul. They informed me I was mistaken. They insisted my claims were misdirected and illusory. But I frequent this area. I talk to the farmers. One told me he saw a police boat anchored here. A diver worked over the side while other men looked on. They were searching for something at the bottom of the ocean."

"Did they find anything?"

She pursed her lips. "My friend didn't think so. They packed up and left."

Aiden trudged back up the steep rise to join us. "I got the gist of her story and thought I'd scratch around," he explained. "There's all kinds of trash on the beach. I found this." He held out a white plank a foot long. "It could be part of a fishing boat, or something else altogether."

I took the plank of wood and examined it. "I doubt we'll discover anything of real value. Whatever the killers and the authorities wanted hidden will remain hidden. Even the witnesses."

"*Sí*," Sister Paul agreed with a ponderous sigh, "even me."

She turned to stare at the black water, her body leaning forward as if straining to find something lost and out of reach.

"Even me."

I t grew late on us. Aiden suggested we not try the return drive to Rosarito in the dark on that dangerous road. We signed for separate rooms. Afterwards, I ensconced myself in a phone booth and made a long-distance call to my answering service, but the operator never got through. Aiden had better luck reaching Eddie, but Eddie had no relevant news other than he was swallowing handfuls of aspirin for his foot pain.

Aiden and I decided to have a nightcap. I looped my arm through his and we went inside the brightly lit restaurant attached to the hotel. A guitarist dressed in a blue guayabera played guitar while a lithe Mexican woman in a striking red dress danced, her arms raised. I watched, chin cupped in hand.

"You look lost," Aiden observed.

"I'm wondering if Tamar was the girl on the beach."

"What if it was?"

"Doesn't change anything. I need to find her, regardless. I have more questions than answers, though. Was that Emil Staaken with her? Why did he kill the courier? I know their next stop was Mexicali. Did they cross the border into the States from there?"

"What was in that coffee can?" Aiden said. "That's what I want to know, but I guess we have a notion about that." He sipped his cold Mexican beer. "Artie made it clear I'm here for muscle, not to think. I always let others do the thinking, anyway. Safer that way. When something goes wrong, they get all the blame."

He put the bottle down, somber. "However, if you want my opinion, Tamar and Staaken are playing out their B-movie version of Bonnie and Clyde. She wouldn't be the first girl to go wrong. Staaken sounds like bad news no matter how you cut it."

"I've considered that possibility." I chewed my bottom lip. "A lot of things don't add up. At least I know she's alive. Or was, four months ago."

"Liable to be a dangerous game with Staaken hanging around," Aiden pointed out.

"It's dangerous either way." I stifled a yawn. "I'm beat, Aiden. Thanks for the drink."

"My pleasure. I like to buy drinks for a lady who can knock me out."

He saw me to the door of my room and we said our goodnights. I brushed my teeth, climbed into bed, and fell asleep.

With the morning sun peeking through a window, I dressed and went downstairs. I tried to put a call through to Sacramento. Then I tried a number I knew in Pasadena and got a connection.

"Hello." Sleepy male voice.

"That you, Lasker?"

"Pixie, you old so and so. How've you been?"

"Thought I'd throw a bit of work your way if you think you can stay out of jail long enough."

Nate Lasker was our second-story man and one of the best B&E men around. We used him for delicate jobs that demanded a bit of finesse, like opening a safe or filching records of illegal tax filings. I didn't need him for that, but he was in Pasadena which was good enough.

"I've got nothing going on," Lasker said. "What do you need?"

"Juanita Drexford, about twenty years old. Married some guy named Thomas Neff." I gave him their address. "I want you to find everything you can on the woman." I told him what I knew from my interview with Juanita which, when you got right down to it, wasn't much.

"Four course meal?"

"Everything. What's her family background. Are they reasonably happy. Are they having money problems. Is there anything going on in their lives that someone could use against them. Chinks in the armor, that sort of thing. The usual drill."

"I'll start on it today."

"And don't hurt nobody."

"Aw, come on, Pix, that was five years ago. You weren't with Valkyrie then."

"One more thing. I'm in Tijuana and I can't get through to Sacramento. Can you call them and let them know I'm moving on to Nogales? In case I drop off the face of the earth."

"You going dark?"

"Yeah. I think so."

"Sounds dangerous."

"Yeah."

"All right. I'll start right away on this. Take care, Pixie."

"You're a champ, Lasker. So long."

I met Aiden for breakfast. He was unusually quiet. We drove back to Tijuana to visit Eddie. When we went up to Eddie's room he said, "Aiden, I got a telegram from Arcadia while you were gone. They have a job for us in Atlanta. We have to get moving."

Aiden jerked a disappointed grin my way. "So much for inter-service rivalry. It was nice while it lasted."

"I'm sorry you have to go," I told him.

"I'm glad to get away from Mexico." Eddie cocked his head at me from the bed. "Dames like you should come with a light and siren."

"I'm going to miss you, too, Eddie." He grinned. At least he was on the mend.

"I'll help you pack the truck," Aiden offered.

"Thank you."

When I was ready to leave, Eddie came down to see me off, too, which I thought a bit odd. He and Aiden had a hurried conference. Aiden faced me. "You have a gun?"

Before I could answer he slipped something small and heavy into my purse. "Take this," he cautioned. "You was a cop so I guess you know how it works. It's a single-shot .45-caliber Liberator. It's not a lot of gun, but, lady, you're sure as hell a lot of woman."

I pulled open the purse to inspect the squat, ugly gun. It resembled a metal toad.

Eddie said his goodbyes and left us some privacy. Aiden cleared his throat. "I'd like to see you again sometime."

"I'm in the book."

"I mean I'd like to take you out to dinner."

I put my hand on his arm. "I'd like that, too, Aiden. Call me anytime. I mean it. Hey, can I ask a personal question?"

"Fire away."

"Are you F.B.I. or some kind of government agent?"

He laughed shortly. "What makes you say that?"

"Last night at the well you mentioned you got the gist of what we were saying, but there's no way you heard Sister Paul from way down there on the beach. Not with those heavy rollers. You already knew what happened and didn't need to listen to her story. Then this morning you hand me a FP-45 Liberator used by the resistance during the war. That's enough to make a girl stop and think."

"F.B.I. ain't got jurisdiction in foreign countries," Aiden said flat.

"They do if they're following up a domestic case that moved to another country, or vice versa, and are working with the host government. French heroin coming through Mexico into the States fits that scenario like a glove."

He smiled wryly. "I ain't no government man. Me, I got scruples."

Without further ado he opened the truck door and helped me climb in. He banged the door shut.

"It's a three-hour drive to Mexicali," he spoke through the open window. "Don't push it. Watch the water in your radiator when you go through the desert. I don't know how you're going to pick up their trail. Maybe you'll get lucky. You always seem to come out on top."

"I'll be careful."

"Stay safe, Pixie."

I felt as if I was being briefed for a mission. Only I didn't know what the mission was.

"You take care of yourself, too, Aiden. And, please, do call me. So long."

I hit the starter and the engine grumbled. I put the truck in gear and backed out of the hotel parking lot. I watched Aiden's tall frame dwindle in my rearview mirror. I liked him. He seemed like a good guy.

But, like Pola Goddard, he was a terrible liar.

PART THREE
MOON PLANE

NINE

FIELDS OF COTTON LINED THE single-lane road leading to Mexicali. I found a clean hotel not too far from the border station. I booked a room for the night and went to work tracing the cold tracks of Tamar through streets lined with souvenir shops, food stands, dingy night clubs, and raucous, smoky dives with dirt floors and stinking of cheap whiskey.

First places I checked were the hotels, then the bus terminal, following up with car rentals. I'd realized Staaken had a habit of changing transportation whenever he was in a new place. I wasted most of the morning and afternoon on this Sisyphean labor before calling it quits. I stopped under a mesquite tree in a stone plaza to remove my shoes and massage my sore feet. I'd need Patton's army to canvass Mexicali, not to mention that most cars around here were rented out of a parking lot or a private garage which didn't bother keeping records or advertising themselves. It was a lost cause.

I had to be smarter than this. No sense poking around the border station, either. People crossed back and forth between Mexico and the United States whenever they wanted. There were no records kept there —at least, not the kind I wanted.

All I knew was Tamar's next destination: Nogales. It was hard to believe they drove all the way to Nogales, though. It wasn't a straight shot from Mexicali, even if they crossed the border here and stuck to highways inside the United States. If they made the trip inside Mexico, they would have to detour south to Caborca and wend their way northeast on very suspect roads. A trip like that could take days, depending how sturdy your vehicle was, and how ready your access to food, oil, water, and other supplies was.

Staaken didn't strike me as the stupid type. I couldn't make myself believe he would risk a trip like that. Not with that coffee can in his possession. He'd killed for it. Whatever was inside had to be compromising as hell. He'd want to travel safely, but fast.

That was the key. Safe but fast. Forget Mexicana Airline or any high-profile carrier. Staaken wouldn't risk losing his coffee can (with the heroin inside) passing through customs. He would want to protect the product.

I had the glimmer of an idea how he could accomplish that and reach Nogales.

I hit the charter companies and I even called one or two back in Tijuana. Some independent airlines were not above taking on shady business dealings long as they didn't risk losing their pilot's license. I was looking for an operation that existed on the back burner, so to speak. Not entirely honest, but not entirely crooked. An airline, or better yet a freelance pilot, who wasn't squeamish if the pay was commensurate to the risk.

I knew I was getting close when I found Garza Air, a fly-by-night outfit run by two brothers. They took my measure over coffee and whiskey and found me to be as greedy and crooked as they were. I wasn't playing a role. I wanted to get to Nogales and do it black. Which is to say, without filing an official flight plan or any record of manifest.

In an airless office with pornographic pinups plastering the wall and filthy fly tape flapping from a metal fan, we talked business.

"We freight everything," Jorge Garza, the oldest brother, said. He had longish black hair with comb marks in it and a white scar across his broken nose and was dressed in oil-stained coveralls. "Gold, spices, liquor, all kinds of contraband. We've flown chemicals, and stolen jewelry, if the price is right."

The other man, Silverio Garza, was heavy around the waist and taciturn. "You tell us what you want moved," he prompted, "and we will tell you the cost."

It had taken no little effort to reach this point in our conversation. These weren't the type of businessmen who opened up to anyone off the street. This was Mexico. You had to build slow and respect their culture. These men were hard professionals. They didn't do anything half-ass.

Jorge tossed off his coffee and poured another before splashing it with whiskey. "We've worked for special interests on both sides of the border. Our clients insist on secrecy and dependability. When they want that kind of service they come to us."

"What kind of special interests?"

"Men who, shall we say, live outside the lawful bounds of society."

"The underworld."

"I didn't say that."

Silverio nibbled a slice of salami. "People who want discreet professionalism always come to us."

I thought these two were overselling themselves, but I sensed I had something ineluctable I could work with. "I'll lay it on the line," I began. "I'm looking for someone, actually two someones, who may have used your services in the past. I will pay handsomely if you help me find them."

Jorge pulled his earlobe and grimaced. He had a gold tooth in front. "We never give out the names of our clients," he said. "I am sure you can appreciate that. You must understand our position. On the other hand, if you tell us what these people wanted transported, we may be able to guide you to the right price."

"What he's saying," Silverio broke in, "is we aren't going to commit to a goddamn thing until we have proof positive of your intent, and the money safely deposited in a bank."

"I understand. That's exactly what I am looking for. All right. It was two people. A man and a young woman." I described Staaken and Tamar. I passed them my photograph of Tamar. Jorge's eyes clouded when he looked at the dog-eared photograph. He recognized her.

"They drove from Rosarito to Mexicali in a green 1946 Ford with a white fender," I elaborated. "They wanted to get to Nogales with as much security as humanly possible. That's why I think they might have chartered a private plane."

"What were they carrying?"

"Only themselves." Staaken would never tell anyone he was smuggling heroin. He wouldn't go to all this trouble to risk a bullet in the brain and his treasure stolen.

The brothers looked at one another. Jorge gave a guarded shrug.

The younger pilot, Silverio, put a match to a maduro cigar. It was a long production and he made quite a show of it. "We can't help you," he said at last. "Not because we don't want to, you understand. We never transport human cargo. We had. . .an incident. Since that time, Jorge and I avoid taking passengers."

"It's one of our Hard Rules," Jorge broke in. "We're not talking white slavery, which pays extraordinarily well. We don't do that anyway. But regular passengers are quite out of the question. Dealing with human beings as cargo is a whole 'nother variable and a huge complication. I'm sorry, but like my brother said, we can't help you."

He rose, followed by Silverio. The meeting was concluded.

"I'm sorry to hear you say that," I said. "I hoped you gentlemen could help me. I guess I've hit a dead end. You were the last names on my list. Thank you, anyway. I'm sorry I took up your time. I'll see myself out."

I was laying it on thick as wax. *Poor little me. If only somebody in this macho country would take pity on me. I'm only a helpless girl.*

"Wait a moment," Jorge said, coming forward. "You said two people?"

I dared not breathe. He raised his eyebrows in inquiry.

"Yes, a man and a young woman. This is the girl." I showed them Tamar's photograph once more.

Jorge turned to Silverio, pulling his earlobe so hard it reddened. "What do you say?"

Silverio smoothed his moustache with his fingertips. "If it's the same couple. Girl matches the photograph. Their car checks out. Might be who this young lady is looking for."

Jorge beamed at me. "We've decided you are in luck. These two came to us but we turned them down." He shook his head regretfully. "We don't move human cargo. Too risky."

My mouth was dry. "I'm open to suggestions. Naturally, I am willing to pay handsomely for your expertise regarding this matter."

"Our professional advice comes at a premium."

"Would one hundred American dollars suffice?"

"We are a small and insignificant outfit, *senorita*. We must make bank when the opportunity arises."

"One hundred fifty."

"Two hundred twenty-five. Cash."

"Two hundred."

"That is acceptable."

The money exchanged hands. Jorge folded the bills in a Bible and placed it in a desk drawer.

"We know someone," he said tentatively. "We sent these two people you're looking for with a. . .let's call it a letter of introduction. Perhaps they found what they wanted there. Perhaps not. I cannot say because I do not know. When they left I no longer had any business with them."

"What's the name of this pilot?"

Silverio spoke. "That person is known around here as the Wasp."

My "letter of introduction" was a silver dollar sawn in half. Painted black on one side, yellow the other. The Wasp, whoever they were, only accepted business through word of mouth. The introduction was the presentation of this peculiar half coin. How the Garza brothers came by it I daren't ask, but I felt I'd come one step closer to finding Tamar.

I got in my truck and drove. The airdrome wasn't easy to find and my directions weren't the best. I knew I had the right place when I saw an ungainly black plane with a cartoon black and yellow wasp painted on its nose. It was a monoplane, chocked and lashed down. There was a Quonset hut with open windows to battle against the enervating heat. A limp windsock and a dirt runway grated out of the hard pan desert completed the basic, and to my eyes barely functional, airdrome.

The plane looked rough and hardly what I'd consider aerodynamic. I'd never seen anything like it. The stubby wings supported by struts had a reverse taper. The wheels were faired. It was held together with baling wire and house glue, its tires were balding, its cabin windows caked with layers of dust. The stubby fuselage joined with plates and brackets gave the impression it could collapse without warning. The three-bladed prop didn't look like it could pull a balsa plane through a summer zephyr.

But when I got close, I found looks were deceiving. The air-cooled radial engine inside the cowling was pristine. The ailerons were in smooth working order and there wasn't a single spot of oil on the ground beneath the plane. Even the tires were in solid shape, what I'd taken for balding rubber was caked-on mud and clay from an earlier expedition. As a whole the aircraft remained an ungainly sight. It was never going to be a beautiful machine, but maybe it could fly after all.

"Fuck do you want here?"

I turned. A stout woman dressed in a gored skirt and gabardine jacket occupied the doorway of the Quonset hut, fists on hips.

"I brought you this." I held out my palm holding the half coin.

She gave no reaction. "Come inside. We'll talk." She melted away into the interior shadows of the Quonset hut.

I girded my loins and followed. I had found the Wasp.

TEN

S HE KEPT AN IMPROVISED OFFICE in back of the Quonset hut. A canvas hanging from the metal rafters blocked off an iron cot with a wooden footlocker. Everything was neat and orderly. The solid floor and metal furniture were spotless. Clothes, washed and ironed, hung inside a cedar closet with military precision. She had a Hammarlund short wave Super-Pro radio for military and commercial use. A record player on a windowsill played a violin concerto by Shostakovich while a black Abyssinian cat washed its paws and eyed me speculatively.

"Grab a seat," the pilot directed. She had a hard Eastern European accent. I thought it might be Russian.

I took a seat on a metal folding chair in front of a surplus Army desk. A wooden tray from a Scrabble game served as the base for her nameplate. The letters were arranged to read: SASKA PINE.

The pilot—Saska—was a heavy woman with a broad, red-cheeked face. Freckles sprinkled her nose. Her short red hair was graying in patches, and when she stared at you her no-nonsense electric blue eyes x-rayed the hidden frontiers of your soul, stripping you bare.

She opened a glass cabinet and took out a bottle of Russian vodka and two shot glasses. The glasses could have been cleaner, but I didn't say anything. She splashed vodka into each and finished by sprinkling a pinch of black pepper into them.

"*Vashe zrodovie.*" She knocked her drink back in one toss and slammed the glass down.

"To your health," I repeated. The vodka was raw with fusel oil. It burned like lava going down and I coughed, eyes watering.

While I regained my composure, I looked at the framed pictures on the corrugated walls around us. They were groups of women in flying gear standing on a tarmac or sitting at the controls of B-26 Marauders and P-51 Mustangs. Some played cards or were drinking and dancing. Many were single photographs of female pilots long dead but never forgotten.

By their uniforms I recognized them as Women Airforce Service Pilots who flew American military aircraft during the war—WASPs.

Saska marked my curiosity. "I was a service pilot with the U.S. Army Air Force. We only flew non-combat missions, but we did it all. Ferrying aircraft from base to base or to staging points and task forces assembling for invasion. Training other female pilots. Calculating flight plans and stage times. Before the war I had over five hundred flying hours and a two hundred horsepower engine rating. I'd been flying since I was fifteen, you see. Even though I was Russian I was married to an American businessman, Oscar Pine. I got accepted into the new program without too much trouble."

"What happened to your husband?"

"Oscar was helping expedite the Lend Lease program. He was killed in the London Blitz. I stayed with my flying group. I had nowhere else to go. No children. No family. I flew everything they gave me—if it could get off the ground, I flew it. I worked with radar-controlled targets, towing them behind my plane so naval guns could have a crack at them. When the war ended, I was able to pilot a jet-propelled plane. We were testing hydraulics on the new landing gear and no one else was qualified at the time."

Her smile was pensive. "That was a lovely, marvelous time of war. Believe me when I say war can be beautiful. I don't mean the savage horrors. Horror is only horror and has no other permutation. There is no poetry in mechanized death. The insensate statistics of wiping whole populations off the map holds no pleasure for me. But I loved watching a sunrise from ten thousand feet. The horizon of the earth flaming red and pink and gold. I could look out my cockpit and from the contrails of the other planes I knew at what altitude they flew. Or standing on an airfield at dusk watching a fleet of B-17s come in from the factories, all of them flown by women. Watching them find the searchlights and circling low enough to touchdown, one by one, and taxi like ducks to park wingtip to wingtip. The cough and splutter of the engines when they switched off. A girl swinging out of the bottom hatch with her kit slung over her shoulder and signing up for another flight the next morning. It was a good and happy time, but like all good times it won't come back so I am left with memories, and Omicron, my cat."

She poured herself another vodka. I placed my hand over my glass. "No, thank you."

She drank off the vodka and slammed the glass down. "Where did you learn Russian?" she asked.

"My grandmother was born in Albania."

"You should watch that kind of thing. Dangerous these days."

"We're in Mexico."

"Even so." Without warning she slapped her hands together and held out them out. "*Documenty.*"

I handed her my identification and investigator license. She barely glanced at them before she tossed them back at me, and steepled her fingers under her chin. Her eyes narrowed. "What do you want here? What is your business?"

I took my creased photograph of Tamar and slid it across the desk. "I'm looking for this girl. She came through Mexico accompanied by a man named Emil Staaken. He's a piece of work. They wanted to get across the border by way of Nogales. I don't think they drove or used any public transportation, so I started hitting the airfields and private planes. You're my last stop."

Saska held Tamar's picture in both her hands. She tapped it thoughtfully. "Who is this girl to you?"

I saw no reason to lie. "Her name is Tamar Bandesi. She's going to inherit a lot of money one day. I must find her and bring her home."

"If she's going to inherit money then why is she on the run?"

"That's a question I'd like her to answer."

"How much money?"

"Millions."

The pilot plopped her boots up on the edge of her desk. "Let's say I saw these two. And, for the sake of argument, listened to what they proposed. To further this rather useless thought experiment which has no basis in fact, let's pretend I took the job. What do you mean to do about it?"

Before I could answer her hand dropped. When it came up, she was holding a .45 Webley Service Revolver. Its barrel pointed straight at me.

"I warn you I am not without protection," Saska said.

My stomach crawled. "My quarrel, if I have one, is not with you, Saska. I'm looking for Tamar Bandesi. She is my first and only concern. I certainly have no intention of injuring the one person who can help me find her."

"Is that so." The gun barrel didn't waver.

"Put the gun away."

A slight wind billowed the gauzy white curtains. Outside, the vast desert was cooling.

The pilot's face was hard. "I am not sure I should trust you."

"Stop being stupid. Put that gun down and let's talk business. Or you can take this foolish fucking half coin and shove it. I don't care either way."

Saska frowned. She lowered her pistol.

"Either you are very brave or an unconscionable fool," she said.

"Why can't I be both? Besides, that's not the first gun I've had pointed at me. That sort of thing loses its potency after a while. Are you ready to talk? If not, I'm wasting my time."

Her eyes narrowed again. "You are on a mission. Nothing can deter you."

"If you want to couch it that way."

"That is how I classify it. I have met many professionals over the course of my career. Worked with them. Killed one or two from time to time. Dedication like yours stems from a deep purpose, but that purpose is not always noble. It can and often does lead to mania." She x-rayed me with those remarkable eyes once more. "I ask you again. Who is this Tamar to you?"

The question put me back on my heels. "I'm not sure what you mean."

"Is this a private vendetta?"

She had hit too close to the mark. "It's not a vendetta. I want to find Tamar because I think she's in trouble and she reminds me of someone I knew long ago."

"Yourself."

God, what marksmanship this woman exhibited.

"I want you to take me where they went and by the same route. It's the only way I can make up time on their trail. The more I learn about how they travel and where, the more I learn about them and how they think. I'm hoping that will give me a tactical advantage when I confront them."

"To get to Tamar you think you may have to go through this Emil Staaken?"

"I wouldn't be at all surprised."

"I can tell you he is not an easy man to deal with. He will not walk away without a fight, and he will not stand idly by while you abscond with this Tamar."

"No. I expect he won't."

"You will have to kill him."

"I hope it doesn't come to that. Perhaps I can find another way."

"You will have to kill him," she repeated.

"If he stands in the way or makes trouble, I will do whatever is necessary to get Tamar away from him."

"What if Tamar decides she doesn't want to go with you? What then?"

"I'll cross that bridge when I come to it."

"Do you want another drink?" Her hand moved for the bottle.

"No. I want to talk."

Saska leaned forward and clasped her hands on top of her desk. Her demeanor was stern. "You will listen to me, private investigator. I do jobs. Jobs for people who don't accept the cost of failure. I have a repu-tation to uphold. The kind of reputation that must be protected or I could lose my life. I don't want to be shot in the head and dumped in a hole in the desert. Understand?"

"Sure. You're a bootlegger. You fly contraband across the border. Both ways if I don't miss my guess. You live a solitary life in the middle of nowhere remembering your glory days as a pilot in the Army. That's the reason behind the secret squirrel bullshit with the coin. You want to relive that great adventure when you were young and vigorous and part of something bigger than yourself, something so big it could swallow you whole and the world would never know you disappeared. But there you were standing against it, two-fisted and ready to brawl. I understand. Hell, we all get old. No one is immune to that. I used to be on the police force in Santa Monica. Some days I thought the crooks were the only good guys around. I've seen this setup before. I don't care what you smuggle in that clapped-out Tinker Toy parked outside. I have one interest and that's finding the girl. I don't care about any other *maskirovka* you're running. It's not my business. *Mnye vsyo ravno.* Now, I'm ready for that drink. Pour us another one and answer my question. Will you help me, or not?"

Her hard demeanor thawed. A reluctant grin appeared, then a genuine smile which warmed over time. "*Xoroso.* I'm starting to like you, private investigator."

"I was hoping to make an impression. Thought I'd have to start busting up furniture to get through to you."

She poured the vodka and pushed the glass across the table. "Not many do since the war ended. The world disappoints me more every day. What is left but to drink? Until a new purpose enters one's life. Today, I believe that purpose is you."

With a wolfish grin Saska raised her glass in a toast, then drained it.

"I will work with you," she said.

～

Saska put a pot of *zharkoye* on a gas stove. While the thick stew bubbled she sliced black bread and laid out a plate of fresh butter and bowls of pickles, salted herring, and chives.

"I confess I thought things would be different after the war." She lifted the serrated bread knife. A cigarette smoldered in the corner of her mouth. "I thought society would change for the better. We had to adapt while the globe chewed itself inside out, didn't we? But when the war concluded everyone went back to their respective corners. I hoped I would keep flying for the Army. One morning my commander called me into his office. He didn't beat around the bush, let me have it right in the gut. I got the feeling he wasn't happy about the new directives coming down from Washington. He was losing a lot of good fliers."

She stirred the stew. Steam broke over her face. "*Da*, during the war I felt I was part of something. I *was* part of something. I tried to pretend we were chosen solely because of our talent. Long story short I got put out to pasture. We all did. All the women, everywhere. The skilled factory workers, the nurses. But for that brief time, a handful of short years, we were equal. Or as equal as we were ever allowed to become."

She puffed her cigarette, tapped the ash into an empty tin can. Her eyes were hazy with remembrance. "I flew *jets*. They wouldn't let just any male pilot do that. Some mornings I'd stride out on the cold tarmac while the eastern sky was pink and yellow and the male pilots gathered to watch me crawl into the cockpit of a B-29 Superfortress. The men didn't trust that plane. They said it was too dangerous to fly. The generals wanted to show them if a woman could pilot the damn thing they could, too."

I helped her lay bowls and silverware on the table. "There's no finer way to shame a man than to show him a woman isn't afraid to do the job he's afraid to do. After I landed and taxied up to them, those pilots had no qualms about climbing into a Superfortress and going to bomb Japan. Like I said, I even flew *jets. Bozhe moi*. How can I describe in words what that was like? Lighting that engine and feeling that sharp kick in my back. I was only wringing them out a bit—testing landing gear, that sort of thing. Nothing too dangerous. But I was able to slap my ass in the pilot's seat because the men on the ground were too green."

Her voice was small and thin. Barely above a whisper. "It was a great and beautiful time to be alive."

She suddenly remembered where she was and pointed her spoon at me. "That's no Tinker Toy. It's a Westland Lysander. They were used for top-secret missions overseas. They became obsolete after the war. A few of us found other uses for them. It's *not* a Tinker Toy."

"The stew is bubbling over."

She swore in Russian and turned the gas ring down. We sat to a hastily drawn meal washed down with dry red wine.

"My point being," Saska said, regaining her thread of thought as she buttered a slice of black bread, "I know the pair you are talking about. The man I quite liked. Oh, I marked him as a killer the moment I laid eyes on him, but even a killer can have positive qualities. He was well-spoken and possessed manners which far too many men have forgotten since the war ended. The girl. . .I did not like. She was withdrawn and spoke little. Kept her thoughts to herself. One of those women who are always quiet, but wounds."

Always quiet, but wounds.

"She didn't have an easy background." I crumbled bread over my stew.

"The girl, or you?"

I fidgeted. Damn her eyes anyway.

Saska drank wine and resumed spooning *zharkoye* into her mouth. "I thought she was a lamprey."

"What do you mean?"

"Those parasitic fish that attach themselves to bigger fish." She sprinkled chives over her stew. "It was hard to pick out the relationship between the two. I thought maybe she loved him, and he not so much. But I'm an old woman and too often mistaken about things like that."

"I must find them."

She stared across the table. "So you said."

"I'll keep saying it until you believe me."

Saska wiped her mouth with a napkin and fished out a cigarette. She struck a match and lit it. A shadow of doubt cleaved with caution flitted behind her eyes. "All right. Let's discuss the business at hand. You want to go to Nogales? I can take you to Nogales."

"Tonight?"

"Nogales is easy. We fly over the desert. There's nothing down below so it's a safe run. I know a place to put down outside Nogales this side of the border. You won't have to walk far."

"That sounds all right." I wasn't looking forward to walking through the desert at night.

Saska smoked. Her eyes narrowed to slits. "Gonna cost you a lot."

We arrived at a price. Fifteen hundred dollars. That nearly wiped out my current cash reserve. But I kept thinking about that shadow flickering in her eyes.

"Saska, where did you take Staaken and Tamar?"

"You said you wanted to go to Nogales."

"Where did you take *them*?"

"Well, it sure as hell wasn't Nogales." Omicron jumped into her lap and she stroked him head to tail. He purred.

"Can you tell me where?"

She looked at me. "It was Tucson."

"So you did fly them across the border."

"You're a detective after all." Her face lit up. "How'd you catch on?"

"If going to Nogales involved flying across an empty desert to land on this side of the border, they wouldn't need someone with your expertise. Anyone with a Piper Cub could do that. But if that's a Westland Lysander you've got that means it's what used to be called a moon plane, one of the special aircraft the British used to put agents down in occupied countries. Tamar and Emil wouldn't need a plane like that to reach Nogales. But to cross the border they would need the Wasp. That's you."

Saska stubbed out her cigarette. "Yes. They would need the Wasp."

"How hard is it to fly across the border to Tucson?"

"Not difficult. But not easy, either."

"Does your plane have that range?"

She simpered. "Oh, yes, and much more."

"Have you made that flight before?"

She shrugged. "Across the border? Now and then on special business. You know how it is."

"No, I don't. But Tucson is where I want to go. I want you to put me down in the same place you left them."

"I don't know where they went after I saw them off. They never told me and I didn't ask. There were lights glittering on the horizon. I told them it was Tucson, which it was. I can only assume they walked because no one was waiting to pick them up after we set down."

"I'll make my way. Tucson isn't that big and I have sort of an idea how they operate in a city. I think I can find them." I was eager. "When can we leave?"

"Let me do the dishes first. Then I must precheck the plane. You can help with both of those tasks. I use a special route to avoid border radar. I'll kit you out with a canteen and snake bite kit. You will have a hike ahead of you. Do you own a gun? Staaken had a gun."

"I do. Of sorts."

"Better safe than sorry if you run into something, or someone, in the desert you can't handle."

"I'll pay extra for the job."

"Forget it. I'll only charge you for fuel." Holding Omicron, she got up from the cluttered table and I followed suit. "I like you, private investigator. Even if you do have a snide-ass mouth. You brought something back to my world I thought I'd lost. Trust me when I say that's payment enough these days."

Her eyes were hard and frank. "Oh, yes, it is."

ELEVEN

THERE WASN'T A LOT OF room in the Lysander's cabin; no one would be spinning a tarantella in here. The plane had a storage bin in the fuselage where I stowed my overnight case. Anything I needed down the line I could purchase in Tucson.

When we were ready to leave Saska rolled out a map of the Sonoran Desert.

"We don't have to worry about the American Pinetree Line of radar defense stations down through here," she said, running her finger along the border. "The United States Air Force worries what comes flying over the North Pole and through Canadian airspace. Soviets aren't out to bomb Washington, D.C. from Mexico. Though I daresay they may wish to one day. However, there are radar spots from American commercial airports we'd do well to avoid. I've marked them down here. I can weave the Lysander along between them and dip through this valley. There's an elevation rise to the north to mask our signature. Then we jink south before swinging back north for the final run in."

She stood looking at the map, arms folded. "You were right to catch on that those two weren't interested in Nogales. We can't fly over the city because of radar, and we won't have filed a flight plan. Before you know it, they'll scramble a jet to force us down, but if we continue a north-northeast course we can thread the line between Sells, Arizona and Nogales for the final leg to Tucson. There's an ancient salt flat west of Tucson. Here. Nice, level terrain. I'll put you down there. You'll have a five- or six-mile hike to the highway where you can hitch a ride."

She folded her map. "The moon tonight waxes gibbous. There'll be plenty of light for you to make your way and for me to see the landmarks I need to hit. That works both ways, of course. Fortunately, most of our journey is over barren desert. No one will spot us."

"What if we have an emergency and need to put down?"

"Then we're fucked." Saska arched an eyebrow. "Losing your nerve, private investigator? You can always back out."

I shook my head, temporizing. I'd pushed things and acted tougher than I felt. I'd never done anything like this and wasn't sure I wanted to try the first time. But I had no other choice.

"Let's get going before I do lose my nerve."

While she finished her pre-flight check I filled a thermos with coffee. This small chore did not take my mind off what was looming ahead. I was scared silly. I tried not to think of all the things that could go wrong and concentrate on what could go right. There weren't many points in that column, but Tamar had made this trip. If she could do it so could I. That's what I kept telling myself, anyway. It didn't do much to alleviate my apprehension.

I met Saska outside the Quonset hut. She was enjoying a last cigarette. "Aren't you going to lock up?" I asked.

She cast a side glance at me and laughed under her breath. It wasn't a good laugh. It was the sound you hear when the executioner trips the gallows. "No one around here is that stupid."

Saska was dressed in khaki flight coveralls, goggles, warm fur-lined boots, and a brown leather flight jacket. Tucked under her arm was a metal clipboard with ruler, maps, extra compass, protractor, and sharpened pencils.

The plane was no longer tied down and the wheel chocks were removed.

"There's a Navajo blanket in the back seat to keep you warm," she said. "Nighttime in the desert is cold. Are you ready?"

I took a deep breath. "I guess so."

"All right then, up you go. Put your left foot on this rung of the ladder and climb. Careful, now."

The Lysander had a fixed ladder on its port side. I scrambled into the back cockpit and strapped myself in while Saska settled her bulk up front with the controls. She closed and locked the canopy overhead. I stared at the short runway. It didn't look like it could adequately handle takeoffs and landings from an airplane, but I didn't mention my concern to Saska. I had to trust she knew what she was doing, and I was frightened enough already.

Saska tested the ailerons and rudder. They were in working order. It was black outside. The sun had set and the moon was rising over sculpted sand dunes and outcrops of bare rock and wraith-like scrub bushes.

Saska started the engine. It fired and caught on the first try. She gunned it, letting it warm up while she checked oil pressure and the RPMs of the prop. The engine was loud and powerful and shook the Lysander's light frame. Revving the engine, Saska kicked the rudder over. We spun 180 degrees and taxied over bumpy earth to the edge of the makeshift runway. She set the wheel brake.

Once more, Saska let the engine idle smoothly while she watched the gauges and made calculations on her clipboard. Then, without warning or a word of caution, she released the brake and gunned the engine hard. I was slammed backwards in my seat. We rocketed down the runway, wheels and undercarriage jolting alarmingly on the uneven surface until it felt like the plane would fly apart and I'd be flung screaming into the desert.

I should not have worried about the length of the runway. Saska didn't need half its run until we were airborne. She banked sharp over the airdrome and climbed to altitude. Saska's cabin was in front of the center of the main wing, and I sat close enough behind we could converse easily.

"How are you doing back there?" she asked once she brought the throttle back and leveled us off.

"My stomach sank to my feet when we took off."

Saska grunted. "The Lysander can jump if she has to." She banked the plane anew until the moon lay off our starboard wing. Its pale cold light broke through the canopy into our cabin. We leveled again. We were on the first leg of our flight path.

"It's that big Bristol Mercury engine," she went on. "Taking off in this thing is like riding an escalator. You ought to see this plane descend and touch down in a field. Like a raven dropping from the sky and alighting on a twig. Most wonderful thing you'll ever see. I'll show you sometime."

"I'll take your word for it."

She laughed and fiddled with her instruments. "How about some of that coffee?"

I passed her the thermos. There were tea sandwiches, too, but I wasn't hungry; my stomach was back at the airdrome. I watched the empty desert crawl beneath us. There were deep shadows and unfamiliar bits of fluted sand and rock and alien black objects which might be cactus or plants or something else altogether. To the south, I made out the winding rill of a dead creek and the salient of a dry wash and then nothing at all but more desert. The lifeless surface of the moon had more landmarks than this grim and inhospitable landscape, made all the stranger by the cold moonlight.

I remembered Saska's remonstration if we had to put down in an emergency. I don't know how long we'd last down there, but it wouldn't be long.

Peering over Saska's shoulder I spotted a black and white photograph. It was a group of women flyers. The photograph was taped to the inside of her canopy.

"Are those WASPs?" I pointed.

"*Nochnye Vedmy*. Night Witches."

"Who?"

"An all-female Russian bomber group from the war. They flew their sorties at night. They'd cut their engines and glide to the bomb's release point. The Germans said the wind whistling through the wing wires sounded like witches' broomsticks. Scared the hell out of the Germans. The pilots didn't carry parachutes. Too much extra weight. They were tough women, let me tell you. You talk about Tinker Toys." She nodded with respect at the photograph. "The flimsy biplane they flew was one. Darkness was their only defense. I keep that picture around to remind me. . . Well, let's say I think of them when I'm on a job. They had it harsh. A lot of them died but a lot of them made it out alive, too. That's worth remembering when you find yourself with your back against the wall."

She said nothing more after that. We flew with only the drone of the engine accompanying our separate thoughts.

"We're coming to the valley I showed you on the map," Saska said a while later, breaking the silence. "Hang on back there. I've got to do some tricky flying."

We lost altitude fast, and before I knew it, we were terrifyingly close to the ground. Rock and sand flashed underneath. We followed the snaking valley until Saska pulled back on the yoke. A long hour passed. I'd started to doze when I awoke with a start. Sometimes I amaze myself with my stupidity.

"If this plane carries one passenger, how were you able to fit both Tamar and Staaken inside?"

"There's a hatch behind your seat. It opens into a space inside the fuselage. The girl rode there. She was the only one who could fit. It couldn't have been comfortable, but that was her problem. She looked a bit creaky when we set down, but she was alive."

I didn't speak. I was learning a lot about what kind of woman Tamar was. She had nerve, and she wasn't afraid to take an awesome risk if need be.

I stared at the back of Saska's head. Tumblers fell into place. We're not talent spotters—while on a case we have plenty of other things on our mind, like solving the problem in front of us and not getting our heads bashed in—but occasionally we run into someone who might be a good fit with our recommendation.

She shook her head when I made the offer. "I like what I do and where I am. I'm not looking for a change."

I left it alone. Time crawled. I remembered the stupid little gun tucked away in my overnight case. Three days ago I'd met Pola Goddard. It felt like three years. I'd learned a lot since that interview with Landers Shavin. I had more questions than answers but that's always a problem at this stage of a case. I still hadn't a clue as to who murdered Tegel, or why.

. . .Arctic expects loyalty.

Once more I got the uneasy feeling I knew something about the phrase, but I couldn't place it. I tried association and word play hoping it might lead me to something concrete, but it always lay just out of reach, and I don't mind saying it left me feeling frustrated.

Saska interrupted my thoughts. "We'll cross the border soon."

I glanced out the canopy. The ground was as featureless as ever to my unpracticed eye, but Saska had kept our airspeed and heading constant while noting the passing time from the plane's chronometer. By this method she could plot our position on her map with reasonable accuracy, even in pitch dark.

When Saska notified me we were over the international border, I looked down. It was something of a defining moment in the context of my case, but I couldn't discern anything in that infinite darkness below. However, after a short while I saw a flickering light. I thought it was a star on the horizon until it split into several stars.

"That's Sells, Arizona," Saska said. She made a slow banking turn to starboard. We were on the last leg of our nocturnal flight.

After another half hour we descended and went through a series of quick turns, this way and that, until I was thoroughly turned around. Up ahead I saw the white salt pan surrounded by low lying hills and saguaro cactus and other desert plants. Saska banked the plane to get a good look at our goal. She leveled off and muttered in Russian under her breath.

"What's wrong?" I asked.

"Must have had severe winds here recently. Sandstorms. Those dunes from the edge have slopped onto the salt pan. We better circle a few times so I can find a safe area between them to set down."

The salt pan looked plenty large to me. It was an oblong rectangle three hundred yards wide and twice as long. But when Saska throttled the engine back and we came over low I saw what she meant. A series of sand dunes had crept across the open area leaving little room to touch down safely. If we hit it wrong, they'd tear the undercarriage right off the plane.

Saska put the plane in a broad circular arc, intently studying the ground below.

"All right," she grumbled at last, "we're going in. Hang on. It'll be tight."

She flew away from the landing site and then turned back in. We came in low while she cut the engine until the propeller windmilled in the airstream. She blipped the engine once or twice, so we'd maintain lift, and then the wheels of the undercarriage touched down and I was flung forward in my seat. I gritted my teeth. It felt and sounded like the wheels were coming off the plane as the tail yawed sickeningly, but Saska kicked the rudder hard the other way and we straightened out.

Next thing I knew everything was silent. We were down and safe. It was that fast. The only sound I heard was my heart beating in my chest.

Saska unbuckled her restraints. "Let's get you up and moving,"

She unlocked the canopy and slid it back over our heads. The night sky was thick with stars even though the moon was bright. I climbed down the ladder, glad to have firm earth under my feet. The salt pan was hard as stone. Saska handed me my overnight case and small bag of extra clothes, along with a canteen filled with water. There was a faint glow of light beyond the distant hills.

"That's Tucson," Saska said. "Snake bite kit is in your overnight case. Walk towards that pointed hill to your left. When you top it, you'll see the lights of the city. Keep heading east through the heavy brush and you'll strike the highway. There's not a lot of traffic this time of night but you might get lucky."

"Got it," I said.

"Well, that's all I can do for you here, private investigator. Good luck." She pulled a glove off and held out her hand.

"Thanks, Saska." We shook. "I appreciate all you've done."

"Watch the prop wash when I take off, or you'll get sand and cactus needles in your eyes." She gave a brisk salute. "*Dasvidaniya*."

She climbed into the cockpit and rolled the canopy closed, waving a final time before she started the engine. She ran the engine up high with the brakes on. It was like a banshee screaming in the arid night. When she released the brake, the plane jumped forward and, before you knew it, was climbing high into the air. It circled once and then flew off.

I listened to the drone of the plane's engine until it, too, was gone. It felt like my last contact with civilization. The desert was eerily silent and vast and alien. Almost oppressive. I didn't like the feeling of vulnerability taking hold. I was out here, miles and miles from nowhere. I found myself wishing I was back with Saska, flying to Mexicali.

I took a deep breath and started to walk. My boots scuffed sand. I took a long detour around a deep dry wash. I didn't want to risk traversing it in the dark and breaking my leg. When I came on the figure of a man with his arms raised, I stopped, heart pounding. I closed my eyes and let out a long sigh. It was a saguaro cactus, distorted into human shape by the shadows. I kept on walking, keeping an eye out for snakes.

True to Saska's word I saw the city lights of Tucson when I crested the hill crowned with cholla.

I'm coming for you, Tamar, I thought. *Damn you for making me do this. But I'm coming after you.*

I started down the far side of the hill, slipping and sliding through loose sand and shale, cutting my hand on some of the rock. When I hit the highway, a pair of yellow headlights shone in the far distance. I hooked my thumb. A truck hauling vegetables and driven by a young skinny Mexican man stopped for me, engine idling.

He leaned his head out the window and spat. "Where you headed, *senorita*?" He wore a faded blue shirt and chewed the end of a cigar stub.

"Up the road to Tucson."

"I'm not supposed to take passengers. Company policy."

"It's only a couple miles. I'll hoof it."

He took the cigar out of his mouth, looked at the chewed stub. "More than a couple miles. All right, it'll be our little secret. Hop in."

I climbed into a cab stinking of sour sweat and stale cigar smoke. The floor was littered with week-old hamburger wrappers, empty soda bottles, and yellowing newspapers.

He dropped me off on Congress Street. I found a hotel whose claim to fame was Dillinger and his gang were arrested there in 1934. I've stayed in worse places, but this was pleasant enough despite its questionable historical value.

I paid cash for a room and followed the valet. My funds had taken a beating these last couple days. I'd have to wire Pola Goddard for more money tomorrow morning.

While unpacking I came across a half coin from the Wasp. She was telling me I could contact her again if I needed her assistance someday. I stared at the broken coin in my hand. I don't come by friends easily, and when I find one it's a tender feeling. I tucked the coin away for the future. After a much-needed shower, I brushed my teeth and collapsed between the harsh sheets.

In the morning I dressed and descended to the lobby. I had a headache and could have used a lot more sleep. But I had to start working.

My room didn't have a private telephone, but there was a row of phone booths in the lobby. There weren't many people about this early. Only the desk clerk, and what looked like a stone-faced hotel dick perusing the morning newspaper. The headlines were screaming something about North Korea. I placed a call to my answering service. The local operator warned it would take several minutes to route the call and she would ring me back. I used the time to grab a hot cup of coffee and parked myself inside the booth to wait.

The first message I took was from Vera Smalls. I got through and she answered on the first ring.

"Hi, Pixie," she began. "I dug up the dirt you wanted on your Warden Krille."

"I didn't know he was my Warden Krille but go ahead."

I heard papers rustle. Vera always kept copious notes. "There isn't a lot of hard information on him. Warden Kevin Krille was born Valentin Korov, 1893, Leningrad. It was called Saint Petersburg at the time. He emigrated to Paris during the Russian Revolution accompanied by a five-year-old girl believed to be his daughter. Name unknown. That information is lost to time. From here he disappears, thought to be living in Orlando, until he resurfaces in Hollywood under the name Warden Krille."

"I knew he had a daughter, but I thought she was from a woman in Orlando. Wait. You said she's believed to be his daughter. Maybe she's not." It was possible Irene had got the timeline mixed, I thought, though it's not like Krille would have advertised his personal life, from what I knew about the man.

"Either way, not much is known about her. We don't have anything at all on the mother. But the girl must have meant something to Krille since he brought her out of Russia during the Revolution. He was a Bolshevik, but his daughter, if she is his daughter, came first. There's no way of knowing more without asking Krille, and I doubt he'd be forthcoming."

"That's an interview I wouldn't want to conduct," I agreed.

"Where was I? Oh, yes, 1919. That's the year Krille and Tegel start their partnership. Independent contractors farmed out to the studios to solve problems. There's nothing they wouldn't touch. From drugs to union busting, you name it." I could hear the disfavor in her voice. "It's as sordid as you can imagine. That brings us to 1929."

"Okay, let me get this straight. We're in 1929 in Krille's life. That makes the girl what, sixteen or seventeen?"

"Thereabout. If we take the Russian Revolution as a baseline in 1917 when she was five years old."

"All right, let's go with that."

"It's difficult pinning down exact dates," Vera dissembled. "There's no paper trail and what I have is cobbled from faint memory and wild supposition. Nothing that would pass muster in a court of law."

"No need to apologize, Vera. You've given me a lot to think about."

"That's all I've got, Pixie. Then we have Tegel and this young girl who start to carry on, and she becomes pregnant. Mother and baby die in hospital in Orlando. That's when the friendship between Tegel and Krille begins to dissolve. I can keep digging, but to tell the truth I was fortunate to pry what I could from my contacts in Hollywood. There is one last item. I don't know how much credence to give it, but I can throw it out there."

"Throw."

"Krille is no longer associated with any movie studio," Vera continued. "He's considered box office poison. *Persona non grata*. Too many papers and magazines have taken a modern interest in all that sordid business studios would rather keep hidden. That's why he and Tegel were cut loose. We know what happened to Tegel, but with his background a man like Krille is never long without work. He's now an independent problem solver—his *métier*—for a mobbed-up guy in Junction City called Anthony Ardak."

...Arctic expects loyalty.

The name I heard on Tegel's tape machine could have been Ardak.

"Ardak," I repeated. "I came across the name in police reports years ago. He resides in Junction City?"

"Honey, he *owns* Junction City," Vera emphasized. "He has the District Attorney and police rolled up tight. That's for starters. His fingers are in a lot of pies. Some are legitimate businesses, but he's known to front money for illegal drug deals."

"Then it would come as no surprise Krille and Ardak found one another. Real kindred spirits if what you say is true. I'll look into that. Any lead where Krille is now?"

"My contacts couldn't, or wouldn't, tell me. They are relieved he fell from the face of the earth and disappeared. A man like him is dangerous to keep around." The tone of her voice changed to one of deep caution. "But, Pixie..."

"Yeah?"

"Everyone I interviewed swears Krille would never kill Elgin Tegel. Not for any amount of money. These men had their disagreements, and a big falling out over a woman, so they went their separate ways. But they shared a past. Neither would betray the other, and they had plenty of opportunities over the years. Those two are—well, were—old school. *Omerta* and all that shit, even though they're not Italian. Krille has principles, such as they are, and lives by them."

"Maybe he's in Junction City with Ardak."

"Anthony Ardak is smarter than that if you can believe what you read in the newspapers, and I do. Ardak has a public position to maintain. He wouldn't keep a weapon like Krille close at hand. Krille is a double-edged sword, Pixie. He's best kept at a distance. To further mix my metaphors, he's a ticking grenade. You toss him at the opposition when needed. You don't keep him in your back pocket. While I'm on this rant, let me say something else. Don't go poking around at Anthony Ardak. Or Warden Krille. They're not our bailiwick. We're looking for a missing girl and that's all. Remember that."

"Maybe so. But Krille must be somewhere close by so Ardak can contact him. I'm just thinking out loud. I have no reason to meet either man and hope I never do. Anything else?"

"I can keep digging but I'd be stealing your money. The studios don't know where Warden Krille is and they don't want to know. They're not crying over the demise of Tegel, either. They view his death as a way to slam doors on an ugly past."

"Vera, if Krille didn't kill Tegel, do you think a studio, or some aggrieved actor, had him iced? A man with his reputation leaves a lot of bad blood behind."

"No." She was firm. "Krille is alive. A studio would want to slab both men in the scenario you describe. Ticking grenade, remember? Do grenades tick? Anyway, killing Tegel but leaving Krille alive is tantamount to signing a death warrant. Studios chew people up and spit them out, but they're *survivors*. No one in the industry is idiotic enough to put a hit on Tegel, even in Hollywood. That's about as fucking dumb as you can get."

"I guess you're right." I heaved a sigh. "Sounds like you did everything you could, Vera. Submit your expenses to the main office in Sacramento. I'll sign them when I get back."

"Hey, sorry I couldn't be of more help."

"Thanks again for everything. *Ciao.*"

"*Ciao.*"

The next message was from Artie. He wanted me to call at noon his time. That gave me a couple of free hours, so I took a taxi to the Lucky Clover Dress Shop. I pretended I was there to buy a blue jean skirt for my niece. Could they look up this tag number and tell me what she wore so I could purchase another? The lady behind the counter fulfilled my request. She cross-referenced the tag number and said Juanita Drexford bought the skirt last year. I purchased a new one and had them wrapped and left the store wondering why Tamar used the alias of her friend.

When I returned to the hotel I phoned Artie. He had preliminary data on the financial situation of Landers Shavin and Dolores Bandesi, but he wasn't going to give it to me without griping first.

"I spent a weekend scrounging this information," he growled. "I called in markers I've been saving for years. Felt I like I wasted a lot of time, energy, and shoe leather for what little I recovered."

"Aw, poor baby. Does hims want a hug? I know how you work, Artie. You hang around yacht clubs and five-star restaurants drinking champagne while schmoozing with the *hoi polloi*. It's a nice gig for a man who grew up as a Kentucky sharecropper. Now quit bitching and tell me what I want to know."

"Always the same Pixie. Sugar and spice and everything *ice*."

I told him to go do something a good Catholic girl shouldn't say.

He cleared his throat. "All right, here's what I've got so far. As of now Landers Shavin has a net worth of twenty-five million dollars, give or take several hundred thousand lying around. He's diversified in real estate, oil, and blue-chip stocks. He owns a couple of downtown restaurants, the odd racehorse or two. Now, I know a fellow who is deputy chief in the trustee department at the Bank of America in Los Angeles. That's where Shavin does his primary banking. Shavin made deposits of five hundred dollars every month into an *inter vivos* trust account with Elgin Tegel as trustee. But there was a second, secret, testamentary trust Tegel controlled. Can you guess its sole beneficiary when Shavin dies?"

"Tenner says it's Pola Goddard."

"I'll happily take that ten spot off you. Frankly, I thought so, too, at first. Makes sense, doesn't it? But here's how everything worked. Shavin paid five hundred dollars a month into maintenance and upkeep for the house. Dolores and Tamar lived off that stipend, and from what I could gather it was more than enough to cover their expenses. When they did fall short for whatever reason Shavin cut them another check. But there is a different beneficiary for this testamentary trust. This trust has received quarterly deposits of five thousand dollars since Tamar's birth. Six years ago these deposits jumped to ten thousand dollars a quarter."

"Jesus. Quarterly?"

"It's currently sitting at around half a million dollars."

My mind raced. "Who gets that money if it's not Tamar?"

"When Shavin dies the testamentary trust goes to Dolores Bandesi. But if she dies it defaults to one Wanda Zipes, who was Wanda Bandesi before she married. You heard that right. Wanda Zipes is related to

Dolores Bandesi. Furthermore, Shavin set up this trust in the name of Pola Goddard, so Pola is the one who really controls it."

In an investigation you can reach inflection points where the case flies off the rails into undiscovered territory. Or opens up unexpected avenues you never saw coming. I was hitting both of them at the same time.

"Why would Landers Shavin place half a million dollars in a trust fund that defaults to Wanda Zipes? Why would Pola Goddard want him to?" I wondered aloud. "I knew Wanda was Tamar's grandmother. But why is Zipes acting like she's just the housekeeper?"

Artie grunted. "Apparently she's more than that. You find the answer and you will be at the end of this investigation. Just make sure you reach it in one piece. These people sound plenty dangerous. Whatever's going on I'm willing to bet it's sure as hell not legal."

I thanked him and hung up the phone.

Part Four

Desert

TWELVE

MY BLOOD WAS UP. ARTIE'S phone call had galvanized me. I went down to Tucson City Hall and spent way too many hours digging through dusty public safety reports, land permits, tax records, and other financial disclosures. This was Artie's expertise, and he could have done the job in half the time, but nevertheless, I got one hit on a Juanita Drexford from Los Angeles. Tamar's Tucson alias. This led me to a realtor's office downtown who liked to gab about his stint as a marine lieutenant in the war while staring at my legs. He kept talking while I pumped him for information, so I let him stare.

The realtor's name was Glendon Milton Baye. Prematurely balding, he was dressed in a striped western shirt, string tie, tan slacks, and a brown Stetson hat cocked back on his head. He chain-smoked Lucky Strikes, lighting one from the other. The windows of his office were flung wide open. The traffic noise was loud and heavy.

Baye liberated a file from a metal cabinet. He opened it and perused the contents while standing near the window with a fresh cigarette smoldering in his mouth.

"Yes," he said. "Here we are. Juanita Drexford and Neff Waverly. They bought this listing at the Top Ring Motor Court on Highway 39." Baye showed me the bill of sale. "Number 17. It's a good motor home and a great deal. They paid cash. I handled the purchase myself and my secretary's grandson helped them move in. They didn't have much seeing how the home came furnished."

"What does this Juanita look like?"

"Thin, short black hair, darker eyes. Bit of a looker. Doesn't talk much, but she sure as hell has a lot to say."

That sounded like Tamar. Juanita's signature on the bill of sale matched samples I had of Tamar's handwriting. Staaken had co-signed as Neff Waverly. They'd changed identities when they crossed the border. They wouldn't have gone to that much trouble if they weren't planning to stay in Tucson.

"Where is this place?" I asked. "Top Ring Motor Court, you said?"

"Out on Highway 39." Baye returned to his squeaky chair behind the beat-up metal desk. "It's out near the Japanese internment camp at the foot of the Catalina Mountains. Or what's left of the camp. There's nothing there now except strands of rusted barbed wire and broken concrete. But you can't miss the motor court. Got a big yellow sign. Take the turn and follow the road. Old Miguel watches the place. In fact, he owns it."

"Miguel?"

"Miguel Morgan. He's quarter Tohono. Been around these parts long as I can remember. Everybody in Tucson knows Miguel. He bought that land before the war and made something of it. Guess he deserves it seeing how we treated all the Indians. I won't judge a man making his way in the world. Some prejudiced people around here don't like hearing that, but truth's truth."

He lit a fresh cigarette and flipped the old one through the open window onto the sidewalk outside. "If you stop by tell him Glendon Baye says hello."

I love little towns like Tucson. They throw information at you left and right if you finesse it right. You hardly have to lift a finger. For all its pretense, Tucson was not much more than a cattle town living off its reputation as a Wild West city.

Following a bite of lunch I rented a used car. I found the motor court without much trouble. There were twenty motor home lots, half of them empty. I drove through the winding lots. I wanted to see where

Staaken's motor home was parked. I found it at No. 17, parked on the edge of the court between a row of castor bean plants and ocotillo cactus. There was a flagpole across the street but no flag. Its steel cable clanked a melancholy knell.

A white A-frame served as office for the motor court. A man dressed in worn blue overalls and a straw cowboy hat watched me drive past. I followed the road out of the court and turned onto an old cattle trail a quarter mile down the road. I found a place to park under a stand of cottonwood trees so my car wouldn't be seen from the road, grabbed my snake bite kit, and hiked several hundred yards up the face of a bald hill and around a big empty hole in the ground where someone had tried to dig a water tank for cattle but given up. Beside the dry tank was a broken and creepy looking chicken coop bound with rusted wire and weathered slats. I had a new hat to shade my face against the desert sun, so I climbed to the top of the chicken coop and got settled. From here I could watch the motor court through a pair of 7x50 binoculars I had purchased in a hardware store.

Stakeouts are part of the job. I approach them as you would an endurance contest. You learn to pace yourself. Impatience never gets you far no matter what line of work you're in. To tell the truth, a private dick does more waiting and watching and digging through public records than anything else. Most of the time it never pans out, but you must make the effort.

Around four o'clock the door to the trailer banged open and Tamar stepped out. I'd seen her photograph, but I would have recognized that lithe form and intense face anywhere. She was taller than I expected, and I thought she had her father's profile. She stood under a eucalyptus tree sipping lemonade. It was the first time I'd seen her in the flesh. I watched her as avidly as a cat watches a canary. I'd traveled a long way to reach this moment. I wouldn't lose her again.

Not that I planned to. My part in this investigation was complete. All I had to do was walk down there, introduce myself, and relay the message from her father. The money, too, if she wanted that, and who wouldn't want a free fifty grand no-questions-asked? All the drama of Tegel's murder, Dolores's strange death, the testamentary trust, and why

Tamar and Staaken took such a roundabout way to Tucson had nothing to do with why I was here *now*.

Shavin had hired me to find Tamar and I'd done it. Pixie solves another tough case. Nothing gets past ol' Pixie.

All I had to do, I kept reminding myself, was introduce myself. I could wire for the fifty thousand dollars and hand it to her in the morning.

But I didn't move a muscle. I watched Tamar through the binoculars. There was too much I didn't know. Tegel's death had something to do with it, but so did the missing boat, the cold-blooded murder of the boat pilot, and ostensibly a coffee can full of French heroin. It was down there, too, probably inside the motor home with Staaken.

Which had nothing, I repeat, absolutely nothing to do with why I was hired. I'd found Tamar. Time to wrap this up and head home. Maybe call my dad.

A man emerged from the motor home next. I looked him over and straightaway pegged him as tall, dark, and mobbed up. I'd seen faces like his in hundreds of police files. After the war, when the men came home, you could spot a veteran a mile away with that thousand-yard stare. Gangsters have the same countenance, but I'd call it a thousand-yard stare *inward*.

Staaken and Tamar passed a few words. There was no tension, no body language which told me there was any stress between the two. But there was something else. I'd bet a century note these two weren't lovers. I don't know what their relationship was, but they weren't sharing a bed. Not that way.

Look, you have to understand what we do in this job. We always watch people. We watch everything about them, day and night, hour by hour. The way a person walks, speaks, and moves tells you more about them than they know themselves. Couples approach one another differently than friends; there is a loose but intimate familiarity between people who love one another or are lovers. Their tiny gestures and their outward demeanor reflect that. They often touch one another while speaking, and they absolutely stand closer together than these two were doing. I'm not saying Tamar and Staaken didn't like one another or weren't close. I didn't know what their relationship was. I just knew what it *wasn't*.

That made all the difference in the world. That's why I didn't go down there and chose to stay perched on my chicken coop. Watching.

They were conversing, with Tamar walking back and forth under her eucalyptus tree and sipping lemonade, when I heard a rustle behind me. My first thought was I'd been set up. They'd pitched Tamar out there as bait so I could be trapped. I whirled and stared down the twin barrels of a shotgun and thought I was dead. The man at the other end was the one I had seen rocking outside the motor court.

"Why are you spying on my place?" he demanded.

I swallowed my fear and raised my hands slow. "Put the gun down, Gramps. You've got it all wrong. I can explain." I smiled, knowing it came off as nothing more than a frightened grimace. Charm wasn't going to work with this guy.

"I'm not your gramps, young lady." He had a broad, strong face and bushy white eyebrows under his frayed straw hat. The twin barrels remained rock solid. "Spill it. What are you doing around here?"

"You're Miguel Morgan, I take it?"

"What business is that of yours?"

"You own that motor court down below. I'm a private investigator out of Los Angeles. Don't panic, I'm reaching for my identification. My name is Pixie Parrish. That's the number for my employer, Landers Shavin. You can call him and confirm. I was hired to find Tamar Bandesi. I guess you know her as Juanita Drexford. She's living down there with that other man, Neff Waverly. His real name is Emil Staaken."

Morgan lowered the shotgun. I took that as my cue to lower my hands. I took a deep breath and let it out slowly. Christ, that had been a close one.

"This Waverly isn't her husband?" Morgan asked.

"No, sir. His real name is Emil Staaken."

"Staaken, you say?"

"Yes, sir. He's from Los Angeles." It's smart to throw in a few "sirs" now and then. You catch more flies with honey and all that jazz. But you have to be careful. Older people have a bullshit detector that's always operating, and it's usually in top-notch working condition.

"Staaken's not his name, young lady. Nor is it Waverly. I can't speak to the girl, but I've known him a long time. Probably longer than you've been alive from the looks of you. He used to come out here before the war. There was no motor court then, but he'd camp by the stream and do a little fishing before I proved the place up. Said he wanted to get away from the big city life of Los Angeles. Said the city demanded too much when he worked those jobs for the studios."

My heart felt like it was going to bang out of my chest. I felt the blood leave my face. *Oh my god.*

"Well, if his name's not Staaken or Waverly or Mickey Mouse what *is* his name?"

"His name's Krille. Warden Krille."

I stared at Miguel Morgan. The truth was out at last. She had crawled out of her well. Bright and awful and it changed everything I ever thought I knew about this whole damn thing.

I licked my lips. "Mr. Morgan, please trust me when I say we'd better talk."

He thought a while. He broke the shotgun open, removed the shells, and dropped them in the pocket of his overalls. He pointed back down the hill.

"That your car back there?"

"Yes, it is."

"All right, let's talk."

THIRTEEN

"THERE'S A PLACE UP THE road a piece," Morgan said. "They've got gas, too, if you need it. We can grab a cup of coffee and something to eat if you're hungry. Turn here and follow the highway north."

Five miles up Highway 39 was a roadside cafe with a kiddie playground. It looked like a popular place. It had a patio with a wooden deck and colorful umbrellas that resembled secondhand purchases from a defunct circus. We commandeered a picnic table in the back corner. I waited for the waitress to bring us coffee and a slice of apple cobbler for Morgan before I started laying the background of my case out in front of him.

I didn't tell him everything. Nothing about the heroin. Just what he needed to know about Tamar and her mother's death and the fortune waiting at Summerchynne. There sometimes comes a time in an investigation when you throw the dice. Morgan could have killed and buried me under the chicken coop. He could have done a lot of things. But he didn't. I felt he was someone I could confide in, and maybe elicit help from. But only after a fashion.

After I put the bare bones of the case before him and let him see how big it was and what was at stake, I asked: "Where did you first meet Krille?"

"During the war, like I said. The first one. We served in the same company. After the Armistice I came back to Arizona to work my land. Krille dropped by infrequently. I won't lie. There were times I felt he was doing more hiding than vacationing. Maybe, from what you say, things got heavy for him in Hollywood. But he never caused trouble and I had no reason to believe he was up to no good. Nothing like the stories you relayed. After a while we lost track of each other. I opened up my place of business. It was, oh, three months ago when Krille popped up with his girl in tow."

"You said *his girl*. You think they are sleeping together?"

Morgan was of an older generation who wasn't comfortable talking so openly about sex. His tan and weathered cheeks spotted red. "No," he said, "that was a figure of speech. I've never gotten the sense they are close in that way."

I questioned him about the day Krille and Tamar arrived at the motor court. The date Morgan remembered fit with the timeline I'd established.

"Krille introduced her as Juanita Drexford?" I inquired.

Morgan was amused by my line of questioning. "Introduced herself, she did. She's not the type of woman who lets others speak her piece for her."

"Juanita is not her real name. That's the name of a childhood friend in Pasadena. Her real name is Tamar Bandesi. Her mother died in February, and I was hired by her estranged father to bring her home."

"This silent film star you mentioned." Morgan finished his cobbler and sat back. "I remember seeing his movies. I rather liked them. Well, I guess you found her."

"It's not that easy, I'm afraid. Krille, his real name is Valentin Korov, used to do dangerous jobs for the movie studios. Squashing scandals and such. It was mostly illegal, and he got paid a lot of secret money for it. He had a partner, Elgin Tegel. Tegel was murdered last Friday."

"I can tell you Krille didn't do it," Morgan stated. "He's been living at my motor court the whole time."

"He hasn't gone anywhere at all?"

"Maybe Tucson to buy groceries. The girl is a different story."

"How do you mean?"

"She takes the Sunset Limited and travels east to Orlando to visit her relatives. Leastways, that's what she told me."

"Orlando."

Morgan shrugged. "Something wrong with that? You look like you swallowed a bug."

"I know Krille has, or had, a daughter in Orlando." Irene Woolfe hadn't said or hadn't known who the daughter was. It wasn't Tamar, because the daughter would be too old now, but it was clear Tamar knew her well enough to visit on a regular basis. "How often does Tamar take the train to Orlando?"

Morgan shook his head. "Couldn't say. I don't keep tabs on my renters. But I do remember her mentioning it this one time."

"Have you talked to Tamar often?"

"Not what I'd call often. A passing hello. She'd drop by to pay the rent. Cash. Maybe it was then she told me about Orlando. I honestly can't remember."

I looked around the patio and spied a telephone booth beside the diner. "I need to make a phone call or two. Will you wait for me?"

"You've got the car," he said.

I tried not to run to the phone booth. I got the operator and minutes later I was connected to Summerchynne.

"Hello?" The connection wasn't great. Goddard sounded tinny and far away.

"Pixie here. I've found Tamar. She's in Tucson. I haven't approached her because I want to tie up a few loose ends. I'd also like to get her alone when I talk to her. She's with someone right now."

"My God," Goddard breathed, "you've found her at last."

"You can tell Mr. Shavin the news, but if you want my advice, play it close to the vest. Like I said, I can't go right up to her until she's alone. There's one more thing."

Pola heard the tension in my voice. It put her on alert. "Yes?"

"Why didn't you tell me Emil Staaken was an alias for Warden Krille?"

"I. . .I didn't know it was the same man. I thought—"

I shut her down. "Bullshit. Stop lying to me, Pola. I know more about this than you probably do. I know Dolores is Wanda Zipes's younger sister. Try this on for size: maybe Zipes and Krille came up with the bright idea to use baby Tamar to burrow their way into Shavin's fortune. Dolores went along with the charade, but she started making money with her paintings and wanted out so someone arranged to have her thrown into a sanitarium and killed because they weren't going to pass up a cool twenty-five million dollars."

Pola's voice was soft but shocked. "You mean she was murdered?"

"A restrained and sedated patient breaks out of her room, over-powers three people, and jumps from a third-floor window. You tell me."

"But that's not true," Pola said. "Dolores was ill. She broke with reality. She was diagnosed as schizophrenic. Her disease was real."

"She was diagnosed by Arthur Hollack, the same doctor who owns the sanitarium where Dolores died. I don't believe in coincidences. I found yellow jackets—Nembutal—and chloral hydrate in her home. You mix those two and you can exhibit signs of schizophrenia. I saw it when I was on the force. It's ugly, but it does happen. Dolores took it of her own accord, or someone fed it to her. I'd bet on the latter."

"God, I can't believe what I'm hearing. You're saying Dolores was murdered in cold blood."

"Along with Elgin Tegel, Dolores turned into a liability and needed to be silenced. I'd like to know who killed them or had them killed. Somebody is shutting down the pipeline and unless I miss my guess it's the same person, or persons, behind both deaths. Where are the paintings?"

"What paint—"

"I told you stop lying to me." My scream rattled the glass in the phone booth and reverberated in my ears. I shut my eyes and took a calming breath. When I opened them, I watched the kids on the playground. One little girl had a bag of corn chips that spilled as she ran around. There was a mother at the bottom of a slide to catch the little ones when they came down. Every time one tumbled down the steep metal slide, she was there. She would always be there, and every kid on the playground knew there was someone to catch them when they tumbled.

Which was a lot more than Tamar had ever had.

I turned away, struggling to control my emotions. My body was quivering. I made an effort to keep my voice level.

"Where are the paintings?" I asked. "There's not one painting in Dolores's house. Not a sketch or a paint brush or an easel. Can you explain that?"

"Pixie, I swear I don't know anything about that. If I must guess, I'd say Elgin had them stored in a safe place. I can ask Landers. . ."

"No, don't do that. You tell him I found Tamar, nothing else. Do you understand?"

"All right."

"Do you understand me, Pola?"

"Yes," she said. "I do."

"I don't know if I can get Tamar away from the people she's associated with. No matter how it shakes out, it won't be easy. I'll try my best."

"I'll hold things down here," Pola promised. Her voice changed. "It's what I've always done."

For the first time, I felt slight empathy towards Pola. She'd been through the wringer with everyone else in this conspiracy. Something like that hanging over your head eats away at your soul.

"One more thing," I said. "Where did you know Krille as Staaken?"

"It was when I was working on a movie. They shot the picture and there was a wrap party. Krille passed himself off as Staaken. He tried to pick me up."

"Did you let him?"

"No. I was in love with Landers, who was in Culver City at the time. It was only later someone told me who this Staaken was. When Landers came home, I asked him and he told me about Krille and what he and Elgin did for the studios. When you mentioned the name I was shocked because I'd all but forgotten it. I. . .I thought I should tell Landers first before I admitted to you I had met Krille."

"I'll accept that as the truth for now."

"It is the truth, Pixie. I swear."

"How is Mr. Shavin?"

"He's doing rather well considering the circumstances. This experience is difficult for everyone."

"Did Quan give him my message?"

"I want to apologize for that," she said. "I didn't know anything about their plans. If I had I would have put my foot down. I had a long talk with Landers, and I told him to let you work without interference. Quan, as you might expect, is a bit shamefaced about it all, but he's not to blame."

"Stay by the phone. I may be in touch day or night. I have a feeling things are coming to a head. Oh, you need to wire me the rest of that money."

At least she didn't ask what I spent it on. "That's no problem," she said. "You can have as much as you need."

"All right, I'll talk to you later. Hopefully, with good news."

I hung up the phone and opened the door to the booth.

Morgan was waiting at the picnic table.

"I need to ask a very big favor," I said.

"I sometimes grant favors."

"Can I stay at the motor court with you? I can pay you for your trouble. I want to keep Tamar under surveillance and pick my time when to approach her. I can live out of my car if I must, but I'd rather have a roof over my head."

He mulled it over. "There's a couch in the back of the office with a sink and running water. How long are you planning to stay? I want it understood I do not want you spying on my other renters. I understand your desire to spirit the girl to safety, if that's what she wants, but I insist the privacy of my other tenants not be interfered with."

"I can promise you that. Does the office have a phone?"

"No, but there's a phone booth outside. It's a party line."

"That will do. Thank you, Mr. Morgan."

He frowned. "I've known Krille a long time. He's not a nice man, but I don't know many nice men. However, if what you say is right, we will be helping the young lady find her own way in the world. That's the least anyone deserves." He stiffened. "Uh oh."

"What's the matter?"

"They're here."

I turned my head and spotted Staaken—I had gotten into the habit thinking of him as Staaken rather than Krille—and Tamar. They went to a table on the far side of the deck and sat down.

"It's all right," I told Morgan. "They don't know me and this place is crowded, but we should leave. I don't want to press my luck."

We took a circuitous route through the crowd of diners and drove back to the motor court. I slowed when we passed their trailer. It looked like they were planning to stay at the diner which would give me time to—

"Forget it," Morgan interrupted. "You're not going inside. I won't allow that."

I gave him my best "Who, little ole me?" look, but he wasn't buying it.

"Park behind the office," he directed. "There's an air and a water pump, too. Gas you'll have to purchase in Tucson or back up the road."

"It's a rental. I've got half a tank."

I parked and we went inside the office. There was a box fan in the corner doing its level best to kick the hot air around. The backroom he promised me wasn't much more than an army cot with a blanket and a horsehair pillow, but was better than the chicken coop. I've pulled stake-outs in frozen doorways, airless warehouses, and pitch-black mine shafts. This was luxurious compared to those places.

I stayed out of Morgan's way. Around midnight I left the A-frame office and stole through the sparse woods towards Staaken's motor home. Coyotes called to one another under the stars, and I spotted a racoon digging through metal trash cans. It was dark. Staaken's car was parked. I tried the door. Locked. I circuited the tiny trailer but didn't see anything out of place. I admit I half-expected to find a brand-new brick barbeque pit built by team Staaken and Tamar. I mean, wouldn't that be the perfect place to hide heroin? Except "The Purloined Letter" is fiction and if you're dumb enough to leave something like that out in the open you probably deserve to have it stolen.

Two days went by. There wasn't much activity out of Staaken. Morgan and I alternated house chores. He cooked breakfast and I'd knock out a pan of hash or fried hamburger steaks with peppers and onions for supper. On the morning of the third day, Tamar drove their car to Tucson. I followed in mine, keeping a discreet distance. Tamar passed the morning window-shopping and browsing an outdoor grocer for fresh fruits and vegetables. I wore my brand new wide-brimmed floppy hat and dark sunglasses, sticking to her like fly paper. I would tag her and follow from the other side of the street. An amateur might think of looking behind them, but they never think to look across the street where someone is on a parallel course.

Tamar never used reflections in the windows or stopped to see what was behind her or doubled back or crossed a street against traffic to flush surveillance. It made my job easy, but I was willing to bet it wouldn't go as smoothly with Staaken, and I made it a point to do those same tricks to try and flush anyone on *my* back while I was keeping an eye on Tamar. It would be like Staaken to push Tamar out as bait and follow behind to see if anyone was after her. But I was clean, and when Tamar went to the train station and bought a sleeper ticket to Junction City I followed after and bought one, too.

Back to the motor court we drove. Tamar went inside her motor home and I went off to find Morgan. He was in the shed repairing a broken stave on a pony keg.

"Tamar's leaving this afternoon for Junction City on the Sunset Limited," I told him. "I'll be leaving with her."

Morgan put the Cooper's hammer down. "She didn't buy two tickets?"

I shook my head. "Either Staaken has one, or he isn't going. Either way I'll be on that train tonight."

Morgan thought it over. "I can telegram ahead and let you know if he does anything here."

"You don't have to do that, Mr. Morgan. I've imposed on your good graces enough. I'll be all right."

"I want you to understand something. This here is my place. I take care of it and I take care of the people who live here. They depend on me to keep the site clean and safe. A man like this Staaken. . .or Krille or whatever his name is. . ." He groped for words. "I don't like how he took advantage of my 'good graces' as you call them. If half of what you say is true, he's a dangerous individual. I'll let you know if anything happens. It's the least I can do."

I met his smile. "Thank you. Here's my card. The number on back is for our Sacramento office. Ask for Artie Glass. He'll know how to reach me in an emergency."

"Will do." He poked the card in his shirt pocket. "Good luck to you, Pixie."

"Thanks, Mr. Morgan, and thank you for everything. I'm on expenses. I can pay you for your trouble."

"Get out of here," he said with a fierce grin, and returned to the broken keg.

I threw together what few items I had in my overnight case. I held Aiden's gun in my hand. I didn't want to carry it on my body. I might be searched. I pulled the hard floor of my overnight case loose and tucked it under there. A handful of newspaper kept it from rattling around. I finished packing and drove to the train depot. The westbound train wasn't due to arrive for an hour and a half. I telephoned Artie.

"You mean you haven't cornered this kid and talked to her? Pixie, you could have closed the case. All you had to do is find her, and you've done that."

"I want to see where she's going," I argued. "There's more to this than a simple runaway. I know it."

"We don't work off emotion and sentiment," Artie reminded me. "That's not how we solve cases. That's Hollywood B-movie bullshit. We use reason and facts to derive our answers. That's what people pay us for, Pixie. To *think*."

"I know, and that's what I'm doing. I'm looking at the things that have happened in this case and I'm telling you, Artie, they don't add up. I have an idea it revolves around the heroin and Dolores's missing paintings and I want to see if I'm right. These aren't separate incidents. Tegel's murder, the heroin, the paintings, and Tamar's disappearance. They're all one thing together. That's not intuition, that's my logical conclusion after examining the facts of this case—coldly and dispassionately."

He wasn't happy, but there wasn't much he could do in Sacramento; he was stuck in the office and I was in the field. My judgement took precedence. The investigator on scene calls the shots while Sacramento provides support and manpower. That's how it works at Valkyrie and Pinkertons and, for all I know, Arcadia. Private one-man operations are different, but for the big investigative agencies with a national footprint it's this format that is used. Only Mrs. DeMoines could order me in from the field, and I'd have to go. But I didn't think Artie would do that to me.

I hung up the phone and walked through a terminal filling up with travelers: men and women, couples and families. There were people running away, and people looking for dreams out west. People with plans, and people who lived life day by day, dream by dream, dollar to dollar.

I stayed put between one of the square concrete columns and a candy-bar machine. Tamar came in carrying a brown mid-size Samsonite suitcase. She sat on a wooden bench with the suitcase by her feet. I remained out of sight, eating a Baby Ruth and watching her from a mirror behind the ticket counter.

The Tannoy announced the arrival of the Sunset Limited in fifteen minutes. I watched it pull in, its big electric-diesel engine chugging a string of cars with black roofs and dark olive-green sides. It had run all the way from Orlando through alligator-infested swamps and cotton fields, and dry Texas plains, with a final stop scheduled for Los Angeles; Junction City was one of the intermediate stops once we got out of Arizona.

People got up from their seats and started for the train. I watched Tamar climb aboard two cars down. Steam from the engine rolled like a fitful specter through the terminal. Black Porters hauled luggage and heavy steamer trunks onboard. One man moved mailbags using a wheelbarrow.

I had no baggage other than my mid-size American Tourister overnight case. I gave it to one of the porters anyway, a middle-aged Black man with close cropped gray hair and clipped mustache. He put down aluminum steps and I went up into his car. He stowed the case in my sleeper, made certain the bed was made and the little overhead fan worked. I tipped him with a five-dollar bill from my purse.

"Thank you," I said.

He knew it was an outsized tip and he knew he'd have to earn it. He touched the bill of his cap and made the fiver disappear. "My pleasure, ma'am."

"May I know your name?"

"Bryson Sheffield. I'm the Pullman porter for this here car, but you can do me the honor of calling me Bryson."

"That's a deal if you call me Pixie."

He smiled wide. "Happy to be of service, Pixie. I'll be on duty until we pull into Los Angeles."

"I'm getting off in Junction City."

"We should reach Junction City around four o'clock this morning. I'll make sure you're up and ready to go before we arrive. Anything else I can do your way?"

"Where is the dining car?"

"Next car down."

Bryson Sheffield moved away down the central corridor of the sleeper car to see after his other passengers. A little boy ran down the aisle with his mother chasing after. A big man stood next to an open window smoking a cigar. Another man lounged in the doorway of his sleeper cabin, holding a bouquet of wilted flowers while a woman inside removed her hat. Outside the door of my berth was a small rack with the name of the Pullman on duty prominently displayed: BRYSON SHEFFIELD.

I lowered the window in my berth and stuck my head out. There was no sign of Tamar or Staaken in the terminal. She was still on the train.

The porters called, "Board," and stragglers hopped aboard while one or two visitors hopped off. People in the terminal waved goodbye. The train jolted and I grabbed a ceiling strap. We started moving slow, carriage wheels clacking in a slow, rhythmic metronome.

Gaining speed, I moved between the carriages, sidling past people who were getting their things properly stowed away.

A cross-country train is like a small city. It consists of working equipment, employees, and passengers. Like any city, it lives and breathes and, if you know the ropes, you can sometimes arrange things to your advantage.

I found the Pullman Dining Car. It was empty and not open for service. A narrow aisle let me walk through it to the next car. I stopped at the galley towards the back and signaled for the steward, a tall man with dark skin dressed in starched white clothes.

"Excuse me," I said. "My name is Pixie Parrish. I'm a private investigator." I slipped him my card with a ten-dollar bill folded square behind it. "I'm in Bryson Sheffield's car. If a young woman by the name of Juanita Drexford comes in for dinner or cocktails I want to know. I'd appreciate it if you could seat me at the same table."

"Juanita Drexford?" he asked.

"Yes, sir."

"I don't want trouble in my dining car," he said.

"There won't be trouble. I simply want to be alerted if and when Miss Drexford comes into the dining car. Can do?"

He eyed me critically. "A private eye? Nice lady like you?"

"I also collect Green Stamps and can change the alternator in a car. What's your point?"

He chuckled good-naturedly, "No point, miss. We get all stripes here." He made the sawbuck disappear. "Okay, I'll see what I can do. But first," he checked his early reservations. "No one listed by that name," he said, "but if she shows up I'll send a boy for you."

"Thank you, very much."

I went to Tamar's car, careful not to be seen or accidentally bump into her. I approached the Pullman porter for the car and asked which berth Juanita Drexford occupied. His eyes slid right and behind my shoulder. She was in the middle of the car. I asked if he could let me know if Miss Drexford changed her itinerary during the trip.

He shoved the ten-spot back into my hand. "No, ma'am," he said, steadfast. "I'm responsible for this here car and I'll not give out private doings. Not for one hundred dollars."

Great, I thought. Of all the porters for Union Pacific I had to find the honest one. But that wasn't fair, I knew. These men took their charges seriously. A momma bear would be easier to get past than one of these professional porters. But I had to give it the old college try.

When I got a good sense of the layout between my car and Tamar's, I returned to my berth and relaxed. I was feeling good. I'd followed and watched Tamar for three days and she hadn't suspected a thing. It would be different if Staaken was on the train. Even so, I reminded myself not to let down my guard. Sloppy people make mistakes, and mistakes can get you hurt. Or worse.

I fell asleep and was awakened by a knock on the door. I checked my wristwatch. It was half past six. I slid the door open to reveal one of the sandwich boys who walked through the train selling cigarettes, chicken sandwiches wrapped in cellophane, candy, and gum. He carried them in a wire basket.

"Excuse me, miss," he said while I bought a pack of Doublemint gum off him, "but the steward said your reservation is ready in the dining car."

I pulled a brush through my hair and headed through the swaying cars. The Arizona sky through the window was purple-black. The desert rolled past while islands of light from the train inflamed cactus, rock, a lone shed, the blazing eyes of a coyote with its legs splayed.

I paused at the door to the dining car. I smoothed my dress and took a deep breath. *Okay, Pixie. You're on. Time to do Irene proud. Make it shine.*

I saw Tamar the moment I stepped through. She wasn't hard to miss. She was seated at a table for two with red chairs. The table was draped with a white tablecloth and next to a window. Silverware laid out shiny and neat. Menus placed to hand.

I'd seen her from a distance and studied her photograph every day, but up close was something altogether different. Her short black hair was brushed until it gleamed, and her bright brown eyes and long lashes were strangely magnetic. They drew you in. Her personality shone like a Klieg light. They call it star power in Hollywood. Irene would fall over herself to sign Tamar to a five-year exclusive contract.

I stopped at the table. She looked at me with polite curiosity.

"Excuse me," I said with a timid smile, as if I wasn't sure of myself. "I think we're sharing this table tonight. If you don't mind my company?"

"Please, do. It'll be nice to have someone to talk to." She had a lilt in her voice, a light Spanish accent. It was a good voice and easy to recognize.

I sat and unfolded a linen napkin on my lap. "I'm Pixie. My real name is Pidge. Friends started calling me Pixie in school because I was so tall. So now I'm Pixie." It's best to use a semblance of the truth when making cold contact with a suspect. The truth is easier to remember, and Tamar wouldn't know me from Adam, or Eve, anyway.

"Thank you for being so accommodating," I said, getting settled. I removed my hat and gloves. "I find traveling so stressful, don't you? Thanks again for letting me join you."

She held out her hand and we shook formally. "No problem at all. It's good to meet you, Pidge. Allow me to introduce myself. My name is Pola Goddard."

FOURTEEN

OUR DRINKS ARRIVED. I HAD an old fashioned. Tamar, a glass of white wine. We waited for the steward to wend his way towards our table so we could order.

My first impression when I sat down was how wrong I was about Tamar. She was an incredibly cautious woman. How many aliases did she have? Juanita Drexford. Pola Goddard. She whipped them out like playing cards.

We discussed the menu. She ordered mountain trout *au bleue* and I got the braised duck.

"Do you travel on trains often?" Tamar asked. Her hand was on the glass of wine, forefinger moving up and down unconsciously.

"Not too often. I'm coming back from Orlando."

She didn't take the bait.

"Is that your home?" she asked in polite inquiry.

"Soledad, California. My father lives there. He used to own a horse ranch. Still does, I guess. He's mostly retired."

"Ah," she said, and raised the wine to her lips and looked at the other diners.

It was that *Ah* that got me. I didn't know if it conveyed skepticism, concern, or polite but dull interest on her behalf. Or all of them at once. There were multiple layers to this girl. She wasn't the fractious flighty runaway I'd been led to believe. She was self-assured and purposeful. Old beyond her years. I had a good decade on her, but she was nineteen going on thirty-five while I was running to catch up.

"Where are you from?" I asked. *Keep the small talk going. Draw her out.*

"Los Angeles." She pronounced it with the hard "g". But saying you lived in Los Angeles was like admitting you lived somewhere on Earth—it was specific and non-committal at the same time.

The food arrived and I dug into my Brussels sprouts. Tamar said presently, "Funny you should mention Orlando."

"Oh?"

"I have family there. My mother and father, and my sister, Tamar. They live on a big, high hill where you can see the ocean. It's a bit of a walk to the beach, but so worth it. I love the white sand and sparkling blue water. There's something primitive and elemental, yet at the same time idyllic, about an ocean, don't you think? I like to stand at the ocean's edge and let the water swirl around my legs while the sand pulls away from under my feet until I'm about to fall. I don't get home as often as I should. My mother's been ill. That's why I was visiting."

"I'm sorry to hear that."

"She's better now." She looked out the window at the darkness rushing past. Somewhere up ahead, the train blew its mournful whistle. "She's in a better place."

I felt gooseflesh. We ate. The trucks for the dining car had rubber-ized springs and sometimes we'd bounce or shake when we went across a bump or a stretch of crooked rail, and a symphony of glassware would tinkle and ring and a wall-fixture would rattle behind me.

I didn't want to say anything, afraid I would spoil the magic seam of gold I was pulling out of Tamar. Pulling, hell, she was tossing it at me with both hands. We're often as much psychologist as anything in the private investigator field. Our workday doesn't revolve around missing jade or Maltese falcons. I wish it were that easy. The moment I saw her photograph I was hooked, and now that I sat across from Tamar my emotional attachment was more than evident. Like a sun expanding to fill the sky until that's all you could see. A blinding reality.

Her story about living on a hill and seeing the ocean from a great height, and water hitting her knees while the ground sucked out from under her feet until she lost balance—that was enough to keep Freud occupied for a month. And the coda about her mother being in a better place...

God, this girl is hurting, I thought.

I knew what that was like. I knew what growing up that way was like.

So why was she hanging around a cold-hearted bastard like Staaken/Krille? I wondered. Was it the danger, the sense of risk and peril that beckoned her? Standing on the edge of an ocean world while daring the water and sand to yank her under?

We finished dinner and signed our separate checks. Tamar put down the number of her berth instead of her name. We rose from the table together and I pulled on my gloves.

"It's been a most pleasant evening," she told me. "Maybe we'll see one another again sometime."

"I hope so, too. Have a good trip, Pola."

"You, too, Pidge." Well-mannered smile. "Goodnight."

We had met and parted as strangers. I stepped into the space between carriages and let the roaring sound of the train's slipstream shout through my head like a hurricane until I, too, had the sense I was lost, and if I wasn't careful, the sand would leave from under my feet and I would be drawn, helpless and spinning, into that awful, elemental void of loneliness.

If I was working with an assistant, I'd have her unlock Tamar's roomette and give it a toss while I kept Tamar occupied in the dining car. That's a problem when you work solo. You have to weigh opportunities and take the one you think will pay off most.

I could stake out her sleeper and wait for her to go to the toilet and washbasin, but that brought its own set of risks. The Pullman Porter would be on duty. He'd want to know why someone who didn't have a berth in his car was hanging around. If things got too hot, he'd call for the conductor and have me thrown off the train. Hopefully while it was stationary but you can't always choose the best outcome.

The train pulled into Maricopa to exchange mailbags. A handful of passengers got off, but no one came on board. We were rolling again before long.

I stayed awake all night. It wouldn't do to fall asleep and have Tamar slip off the train at one of our intermediate stops. I had Bryson fetch me coffee and I sort of moved back and forth through the cars to stay awake. The night wore on. Mesa, Arizona. Exchange of luggage, mail, a passenger or three. The hour turned. The cars rocked peacefully in night's dark nave while we rolled through the wide-open desert. An hour crawled past. Another.

Bryson came up to me. "Junction City," he said in a soft, respectful voice. "Twenty minutes."

"On time?"

"Yes, ma'am."

"Thank you, Bryson. By the way. . ."

"Yes, ma'am, Pixie?"

"Can I get off on the other side of the train?"

"You don't want to get down at the terminal?"

"I'd rather not."

"I'll arrange it for you."

I went to my berth and changed from a sleeveless blouse and skirt to a dark blue shirt with black slacks. I crammed my hat and gloves in the travel case. I'd worn a big noticeable floppy hat and white gloves to dinner so Tamar would associate them with me. Human memory is malleable. People connect a stranger's face with the clothes she wears. It's why police ask witnesses what the suspect wore. It aids the police and helps the witness remember the face. Human nature at work. Changing outfits altered my profile, giving me a chance at trailing Tamar without being recognized. I was wearing the same shoes, but she wasn't a professional stalker and wouldn't notice a detail like that.

We pulled into the Junction City depot. Bryson put down the

aluminum steps on the far side of the train. I pressed more money into his hand and stepped off and moved for cover between the corner of a building and a row of cigarette machines and magazine racks outside a pharmacy.

There was a short wait until the Sunset Limited pulled out, headed for Los Angeles. On the other side of the tracks, Tamar's straight back disappeared into the waiting lounge. I followed after, crossing the tracks. She turned towards a cab rank. A cab driver placed her luggage in the trunk and they sped off.

I went to the next cab in line and jumped into the back seat. I held a ten spot over the seat.

"Follow them and don't let yourself be seen," I said.

"Look, lady, it's a quiet, peaceful night. I don't want trouble. Me, I've got ulcers."

"There's not going to be trouble. Now let's go. They've turned left up ahead."

"I knew you were bad news the minute I laid eyes on you," he growled. He snatched the ten-dollar bill and stuffed it in his shirt pocket and started the engine. "Any idea where they're headed?" he asked. "Alaska, maybe?"

"Not really," I answered. "Watch you don't get too close. That driver can see your headlights. There's not a lot of traffic this late. Keep a car or two between you. Let that truck get through the light and then follow them."

"Lady, you want to do my job, or what?"

"Keep driving. You're doing fantastic."

"They're pulling over," my cabbie said.

"What's up that way?"

"Couple of hotels. Good ones. The St. Regent and the California National. The Regent is better, though."

Tamar's cab pulled to the curb. She got out, paid off the cab, and retrieved her suitcase. She walked towards the hotel lights a full block away.

"Douse your headlights and let me out here."

"Gladly."

I ditched my cab and crossed the sidewalk. There were long deep shadows and black alleyways between shuttered offices and closed restaurants. I was leery, being a woman alone in a strange city late at night. I didn't know which hotel she'd go for, but I rather hoped she'd make a call from a phone booth on the lighted street ahead. I'd be able to tell if it was long distance from the amount of change she shoved in. It's the little things.

Tamar was in no hurry. She ambled down the middle of the sidewalk staying in the wide pools of yellow lamplight. I stayed nearer the darkened buildings, using stairway stoops and rows of garbage pails to keep out of sight.

She turned right, headed for a tree-lined walkway running between the two hotels. I moved after her when I heard a scratch on the pavement behind me.

He wore rubber soles, but he was in a hurry to catch me before I reached the light streaming from the walkway. That's why I heard him.

I spun around, swinging the overnight case at his head. He was ready for that, too. He side-stepped and shoved the blunt end of a blackjack into my stomach. When I folded up, he whipped it expertly across the back of my head behind my right ear. It's true what they say. You see stars.

I hit the ground. Tires squealed and someone grabbed me under my arms, lifted and shoved me into the back of the car, and then I gave up and let myself fall into a bottomless well of black sorrows.

～

I came to lying on a wooden bench. It was two planks lashed together with hemp. I swung my legs over and sat up, clutching my head in my hands. My face hurt. I'm no prize fighter. I can be hit, and I hurt.

There was a bright sun floating above my head. I focused and it turned into a naked light bulb hanging from a rusty chain. I looked around. One man with brown curly hair sat at a card table playing solitaire. There was a gun on the table, a .38 Special. My overnight case was on the table, my clothes spilled out in a mess. The case was on its side, but the false bottom hadn't been discovered.

Another man stood with his back against corrugated tin, hands in pockets, a metal toothpick in the corner of his mouth. The lightbulb cast ugly, cruel shadows on his face, or maybe he was born that way. I already knew he was a bastard. He was the guy who hit me.

"Bathroom's that way," he jerked his head. "Or you can use the mop bucket there." He must have seen my face go white.

When you're sapped the first thing you experience when you come to is an overwhelming sense of nausea. They never show you that in the movies. I lurched to my feet and stumbled through the narrow door and fell onto my knees over the toilet bowl.

Every time it came up my head split open like a rotten melon. The pain in my head was as bad as my stomach, and I coughed and spit and wiped my mouth with the back of my hand. I stayed down there until my stomach was empty. I flushed the toilet. The swirling water made me sick again, so I shut my eyes. When it stopped, I grabbed the washbasin and pulled myself up. The little washroom spun and yawed and turned upside down, but I stayed upright until it passed in subsiding waves. I ran cold tap water and splashed my hot face and rinsed my mouth out with Listerine. When I looked in the mirror over the metal basin, I didn't like what I saw so I stopped looking.

I came out rocking on my feet and feeling tremulous and weak and vulnerable.

The standing man met me. "You try anything funny I'll put a slug in your guts. It won't kill you, but you'll wish you were dead. Get me?"

I nodded wordlessly. I crossed the room to sit on the bench. My breath was heavy as if I'd run a mile.

"You've caused a lot of trouble," the curly-haired man at the card table said aloud. When he talked the cigarette in his mouth jerked side to side. He shuffled the card deck and started a new game of solitaire. "I hope the boss gives me the job to put you down. You've caused a *lot* of trouble."

"We'll wait for the call," the standing man said. His voice sounded like pebbles rattling in an empty can. "She's not in any hurry to leave. You're not in any hurry, are you, lady?"

I forced myself not to look at the open overnight case. They might realize what I was looking for. People can figure out what you're thinking if you think about it too much; I don't really believe that, but I was desperate. They hadn't found the gun, and I didn't know what that meant for me, but it was something to cling to.

"Hey," the man at the table snapped, "Carino asked you a question. When Angelo Carino asks a question, you answer him. You don't want to make Angelo mad."

"No," I said. "I don't want to make Angelo mad."

He pointed his finger at me. "You do what we say and he won't get mad. Will you, Angelo? Will you get mad?"

"Shut up," Carino said low. The man at the table laughed and went back to his card game.

I took in my surroundings. We were in a garage. An infamous black and white photograph of Carmen Miranda was taped to the wall. This room was attached to a big bay where a Chevrolet sedan stood on jacks. The wheels were off, as were the doors and hood and trunk. The seats were gone. It looked like someone had started to chop it up for parts before being called away. There were toolboxes, an acetylene torch, work lamp, a bench with a vise, and a stack of rubber tires. I smelled old rubber and oil and stale cigarette smoke. My stomach started acting up again.

"A whole lot of trouble," the man at the card table repeated. "Things were quiet before you turned up." He drew a Queen of Spades and placed it on a red king.

Carino opened a bottle of 7-Up and looked at me. I shook my head.

"It's getting daylight outside," the man at the table said.

"It's been daylight outside," Carino said. "You ain't looking. You never do."

A phone in the shop bay rang. It went through me like a carving knife.

"Go answer that, Jimmy," Carino said. "I'll watch her."

Jimmy tossed his deck down. "I ain't got no ace, anyway." He scooted his chair back and left. I looked at Carino wordlessly and he stared back at me.

Jimmy lifted the receiver on the third ring. "Yeah. No. Gotcha." He hung up and came back. As he did, he moved a few tools out of the way, including a striker for the acetylene torch.

"It's time," he said. He took the cigarette from his mouth and flipped it away in an arc.

Carino put down his bottle of 7-Up. "Here's how we're going to play this here," he told me. "You walk between us nice and easy. Jimmy goes first. He'll open the car door and you crawl in the back seat. You be funny, you be funny in any way, and I put one in your spine. You understand?"

"You answer when Angelo asks you a question," Jimmy said.

"Yes," I said. "I understand."

"All right, Jimmy. Let's do it."

Jimmy grabbed rough handfuls of my clothes and crammed them into the overnight case. He closed and locked it.

"Now you follow Jimmy," Carino said in that soft, urgent voice of his.

It went exactly like Carino wanted. We walked into the gray, watery light of dawn and I got in the back seat of a midnight blue Packard with red upholstered seats. Carino slipped in after me and Jimmy slid behind the wheel with my overnight case on the seat beside him.

"All right, Jimmy. Drive."

Jimmy cranked the motor, engaged the clutch, and put the car in gear. We made a half circle on the bare yard and bumped across a shallow ditch onto a lone country dirt-top covered in loose gravel. There was a bar ditch on one side of the road and a clumsily made stone fence on the other that opened onto a stinking onion field. I could smell it through the closed windows of the car and it was awful. The garage was surrounded by a few twisted trees with a barbed wire fence down one side. Jimmy drove, and no one said anything because it had all already been said.

I tried to think. There was no way I could reach the case and open it and pry the false bottom loose and get the gun and turn it on Carino before he killed me. I didn't have a chance to grab the soda bottle back there in the garage and smash it in his face. I was in the hands of professionals. I made myself remember that. They were professionals and would behave as such. That was my last hope. Professionals don't chatter how they're going to shoot you and make you hurt and scream when they want to kill you. Professionals just do it. There's nothing to talk about. If they wanted me dead, they'd have killed me in the garage. With no one around. No one to hear the gunshot.

They were taking me somewhere. To someone who wanted to see me.

Jimmy turned onto a blacktop highway and we motored through mile after mile of orange groves. We were headed for Junction City.

We went through the business section of the city and climbed through rolling desert hills covered in manzanita and purple sage. There were houses up ahead. I was reminded of when I drove through Beverly Hills to Summerchynne. That felt like such a long time ago.

Jimmy swung the big car through the opening of a driveway, and we took it all the way into a semi-circular drive in front of a big modern house in the style of Frank Lloyd Wright. Jimmy switched off the engine.

"Get out," Carino directed me.

I opened the door and stepped out, Carino sliding along the seat after me. Jimmy locked the car. There was a flatbed truck with an iron tow hitch and a powder blue Lincoln Continental farther along the driveway. We walked single file towards the front of the house.

Jimmy opened the door and we entered a big, airy vestibule. The men bracketed me as we went deeper into the house, where three people waited at the top of shallow stair leading to an open sitting room with very expensive and opulent furniture. On the walls were paintings. A lot of them. They were done in oil and acrylics, but most were watercolors. They were framed. No, not all of them. Some had been removed from their frames. There were canvas rolls stacked on a coffee table between a divan and a pair of sitting chairs. Somewhere in the house a violin concerto by Mozart played.

I looked at the three people waiting for me. One man, two women. The man I didn't recognize until I remembered coming across his mug shot in Santa Monica. Anthony Ardak was of average height and weight with a fine head of hair and a brown mustache and eyebrows. His face was lean, hungry. This was the man who owned Junction City lock, stock, and barrel—well, he owned the police and district attorney, which was as good as.

One of the women was Wanda Zipes. She watched me with a face closed like a fist. She wasn't dressed like an ordinary housekeeper anymore. She wore an expensive red gown with gold jewelry on her wrists and around her neck. Her hair was marcelled, and her makeup picture-perfect. She resembled a beautiful cobra.

The other woman was Tamar. She turned and said quietly to the man: "That's her, Mr. Ardak. She was on the train."

FIFTEEN

WANDA CAME DOWN THE SHORT flight of steps towards me. Her red gown fit her body like a knife sheath. She snapped her fingers impatiently. "Jimmy, hand me that overnight case."

He did. She carried it with both hands like it was a religious salver. She set it on a table made of glass and steel beside the open fireplace.

"We checked that already," Jimmy said with annoyance.

He could have been a bug for all the attention Wanda paid him. She opened the case and took out the clothes, leaving them in a pile. She upended the case and shook it hard. When she was done, she tossed the case away and it spun across the waxed floor and crashed into the wainscoting. She picked through my clothes, feeling the hems and testing the stitching and the lining.

"Where is it?" she asked me without turning around.

"I don't know what you're talking about." She wasn't looking for the gun, and I had lied. I had a pretty damn good idea what she wanted. But she hadn't found it which was why she was searching my clothes, hoping to find a key or a tag or a chit to a safety deposit box or a bus locker somewhere.

"She doesn't have it, Wanda," Ardak said. "That's what the girl says, and I believe her."

"You'd believe any woman who smiles at you," Wanda snapped. She finished searching my clothes and looked at me, eyes blazing like twin funeral pyres. "You're going to tell me where it is," she promised.

"I don't know what you're talking about."

She came straight up and slapped me. "You do know. These men will make you know. I've seen what they do to people. To women. You won't like it."

"She doesn't have it, Wanda," Ardak repeated, calm and urbane.

"She knows where it is," Wanda insisted, half-turning to address Ardak over her shoulder.

I wasn't sure how much I should reveal. The only weapon I had left was information and it was paltry. I wasn't certain how much of it was true or could be proved. But, maybe, if I played things right, I could walk out of here in one piece—with Tamar.

"They're all government people," Wanda said. "The only reason she's here is because she came up through the pipeline. They sent her. She's their agent. Unwilling or not, she's their agent."

"I don't know what you're talking about," I said again.

Wanda slapped me again, hard.

"That's not going to get you what you want," I said. "I don't have the heroin. Staaken, or Krille, or whatever name he's going by these days, has it."

"You came through the pipeline," she insisted through gritted teeth.

"The Marseilles pipeline is closed," Ardak said. "Staaken—we'll use that identity since that's how he introduced himself—took care of that unpleasant piece of business for us." He motioned for my attention. "Come. Let us be comfortable. I assure you, Miss Parrish, you will tell us everything we want to know. Wanda is correct about that."

I walked past Wanda, my face burning, and followed Ardak. For the moment he was willing to protect me from Wanda's wrath and I was willing to accept his protection while it lasted.

When I mounted the shallow steps, I came upon a lot of hand tools lying around: hammer, pliers, pair of Channellocks, flathead screwdriver. They were being used to dismantle picture frames so the canvases could be rolled. A dozen framed paintings leaned against the wall, and there were stacks of sketches in charcoal, India ink, all different kinds of media. On closer inspection I saw two piles of sketches. One signed, one not. I picked up a pencil sketch to read the name added to the bottom.

"Bandesi." I turned. "They're beautiful, Tamar."

Her eyes dropped in appreciation. "Thank you, Pidge," she said timidly.

"You've been hiding your talent a long time."

Tamar started.

Ardak stood by the fireplace, elbow resting on the marble mantlepiece. "Why are you here?" he asked. "What do you want?"

I nodded at Tamar. "I want her."

Wanda sucked her teeth loud. Tamar started again. She hadn't anticipated that reply.

"Explain," Ardak demanded evenly.

"I'm a private investigator. I was hired to find Tamar and bring her home."

"Who hired you?"

"That's none of your business."

"Landers Shavin hired her," Wanda said. "It's patently obvious."

"We can make you talk," Ardak insisted.

"You can try."

"No," he said softly. "We can make you talk." He thought a moment. "You're not with the Federal Bureau of Narcotics?"

"Of course not."

"You were in their company."

"I didn't know they were government men. I suspected it, but I didn't know it."

"You came through the smuggling route all by yourself?"

"Yes."

Ardak examined me in a thoughtful new light. "Impressive."

"Yeah, she's real impressive," Wanda said with mounting distaste. "Let me have half an hour with her. She'll tell us everything she knows."

"You know why we're here today," Ardak prompted.

"I can speculate." I motioned to the artwork being gathered. "You want to trade the paintings for the heroin."

"That is correct," Ardak said.

"Staaken has the heroin."

"That's what we believe. In fact we know it to be true, because I believe Tamar."

"If he's anything like the stories," I said, "he'll exact his pound of flesh, and a whole lot more."

"You don't know everything," Wanda sneered. "You think you do, but you don't."

"I can make a few wild guesses about you, Wanda. You learned Dolores was sleeping with Landers Shavin. When she got pregnant, you came up with a scheme to blackmail Shavin. Because that's what it was. Blackmail. Dolores went along because she always did what you said. When Tamar got older, she started scribbling pictures. She was good. Then she got better. Then she became amazing. You had another brilliant idea. Let's pretend Dolores painted those pictures, you thought. Dolores was an adult and you could start making money right away. But you lost control. Dolores started to get accolades when the art began to appreciate in value. How am I doing so far?"

Wanda sat on the couch and kept silent.

"Meanwhile," I continued, "Dolores saw a way to become her own person for the first time in her life and crawl out from under your domineering shadow. She was sick, though, and becoming a dangerous liability. She was having unforeseen mental problems. You helped her along. Yellow jackets and chloral hydrate are a lethal mix. You had her thrown into a private sanitarium where she would be out of the way, but she started to improve and she might talk, so that's why you had her thrown out a third-story window."

Wanda's eyes were dark and fathomless and full of rage.

"Tamar saw this growing up. She became involved with Staaken. If I had to guess I'd say he approached her first. She wouldn't have known who he was. They left together after the funeral. You had the artwork. Staaken thought to steal the shipment of heroin coming in from France and trade it for the paintings. With Tamar in tow, he grabbed the heroin and closed down the pipeline."

"I didn't know he was going to kill people," Tamar said weakly. "When he did that, I was so frightened. He said he'd kill me and my grandmother if I made trouble. I believed him. A man like that I had no choice but to believe him."

"No one blames you, Tamar," I said. "You got caught between people who maul and destroy everything around them to get what they want. You're not responsible for their actions."

I turned to Wanda. "Now you have the paintings and he has the drugs and there's going to be a trade. Then everyone will get what they want, and the sun will shine and birds will sing and the world will be a beautiful place. But you'll always be a cold-hearted murdering bitch who killed Dolores because she was a liability."

Tamar's face was bone white. Her mouth was open. "Is that true?"

Wanda challenged her stare. "No, it's not."

"Grandma, is what she says true?"

"Of course not, dear. She's delusional. She wants to throw a spanner into everything and keep you from receiving the recognition you deserve. You know I would never do anything to harm your mother or yourself. That's why I stayed at the house pretending to be a housekeeper. I forfeited my personal life to keep you and Dolores safe. That's the selfless sacrifice I made because I love you and I always will."

The room was full of black ice and raw terror. Tamar took a halting step. Her body was thin and lithe like a drawn, quivering sword. "Grandma. Is what she says true?"

"No," Wanda said with conviction. "How can you ask me that?"

Tamar looked at me beseechingly. She was on the brink of tears. "Pidge. . .?"

"Tamar, I'm sorry. You cared about the art because it was a personal, very private side of you. It was how you communicated with the world and your mother was happy to bring that out in you. But people took advantage of it. Your grandmother was one of them."

Tamar's face settled into carved stone. She neared Wanda, her movements stiff and wooden and unnatural. There was a war raging inside she was fighting to master—and losing.

"You lied to me," she said in a hard, accusing way. "You lied to me, and you lied to my mother. Everything you said was a lie."

"Tamar, she can't prove this because none of it is true. Your mother took her life. I did everything to get her the help she needed. I sacrificed everything I had." Wanda bolted upright. She was losing patience.

"We're family, child. Are you going to believe this stranger over me? Your own flesh and blood?"

Ardak spoke up from across the room. "Tamar. Events spun out of control. We lost the ability to shape the perfect outcome we wanted. We are doing what we can to set things right."

She spun on Ardak. "Why didn't you stop her?"

"Tamar, why won't—"

"WHY DIDN'T YOU STOP HER?"

Carino cleared his throat. "Mr. Ardak, what are your orders?"

"Take Jimmy and finish preparing the truck. We'll close up here."

"Yes, sir." The two gunmen melted away.

Tamar fell across a chair like a broken doll and sobbed. Ardak squared his shoulders. "Miss Parrish, are your services for hire?"

"Why?"

"I want you to make the trade in our stead."

Wanda bit back a scream and flew off the couch at him. "Why her? Why *her*?"

Ardak viewed her with equanimity. "She's here for Tamar. She doesn't care about anything else. If that's true, and I believe it is, we can trust her. Up to a point. She'll make the trade and take Tamar and the paintings off our hands. There's nothing she can prove. It's our word against hers and I have the weight of an entire city at my disposal. She's no threat to us, Wanda. She never was."

"I don't want the job," I said.

"I'm not asking if you want it," he said.

"I won't do it."

"Then you lose custody of Tamar." His eyes narrowed a fraction.

If I didn't do what he asked he'd have Tamar killed.

"Can I change clothes?" I asked. "I'm fairly grim at the moment."

Wanda came down the steps and pulled a blouse and a long skirt out if the pile of clothes and flung them at me. I picked them up off the floor.

"Where can I change?"

"Tamar, show her the guest room down the hall. Leave the door open."

Tamar beckoned and I followed. "There's a bathroom in there," she pointed. I went inside and cleaned up best I could and dressed. My old clothes I tossed into a hamper.

When I came out, Tamar was there to greet me. She started to say something, stopped. She fidgeted restlessly.

"Hey, what's wrong, kid?"

"You look much better." She looked away. Her face was pale.

"I feel better. Hey."

Then it came rushing out in a flood of emotion. "I'm sorry for all the trouble I caused you," she said. Her eyes were red from crying. "They said they would check my back to see if anyone followed me off the train. I thought they were being overcautious and silly. That was before I learned Mr. Ardak and my grandmother planned to trade the art for the drugs Staaken stole. I didn't know they were going to hurt you like that. I guess I've been naive this whole time. You must hate me for that."

"I don't hate you." I tucked my blouse into the waistband of my knee-length skirt. "Is there a phone somewhere in the house?"

"Two. One in the main room where they are at present, and another in the kitchen."

"Can you reach the kitchen without being seen?"

"I think so."

A bureau dresser had a notepad and pen. I wrote a number on a slip of paper and gave it to Tamar. "Call that phone number. It's my office in Sacramento. Tell them who and where you are. Tell them you're with me. Be specific. We're rolling the dice here, kid, and it's our last throw. This isn't much to hang our hats on, but it's all we've got left."

"Anthony said after we make the trade you and I can leave."

I gripped her by the shoulders until she winced. "I want you to listen carefully. Wanda doesn't trust me as far as she can throw me. She's not going to risk a life sentence in Tehachapi. Ardak didn't reach his position of power by being stupid and careless."

"Pidge, you're hurting me."

"Good. Maybe it will drive some sense into that thick head of yours." I let her go and stepped back.

She rubbed her shoulder ruefully. "You mean. . .they will have us killed?"

"You've spent more time with them than I have."

"I don't believe my grandmother would do that."

"I'm sure your mother thought the same thing until she was tossed out a third-story window."

"You don't like her very much, do you?"

"Liking people isn't my job. I was hired to find you. Now that I've found you I'm going to take you to Los Angeles. That's what I mean to do." I ran a comb through my hair and threw it back down. "All I need is for the breaks to go my way. From the looks of things, that's asking quite a lot."

I leaned through the open doorway. Voices were raised in the other part of the house. Wanda and Ardak were arguing. I faced Tamar.

"I don't know how much time we've got left. I want some answers. What were you doing with Staaken? Were you sleeping with him?"

"With Emil? Don't be ridiculous, Pidge. He's more than twice my age. Why would I want to make love with Emil?"

"You went to his bungalow. The two of you left for Mexico."

"That doesn't mean I went to bed with him."

"Do you know who Staaken is? What he did in the past?"

"He worked with Elgin and they did a lot of ugly, hurtful things. The time I spent at Summerchynne I heard Landers and Pola talk about it. They didn't know I was listening. I can't say I was shocked or surprised. I do admit I rather liked Elgin. He was never anything but magnanimous to me and my mother."

"Why did you let Dolores take credit for your art?"

"I thought it was fun. A game. I was pulling the wool over all these eyes. That hoity-toity pretentious art crowd who thought they knew so much about everything. It was a big joke. I liked fooling them. Mom went along with it because she thought it was funny, too. She kept saying someday the world will know the truth and won't they feel silly. Then your art will be worth even more, she said. But I never cared about that. I've seen what money does to people. How it twists them. For me the only thing that mattered was the art and the joke I was playing. Everything else was secondary."

"What was that business with the barbeque pit?"

"Emil wanted to do something nice for Mrs. Sheldon. He said she didn't know about his past and she was one of the few people who treated him with a modicum of decency. He knew he was never coming back. So, one night when we had nothing better to do, we built a barbeque for the complex."

"You're trying to make me believe Staaken is something other than an ice-cold killer?"

"I'm telling you what we did. How you take it is your own business."

Like it or not she had her grandmother's fire.

"Why did Staaken come to you in the first place? Where did you meet?"

"My mother and I were leaving Elgin's office when he met us downstairs. He must have been waiting for us. He said, 'Hello, Dolores,' and she recognized Emil at once. She introduced him as an old friend. Said they met when she was seeing my father. He'd drop by the house sometimes and inquire about my mother's artwork. Or what he thought was her artwork. The paintings were only ever signed 'Bandesi.' He fronted the money so she could hold her first art show in New York."

"Why would he do that?"

"I don't know. I assumed they were friends. That's how they came off toward one another. That's how my mom talked about him. I don't know how she really felt, but she did say that Emil never sold his soul to Landers Shavin."

"Meaning Elgin did."

"I was a little kid when I figured out Elgin was always more interested in the big payout."

"He's dead, did you know that?"

Her mouth clamped shut and she moved restlessly like a young colt in a thunderstorm. "I heard that news." Her voice was flat.

"Where did you hear it?"

Her eyes avoided mine. "I don't remember."

"I'll jog your memory. You heard it when Carino returned with your portrait of Elgin from his office."

Her voice was tiny and afraid. "Maybe so."

I felt sorry for her even though it wasn't my place to feel sorry for anyone. She was stuck between murderers and killers. All she ever wanted was to honor her mother's memory and protect her artwork. That way, something of her mother would always remain and Tamar would have something to hold on to, because there was no one, literally no one at all, in her life who would step up and take charge of that lost and frightened girl who lived in the heart of this young woman.

"Why are you here, really?" she asked.

"I told you. I'm here to take you home."

"I don't have a home."

"It may not be the home you want but it's all you've got. Your father wants to make amends. He's dying and he wants to make right what went wrong all those years ago. It's your decision. I can't make it for you. But you won't have the opportunity to choose if we don't find a way out of here."

"I don't care about the money," she said. "I told you. I've seen how Pola and Landers live. Money doesn't make you happy."

I pointed. "Everyone out there does want the money. That's what you better remember because they don't operate by the same principles you do."

I pried the false bottom out of the overnight case and retrieved the squat, ugly little gun. "Do you know how to shoot a gun?" I asked Tamar.

"I've never shot a gun in my life."

"They're going to search me again, but maybe they won't search you. Here, hold it like this, point, and shoot. There's only one shell so make it good. Tuck it between your waistband and the small of your back. Pull your shirttail down. That's right. Perfect."

"But. . .but my grandmother. . ."

"Tamar," I hissed, "she killed your mother. Or had her killed; it's the same difference. You think she'll have a soft spot in her heart when it comes to you? *There's millions of dollars in heroin out there.* Wanda's not going to turn her nose up at that kind of payoff. Not to mention she's the beneficiary of a secret trust. You've fallen in with thieves and crooks, kiddo. Today, this is as good as it gets."

"You're not like them, Pidge."

Her naivete melted me. After all she'd been through, she was looking for a friend. But it wasn't me. It couldn't be me. It would have to be her family, if that's what she chose.

The raised voices died away. They'd be coming for us next.

"So one day Staaken approached you and said, 'I know who has your paintings. Your mother's dead and can't do anything about it, but I can. Come with me and we will make the people who stole your mother's legacy pay.' Or something like that. Right?"

"It was something very similar," she admitted. "But I didn't know Emil was going to kill that man and blow up his fishing boat. I didn't know anything like that would happen. I thought it would be something like one of those heist pictures. Something exciting and daring. Like me fooling people with my art. I was too scared to run after that. I somehow knew if I didn't do exactly what Emil said he'd kill me, too. I knew it the night he killed that boat pilot."

"Because after that he had what he wanted."

"Yes. He had the heroin. Then I found out *why* he kept me around. I was his courier. I guess you could say I was his mouthpiece. He knew he could send me to Ardak and my grandmother and tell them what the terms of the trade would be."

"What are his terms?"

"The trade is going to happen at—"

I heard footsteps in the hallway and made a motion for Tamar to cease. Wanda came into the room. She ran her eyes over me and Tamar.

"Well, here you are," she said, as if she hadn't known exactly where we were. "Anthony is waiting. There's work to be done. This thing has to run like a Swiss watch, or everyone loses out tonight."

As she said that last bit, she shot me a long, meaningful look. I knew then my future was guaranteed. One way or the other.

PART FIVE
TRUTH

Sixteen

I KNOCKED THE WOODEN FRAMES apart while Tamar rolled canvases. We packed them in excelsior and the bundles went into aluminum tubes and those tubes into refuse cans. Carino and Jimmy lifted the metal cans into the back of the flatbed pickup truck and tied them down. Anyone looking would think trash was being hauled away.

Wanda and I stayed behind the truck while Carino and Jimmy and Tamar stood on the flat bed. I had to watch where I stepped. There was a big oil puddle between the truck and the car behind us, the powder blue Lincoln Continental.

"How much is all that stuff worth?" I asked Wanda. The men and Tamar were pulling a tarp across the bed and lashing it down.

"Like all art, it's market driven," she said. "It's increased in value since Dolores passed away."

"Kind of limits Tamar's output, doesn't it? It would be suspect if more Dolores Bandesi paintings turned up after she's dead."

Wanda had her hands clasped behind her back. She kept silent.

"There's no way it's worth as much as that heroin," I pointed out.

Her eyes were on Tamar. "I didn't say it was."

"Makes no sense. Why would Staaken go to this trouble to get possession of these paintings when he has possession of the heroin?"

Wanda regarded me. "What is he going to do with it? He doesn't have the organization or the chemists to push it out on the streets. He isn't able to pay off law enforcement and move the product in any profitable way. That's not a one-man operation. It takes a crew."

"Ardak's crew."

She met my eyes. "That's right."

I shook my head. "Still doesn't make sense. Staaken shows up one day and tells Tamar, 'Hey, I know who has your mother's artwork.' What he thinks is her mother's artwork. 'Come with me and we will stick it to the people who did this.' But you're not losing anything, Wanda, and neither is Ardak. He's gaining."

"So is Tamar," Wanda said. "She will receive conservatorship of her mother's work. She will be the sole owner and authority of Dolores's legacy even though she's the true artist. And when the truth does come out the price of the art will skyrocket. It will become priceless. Nothing increases the value of art more than controversy and scandal. What Tamar doesn't realize is how Staaken is using her. He's not going to disappear into the woodwork when this is over. He's gone to a lot of trouble to insert himself into her life. She can't move against him. One word, one hint of a threat, and Staaken will throw her to the wolves. She was present when he killed that boat pilot. Not to mention when they smuggled an illegal drug across the United States border. Tamar's in *zugzwang*. She can't make a move on the chessboard without Staaken checkmating her. Tamar has the art but Staaken is set for life, and there's nothing she can do about it."

I frowned at Wanda. "You're not bothered by this one goddamn bit."

"What do you want me to do?" she fired back. "I helped curate Tamar's work in Dolores's name and kept it together for her. When Staaken turned up I had to make a decision. You would have done the same thing."

"No, I would not. I wouldn't dishonor my daughter's legacy."

"You don't have a daughter," she said in a perfect shot across the bow. "Until you do, don't lecture me on what I should do with my family." She turned away from me and watched Tamar.

In all my years as a policewoman and an investigator I'd never met anyone like Wanda Zipes. I had encountered men and women who had no conscience and would do anything they could to escape justice. I'd seen a lot of ugly things when I worked in Santa Monica. They always put female police officers on certain jobs. It's not that men wouldn't touch those cases, but officials believed a woman could deal with some ugly realities better. I worked them all. Child custody cases. Endangerment. Sexual violence. You see what never makes the papers and you go to bed at night remembering the photographs of frightened faces and mouths opened in silent screams. That shit stays with you a long time. There was another female officer I'd worked alongside. She left the force because she said the things she witnessed on the streets no longer bothered her. She couldn't live another day knowing she'd become inured to the grinding violence every police officer sees on a routine basis.

It reminded me of something Rhea Sheldon's husband had said. How we are forced to become something we never thought we'd be or should become.

I had not reached that point yet. I hoped I never would. But I knew I'd come to a crossroads in this case where my emotions and feelings about one of the principals involved was tainting my overall perception.

Ardak didn't trust me, but he trusted me enough not to do anything that would endanger Tamar. That was insurance in his eyes, and he wasn't wrong. All he had to do was agree to Wanda's proposal. Then if he wanted to, he'd kill her, Tamar, and me. Clear the decks. Carino could do that sleepwalking. Ardak would have the heroin, the paintings, everything. He could sell the paintings in private auctions or through a third party. A man like that knew how to navigate the tricky financial avenues which were part and parcel of the underground art world. If that's what he ultimately decided to do.

And, so, this was the dilemma I faced. I had to find a way to keep Tamar alive and go through with the transfer while keeping the artwork safe.

After lashing down the tarp, we went inside. I sat in a chair off to the side and thought and watched for an hour. Then I waited for an opportunity to speak to Wanda alone. When it happened, we were in a hallway leading off the dining room. I stepped in front of her so she couldn't leave.

"Is Tamar your granddaughter?" I asked her.

She froze as if caught in a spotlight. "What do you mean by that?"

"I didn't want to say anything in front of Tamar, but the dates don't work out, do they? Landers Shavin wasn't in the States when Dolores supposedly became pregnant with his child. He was in Milan with Pola Goddard. Which makes me think maybe Tamar isn't Dolores's daughter, either, because she couldn't have been pregnant. But maybe, just maybe, she's yours."

"That's the most insane thing I've ever heard."

"It hangs together. I found a picture of Shavin and Dolores at the Trocadero. She sure as hell wasn't pregnant when she should have been. The problem is Tamar's father. If it's not Landers, and it's not Emil Staaken because I have things all turned around, that limits things. Landers Shavin was committed, in the only fashion he's capable, to Pola Goddard. You've met Pola. But you didn't know Shavin. At least not intimately. That leaves one other person. Someone with a vested interest in all this. Anthony Ardak, perhaps."

Wanda watched me with growing fascination. "You can't. . .you can't prove that."

"No, because you probably had Hollack fudge the paternity tests all the way around. You needed a loaded gun to point at Shavin's head and Hollack gave you one. With Dolores posing as Tamar's mother, you had the freedom to run around behind the scenes doing your own thing. Except Dolores discovered Tamar had genuine artistic talent. She saw a way to slip out from her predicament. Be her own person for once and not something you wanted her to be. She was willing to go along with the gag as long as she had no other recourse. But the paintings were gaining recognition. She was afraid of getting caught and she wanted out. You weren't about to kiss a million dollars in art goodbye, so you started feeding her yellow jackets and chloral hydrate. Before you knew it, she's stumbling half-naked down Sunset Boulevard. She's institutionalized, again by Dr. Hollack, and when she starts showing improvement you have her pitched out a third-story window."

"You can't prove any of this."

"Hester Paige saw a woman get into a taxi that night. If I talk Shavin into taking another paternity test, one not administered by Hollack, will it show him to be Tamar's father?"

She refused to answer.

"Your trouble is you had too many balls in the air, Wanda. The fake paternity test. Dolores wanting out of the conspiracy. Keeping up the blackmail pressure on Shavin. Trying to deal with Tamar's intractable behavior. Seeing a once-in-a-lifetime opportunity to score a big payout while at the same time getting rid of Staaken. Does Tamar know the truth?"

Wanda's face paled. She looked down and then back up. Her lips barely moved. "Of course not. She never will."

"Does Ardak?"

A long silence followed. "He believes Tamar is Shavin's child by Dolores because that's what we wanted him to believe. Anthony isn't the father. It was another man. We spent a couple of weeks together in Orlando. That's all it was, until it became more and that was lovely. But he left me, and I was stuck having a baby alone."

"You never told Ardak."

"No." She picked up a crystal unicorn from a table, looked at it, and put it back down. "Why would I? He wouldn't care." She sighed but it was more the sound of ice cracking.

"I was going to give Tamar up for adoption," she confessed. "I couldn't be burdened with a child. I had no money. Then I saw a way I could keep my baby. All I had to do was pretend she belonged to Dolores. She went along with the idea at first, but like you said, she got cold feet when the screws started to tighten."

She met my eyes. "I didn't have her killed. No one at the sanitarium killed Dolores. She had stepped far to the other side. Hollack couldn't reach her. I went to see her that last day. She didn't recognize me. That. . .hurt. There was a time when all we had was each other. There was no one else. No money. No food. We slept on the streets. When. . .when I heard Dolores killed herself, I phoned Hester Paige and told her to change the record so my visit wasn't logged. I didn't want it to get back to me. I knew if people learned I was there it could lead to too many questions. Questions I wasn't prepared to answer. Or couldn't answer." Her eyes dropped. "Or was unwilling to answer."

"Hester cut the page out of the visitor's book?"

"No. She wouldn't do it, no matter how much I begged and threatened. Hollack did that for me."

"So where is Shavin's daughter?"

Her eyes snapped up. Her mouth slightly parted.

"Because he does have a daughter, doesn't he? Somewhere."

Wanda looked trapped and defenseless. All her armor peeled away.

"It's Juanita Drexford," I said. "Juanita is his daughter, and Pola is her mother."

Having it out in the open was like a crack of thunder.

Her eyes searched my face. "How did you know?"

"When I put forth the proposition to Tegel that Tamar was Pola's child he was stunned. He said something I'll never forget. He said she wasn't, but he understood what was going on. He had figured out what you'd done just that fast. I was going back to hear what he had to say, but Carino got to him first. That was my bad luck."

Wanda's crushed demeanor told me I was on the right track.

"Here's how I think it worked," I said. "You had an illegitimate baby. Pola had a baby, too. She knew she was unable to take care of a child; that woman has all the warmth of a hangman's noose. That's when you saw your chance. You told Pola that Dolores would take care of her baby. You'd be there to see she would do a proper job. Of course, you had other reasons for doing this, but we won't delve into that again. Pola was relieved. Her daughter with Shavin would be well cared for. Shavin sure as hell was no family man, and Pola knew that, but he was decent enough to see that his daughter and her 'mother' were well taken care of so he went along with the charade. So far, everyone is happy with the arrangement. Pola disappears and has her baby in secret. Then she comes back and hands Dolores the baby to raise under your guidance and she and Shavin think everything is fine."

I poked Wanda's chest. "But you switched babies, didn't you? You gave Pola's daughter up for adoption and you let Dolores raise yours. Far as Dolores knew it was Pola's child she was caring for. Pola never found out. Her baby was in an orphanage under the name Juanita Drexford. Shavin never found out. One newborn baby looks like another to most men. Leastways, when they're that old and Juanita and Tamar were born within a week of each other. Shavin provided for Dolores and Tamar with payments through Elgin Tegel. But over the years Pola started to feel pangs of conscience. Maybe she's salvageable as a human being after all. She's not in your mold, anyway. She started putting money into a secret trust fund for Tamar, paid directly to you because she trusted you. You were keeping her Big Secret and she knew she could trust you with another one. Except she was paying money into a secret trust fund for a baby that wasn't hers. But she didn't have to know that, did she, Wanda?"

Wanda took a deep breath and let it out in short gasps. "No. Only I had to know."

"Then somehow, someway, against all the odds, the universe plays a devilish trick on you. Tamar and Juanita meet each other at the S.P.C.A. and become friends. That must have been one hell of a shock."

She gave a humorless laugh. "A last trick of the gods. Fate, or whatever. I kept tabs on Pola's baby, Juanita, over the years. I knew she'd been adopted by a good family. Then, before I knew what was happening, Juanita was standing on my doorstep beside my own daughter, Tamar."

She looked at me in horrified amazement. "It was. . .it was like heaven crashing down. There. . .there wasn't anything I could do. These things simply do not happen. One in a million chance and my number turns up. Sweet Christ in heaven. I can't tell you how I felt when I saw Juanita with Tamar."

"You spread a lot of thick lies over the years. They're coming home to roost and you're scrambling. Trying to catch straws in a tornadic wind. I hope you fail. I hope you fail, and your world, and everything else, crashes down and buries you forever."

She watched me in amazement. "What are you going to do?"

"I can't prove any of this," I admitted. "For all I know a paternity test will show Shavin did father Tamar. Paternity tests aren't that accurate and too often the results are hammered out in court. Ask Charlie Chaplin how that all turned out." I took a breath and ran my fingers through my hair. "Given the convolutions to this case I don't know if it would even get to a jury. A judge might throw it out for lack of evidence. But Pola believes Tamar is her daughter. Landers Shavin believes Tamar is his daughter."

I was frustrated. Do I ruin lives for the sake of truth, or let things run their course? As it was, everyone was satisfied with the results. So far. That might change in the future. But for now the lie held. If no one said anything it would probably hold forever.

"What are you going to do with this knowledge?" Wanda asked me cautiously.

"I don't know and that's the truth. I used to believe the truth was the single most important thing in our lives. Now if I tell the truth, I could ruin dozens of lives. But everything I know was built on lie after lie and all of them told by you. If I could see another way to put you away forever, I'd do it. But, and God help me, I don't. I just don't."

I felt like my heart was torn up inside me. I put my hand on Wanda's chest and stiff-armed her hard against the wall. I leaned forward until we were nose to nose.

"You're going to do what I say from now on," I said fiercely. "Do I make myself clear? Because if you don't, I swear to God, I'll kill you myself."

She opened her mouth to speak but no sound came out. She nodded jerkily. But for all that, there was a light of relief in her eyes.

My face was hard and cold. I wasn't myself, and I didn't care. "I'm going to do you a favor, Wanda. You think you've been a bitch? Well, you've met the Queen. I want to know everything you know. Where is this trade taking place? Who is involved?"

"It's at the garage where you were held. There are two main parties. Anthony and Staaken. Staaken will hand over a sample. Anthony will test it to make sure it's the real thing. Staaken will take possession of the paintings and Anthony the heroin. Then everyone goes their separate ways. There's too much at stake, too much money involved going both ways for anyone to get cute. Anthony has been in negotiations with Staaken for three months. They've decided how this will go down to the second. There will be no mistakes. There must not be."

"What else?"

"No guns. Not at the final transfer point. No one wants to get funny and risk a lifetime in San Quentin."

"Time?"

"Ten o'clock tonight. The garage is neutral ground. Staaken turns over a sample and it's taken to Anthony and verified, like I said. Then the real exchange happens."

"Who represents Ardak?"

"You. He couldn't believe his good fortune when you showed up. You came to him like a bolt out of the blue. He knows you will do everything you can to protect Tamar."

"Otherwise, he'll have Tamar killed."

"He's threatened to do that. I don't think he would."

"Can you stop him?"

She tried to find an answer but couldn't.

"Ten o'clock tonight?"

"Yes."

"With no guns."

"Or it's all-out war and everybody loses."

"Okay," I said, feeling trapped. "At least Tamar can stay here, out of the way. That's something, I suppose."

Wanda gripped my arm. "No, you don't understand. She's the key to everything: the drugs, the paintings. She's insurance for both sides. Staaken doesn't want her harmed and Anthony wants her there because she's his insurance policy, too. She's there to let Staaken know there will be no double cross. Staaken can use her because if there *is* a double cross he'll put a bullet in her head and destroy the heroin."

Wanda led me outside until we stood beside the flatbed truck. "What do you see?"

I shrugged. "A tarp. The cans underneath where the paintings are stored."

She shot me a pointed stare. "Look again. You're supposed to be a detective."

I lifted a corner of the tarp and looked under. "I don—"

"We used four cans. Now there are five. The fifth is filled with six sticks of TNT. It's connected to a radio circuit and a detonator. If anything goes wrong, Anthony will hit the switch on a special walkie talkie and the truck goes up in a ball of fire. With you and Tamar inside."

I won't lie. I'd expected something like it, but when you hear the words out loud it sends an ice-cold shiver down your spine.

"You're going to let that happen?" I asked Wanda. "To your own daughter?"

She looked down. "Like you said so eloquently, straws in the wind. They're too fast for me to catch. There's nothing I can do. You have to take Tamar with you to complete the trade. Any other scenario means Tamar dies. Despite what you think, I don't want that to happen."

She looked into my eyes. Her own were misty. "I'm telling the truth, Miss Parrish. I don't want my daughter to die. But there's nothing I can do to stop it. If I try to get her free Anthony will kill you, Tamar, and probably me. He will still have the paintings in his possession and set up another trade with Staaken in the future."

She drew a ragged breath. "You see, when it comes down to it, he doesn't need any of us."

SEVENTEEN

ARDAK FLATTENED A COUNTY MAP and he and I went over the timetable. He had two men stationed a quarter mile away where the purity of the heroin would be tested. When we got to the part with the garage, he said, "You open the garage door and back the truck in. Turn off your headlights. Staaken will drive his vehicle down this country road from Junction City. He will make the turn at the intersection at the top of this hill, stop, and flash his headlights twice. You respond in kind. That's the all-clear signal."

"There's already a car inside the garage," I said. "The truck won't fit."

"It's been moved," Ardak said, rolling up the map. "Carino and Jimmy took care of that earlier. We will watch everything from our vantage point after we escort you to the garage. Hear me loud and clear, Miss Parrish. Make one false move and Staaken will think he's double-crossed. He'll kill you and Tamar both. Try to cross me and the same thing happens. Go through with the trade. When that's complete Staaken will depart and we will take possession of the heroin. You don't need to do anything else. Don't try and leave prematurely. Wait until we arrive. When we have what we want you and the girl can clear out. Questions?"

"Yeah. About a thousand. Are we switching vehicles when Staaken shows?"

"He will be driving a truck or something similar. All you do is switch keys with him and take his vehicle. He'll take your truck."

"Uh huh. Sure. Sounds easy. Where's the heroin?"

A quizzical frown appeared on Ardak's flesh-colored lips. "I don't read you."

"Don't be stupid, because I'm not. Who's to say Staaken won't have the French on him when he comes to the garage? Or ditch it somewhere else before he pulls up?"

I knew why Staaken wouldn't do that. He would know about the dynamite wired to the truck. It was the only reasonable answer. Ardak certainly knew. That was their mutual insurance policy. Not Tamar. Staaken wouldn't risk having priceless artwork destroyed any more than Ardak wanted his heroin destroyed. Maybe they both had walkie talkies which could activate the detonator. They'd been setting this thing up for three months. They were going through a lot of gyrations to guarantee both parties be on their best behavior. One false move, and either man could hit the doomsday switch. Goodbye paintings. Goodbye French heroin. It was the perfect solution.

"The full amount of heroin will have been confirmed in Staaken's vehicle before he approaches the garage," Ardak explained. "This will have taken place shortly before Staaken hands over his sample. We have built in safeguards on both sides. Nothing is left to chance."

Ardak wasn't going to tell me about the truck being rigged with explosives. In his eyes I didn't have to know. It didn't affect the job I was on, other than I would be driving a truck ready to blow up any second, but who would get nervous about that? Tamar was there to make me think she was the one thing assuring both men would behave. Ardak knew I would do everything I could to keep Tamar safe. He could use that against me, which is why I didn't have to know about the explosives.

I could list a hundred other reasons why this would never go down as smoothly as planned, but I had no other choice. I was going to have to drive the truck and Tamar was coming with me. Ardak played this setup beautifully. It was like one of the Mozart symphonies he listened to: mathematically structured and pure as crystalline ice.

Tamar approached me when we had a moment. "I can't get inside the kitchen," she whispered. "There are men inside I've never seen before. They wouldn't let me through the door."

"It was worth a try."

I'd been allowed by Carino to pick up my clothes and fold them back in the overnight case. After all, I'd be leaving tonight with Tamar, right? Why shouldn't I be allowed to take my clothes. He stood smiling under that thick moustache. *Sure, Pixie. Pack your things. No problem at all.*

I handed the case to Tamar. "Hold on to this. I'm going to be a bit busy tonight, methinks, but I want to keep it around." I didn't need it. It was just to give her something to do. "You've got the gun?"

"Yes," she whispered.

"We're going to do what they say. Then they'll let us go."

"You think so?"

No, I don't. "Yes. They have no reason to keep us around. Everyone will have what they want. Compared to everything else going on we're minnows."

"Except minnows get swallowed by bigger fish, Pidge."

She wasn't dumb. I put my hand on her shoulder and flashed a smile. I hoped the smile looked real because it felt cold as sin. "Everything will be fine. This is what I get paid to do. Don't worry."

I didn't like lying to her, but she had enough on her mind. I was supposed to be the expert around here. The only thing I wanted was to get her somewhere safe and sound. I had to find a way to do that without getting us both killed.

Another hour passed and the house filled with strangers. Well, it didn't fill up as much as there were suddenly a lot of men hanging around. Most were gathered around Ardak. They smoked and talked in hushed tones. No one looked my way. Not one person.

If I didn't already know the truth, that was enough to tell me I wasn't coming out of this alive.

A butler came by with a tray of tuna sandwiches and drinks. I wasn't hungry but Tamar ate a little and I had some tomato juice.

People came and went from the main room and out the front door. Carino sat in an armchair, perusing the evening paper. Jimmy tuned a radio to a local station and did a soft shuffle-step to the music.

I didn't see Wanda anywhere around. Come to think of it, I hadn't seen her for some while. She'd hung around Ardak like a barnacle since I'd arrived, but now she was missing.

I picked a spot where I could observe the front door. I felt a shift of air when Wanda sailed through. I was certain she hadn't gone out that way since I'd started haunting the main hall. She must have gone out another way. The kitchen, maybe, where Tamar couldn't get in.

A door that led into the back parking lot with the flatbed truck.

Wanda favored me with a passing glance and went straight to Ardak. She took his arm and laughed at something he said. She had her back to me. She spoke briefly and the men around her chuckled. Someone handed her a drink and Ardak lit her cigarette.

In my job I have to be able to read individual people really well, but I also have to understand people in the general sense, especially how they react, in general, to stress. There's talk of a sixth sense. I don't believe it. I do know there are cues and body movements and facial prompts which can convey unspoken words. Smiles, gestures, the way someone sets her shoulders or carries her head are the most obvious. But I'm talking about more subtle cues. The kind where if you pick them up you think it's magic because it's like you're reading the other person's mind.

I don't know exactly what it was I saw when Wanda walked past me. Maybe the lock of hair blown out of place by the wind outside, or the smudge of dirt on the back of her hand, or the oil stain on one of her expensive pumps. Collectively, they told me she'd been outside with the truck. Fifteen, twenty minutes tops. Long enough to accomplish what she wanted. That was the look I got. Except I couldn't think of anything she could be doing out there.

But she had passed a look meant only for me.

I went to Carino. "Hey."

He lowered the paper. "What do you want."

"Since I'm driving that truck, I want to know if there's anything strange with it. I don't want to be surprised out there."

"What do you mean, strange?"

"Does it go left when you turn right. That sort of thing."

"There's nothing wrong with that truck, lady. Don't worry your pretty head about it."

"Full tank?"

"Sure."

"Does it have a jack? Spare tire?"

"You're not driving across country. You don't need a spare."

"Yeah, but say the impossible happens, because you and I know it always does."

"There's a jack behind the seat."

"But no spare tire, I take it. Or an air pump, maybe? No, not even that. Christ, what a half-ass outfit this is. Okay, if that's how you want to operate it's fine by me."

"You don't need it." He lifted the paper signifying our conversation was at an end.

I grabbed the top of the newspaper and crushed it down. I leaned in with all my five-foot-nine height. "Look, pal. I'm not the one who's going to get skinned by Ardak if I pick up a goddamn nail and blow out a tire. I thought I'd ask how the truck was and you're telling me it doesn't even have a fucking spare."

I stepped back, ran my fingers through my hair. "Christ, what a shit show. Here I thought you guys were professionals. Come to find out you and Jimmy are nothing but a couple of cheap hoods."

"Fuck off," he snarled.

I slapped the paper back in his face. "I'll ask Ardak to take care of it. He'll want to know anyway, I suppose. Go back to your funnies, Carino."

I turned in disgust and stalked away.

Maybe I laid it on a bit thick, but he hadn't liked my threat of going to Ardak. If it hadn't been a spare tire, it would have been a jack or a tool kit or an oil can or a lug nut or *something*. I wanted to go out there and give that truck the once-over. I wanted to know what Wanda had been doing that got her shoe stained with oil.

Carino flung the newspaper down. "Wait a minute."

I stopped, turned. "What d'you want now?"

"Let's ask Jimmy."

"Okay. Let's ask Jimmy."

I meekly followed him across the terrazzo floor to where Jimmy listened to Dinah Shore on the radio.

"Jimmy," Carino started, "this dame is worried about the truck. She wants a spare in case she picks up a nail. I think it's a smart idea. We can't take chances."

Jimmy didn't bother turning around. "That truck is in tip-top shape, Angelo. She ain't got no worries."

"Say something does happen," Carino barked back. "You want to explain that to Mr. Ardak, maybe?"

Ardak's name carried a lot of weight. Jimmy turned around. He looked over Carino's shoulder at me. "You know how to change a tire?"

I put Jimmy down as a good ten years younger than I was. I helped my old man change tires on the Ford tractor when I was a snot-nosed kid sneaking cigarettes behind the barn with my brother.

"Yeah," I said, "I think I can manage it."

Jimmy looked me up and down. "I guess maybe you can," he admitted with grudging respect. "Most dames can't. Or don't want to. Okay, I'm sold. But goddamn if it ain't one thing it's another. Dames is sure a lot of trouble, I swear."

I didn't answer. I couldn't believe I'd gotten this far. I didn't want to jinx things.

I dutifully followed Jimmy through the dining room and into the kitchen. There were men in dark suits drinking and playing canasta. They looked like torpedoes. The real kind, not the Aiden and Eddie knock offs.

"Where you headed?" one of them asked, gruff.

Jimmy paused with his hand on the doorknob. "Gonna take a look at the truck and make sure nothing is amiss. We don't want some accident happening out there and not be ready."

"What kind of accident?" a second man rumbled.

"The accidental kind of accident," Jimmy elaborated. He moved past them and I went with him. I kept my eyes fixed on his back while they watched us walk out the door into the back lot. Jimmy hooked a thumb. "Yonder she is. I'll roll the spare from the garage."

Hell, I could have kissed him. "Okay."

He disappeared. I popped the hood to check the oil and the water wells in the battery. Fan belt was tight. Radiator full. I shut the hood. I crouched on my hams and looked under the truck. Brake lines good. I straightened and kicked a tire.

I walked to the garage to meet Jimmy, giving the Lincoln Continental a passing glance while watching out for that big oil puddle. That's when I saw the car trunk had a small handprint in the dust. I also noticed a corner of the tarp on the flatbed was loosened. I lifted the tarp and saw the cans and then I tied it down again. Tight.

Jimmy rolled a tire out of the garage. "There's a place under the bed where it sits with a lock nut what holds it in."

"That tire's pretty big," I said. "Can you help me lift it?"

"Sure." We slid under the truck. Jimmy held the tire in place while I locked the nut down with a wrench. Crawling out, Jimmy brushed his hands clean. "That's that."

"You got the keys on you? Fire up that engine. I want to check the oil pressure."

Jimmy slid into the driver's seat while I hovered in the doorway. He pumped the clutch and the engine started smoothly. I leaned through the doorway to read the dashboard. My shoulder put pressure on Jimmy's chest. A woman can tell when a man is watching, or when you're close to him and he doesn't want to move because he's smelling your perfume or the warmth of your hair.

"Gauges look fine," I admitted. "Guess I was worried over nothing."

Jimmy switched the engine off. "Dames is always trouble. Let's head back inside."

I thought my heart would burst when he walked around the bed testing the knots on the tarp. My blood pressure was higher than the Empire State Building. I tried to keep a bored look on my face.

"Everything copesetic?" I asked.

"I'm satisfied if you are," he told me.

He headed for the kitchen door. I skip-stepped around the oil puddle and let my knee buckle while I lost my balance and bumped into him. He caught me around the waist.

I quickly disengaged myself from his embrace. "Sorry," I stammered, straightening my clothes and patting my hair in place. "I was trying to keep out of that oil puddle."

"Yeah, it needs sopping up." He pitched me the truck keys. "Here. You might as well keep 'em."

"Thanks."

"Let's get inside. No, this way. I don't want to cross that puddle again. Let's walk down this side of the house and go through the front door."

"Like you say." I walked ahead of him so he could watch me from behind. I didn't know if he might want to take me by the arms and push me against the house for a quick feel. Whatever happened, I didn't want him looking at or thinking about the truck. I wanted him to think how I bumped into him and how my body felt in his hands. Not that I thought I could seduce him. I'd been through a rough twenty-four hours. If I could throw a rock and hit him in the head to keep his mind off the truck I'd have done that. I'd have done anything.

Inside, Carino and Jimmy passed a guarded word. Carino looked satisfied and returned to his armchair and his newspaper. Jimmy lit a cigarette and went back to the radio.

I found Tamar standing by the fireplace. "Hey, kid, how're you holding up? Still got the overnight case? Good. Hold on to that." I turned sideways so Carino couldn't see my face from where he sat. Now was not the time for mistakes. One wrong blink, one guilty look, and we were cooked.

"I want you to stay close to me," I told Tamar low. "Do everything I say. Don't stop and think about it. I yell frog, you jump. Understand?"

"All right. But—"

"But nothing. We have one chance and I don't want to queer the pitch. We're getting out of here. Don't look surprised, kid. You're not alone in this world after all. You've got a guardian angel."

"Who?"

"That lady over there with men hanging around her like bees buzzing around a flower. Wanda. Your. . .grandmother. She's going to give us a chance to escape."

"How?"

"She's going to blow Ardak to Kingdom Come."

EIGHTEEN

I STARTED THE TRUCK WITH Tamar sitting crooked against the passenger door. We followed Carino and Jimmy onto the road. They were in a different car, a black Ford Super Deluxe, Carino driving. Ardak and Wanda brought up our rear in the Continental.

I half expected Ardak to flash his lights for me to pull over or have Carino wave me down so he could take a final inspection at the tarp covering the truck bed. But we were in a final phase of the mission and headed to the rendezvous point and everyone's mind was on something else. They hadn't noticed the topography of the tarp looked different because a canister was missing. The one thing I worried about was whether Ardak would notice the extra weight in the trunk of the Lincoln. That big car had sensitive shocks and the extra weight might be enough for him to feel a change in the handling or suspension. But, I mean, how much could six sticks of TNT inside a metal can weigh? Chances were he wouldn't realize a thing.

The missing canister was what I had noticed when Jimmy and I inspected the truck. I didn't know what Wanda had done when she was out there, but I'd put two and two together with the splash of oil on her shoe and the feminine handprint on the Lincoln's powder blue trunk. Looking under the tarp and counting the metal cans in the washed-out green light sealed it. She'd removed the can with the TNT and placed it sideways in the trunk of the Lincoln. I'd have liked to pull her aside and question her, but there wasn't time. There was never going to be time. She was in a car with Ardak and six sticks of dynamite wired to a walkie talkie and as soon as he hit the trigger, they would both go up in a crack of thunder and flame.

But she wasn't going to do it on her own. She would want a starting gun. She had to have something, or someone, give her the all-clear signal. That someone was me. I had Tamar. When I made my move to get Tamar away, Wanda would play her part, and then it'd be all up to me. Wanda was going to give me the best chance possible to affect an escape, hoping I'd be able to slip free in the ensuing confusion.

I kept tabs on the Lincoln in my rearview mirror. I didn't know how much damage six sticks of TNT could do, but I was certain it'd engulf my truck if Ardak hit the trigger now. He was barely two car lengths back. Either I had to make a move and try and peel out between Carino's car and Ardak's or wait for a better opportunity to present itself. It was possible Wanda had her own idea when I should make my move, but I had no clue when that should be. I had to drive and think and decide on the fly if the next turn, or the next quarter mile stretch of road, or that banked curve ahead was where I needed to make my break.

Also, I wasn't driving a sports car. The truck's V8 engine had a lot of horsepower, but it was pulling a lot of steel along with it. Call it a ton and a half. My acceleration was severely limited. I couldn't outrun the Lincoln or Carino's Ford. I had to make a move that would use the weight of the truck in such a way that it would give me an edge and I could get away clean. If I couldn't outrace them then I had to outthink and outdrive them.

Ardak wouldn't hit the trigger in the first few seconds. He'd be surprised, shocked, maybe. But he was ready for trouble. A man like that doesn't get where he is by being careless. But he'd be surprised because that's only human nature, and that was the one chance I needed to get loose.

Therefore, I had to wait for my chance, but not wait too long. At the end of it all was Staaken. I sure as hell didn't want to put things off until then. That would be terminal in more ways than one. I had no gun, no weapon, nothing. All I had was—

Tamar said, "Do you think we should try to get away?"

We crossed a gravel crossroads. I geared down so I wouldn't lose the back end on the slippery shale. The Lincoln drew close and Ardak tapped his horn for us to keep moving.

"How do you mean?" I asked.

"We have a vehicle. We may never get another chance. Maybe we can signal the authorities."

I liked how her mind worked even if it wasn't conducive to reality. Her suggestion was pure Saturday matinee stuff. The B-movie between the newsreel and the cartoon. Wallace Beery fighting the good fight against city corruption and wrapping things up in a 68-minute run time.

"I don't think we're going to find any cops out here," I said. "But you can be sure if I do, I'll honk at him."

Her face was downcast. "I'm only trying to help."

I felt sorry for her. She didn't know what her mother, who she thought was her grandmother, was planning. She didn't have to know. That's why I felt bad. Everyone had lied to this girl since the day she was born. Now I wore the liar's crown. She didn't deserve that. Nobody did. I'd been in this business long enough to know nobody deserved anything, but they always got it coming to them anyway. I was more than a bit tired of it.

I reached over to take her hand. It felt cold and dry. "I know you're trying to help, and I appreciate it. Maybe there is something we can do." I had an idea forming like ice on barbed wire. And about as dangerous.

"You have a plan?"

I checked my mirrors, making sure the Lincoln was right up with us. "I wouldn't exactly call it a *plan*."

"Pidge," she frowned.

"Remember that slippery stretch of gravel back there?"

"I don't think so. I haven't exactly been paying attention to the road."

"There's another one coming up at the bottom of the next hill before we reach the garage."

She looked through the windshield at the road ahead. "So?"

I checked the mirrors. "You know what a bootlegger's turn is?"

"No. Wait. Isn't that when a car turns around fast to head the other way?"

"Yep. And that's what I'm thinking." I'd spotted the stretch of gravel up at the next intersection when I was leaving the garage with Carino and Jimmy. Say, a half a mile away from where we were now. Approximately the same distance to the garage. There was a four-way stop at the intersection, too, and it was on top of a steep hill.

The truck I drove had a nice heavy tow hitch that could puncture the radiator if you hit the car behind you off-center. I couldn't ask for better.

They're not terribly hard to execute. Bootlegger turns, that is. My brother and I used to do them in my old man's Flivver. We'd take turns flying down a single lane road into Soledad. We tried to outdo each other, seeing who could make the turn without flying into a bar ditch and overturning the car. The narrow farm road forced us to practice the maneuver until we could do a full 180-degree turn. If you have the horsepower, you can do it on about any blacktop. My truck had the horsepower, but weight was the limiting problem. I'd have to reach speed to pull off a trick like that on a dry blacktop. But not loose gravel. It wouldn't be difficult on loose gravel. Yes, sir, loose gravel would do nicely, and there was a nice long stretch on the old farm road in front of the garage at the bottom of a hill.

All three cars stopped at the four-way, one behind the other: Carino and Jimmy, me and Tamar, Ardak and Wanda. I had the impression we would go at the same time, single file, like ducks. And that's what we did. We started through the intersection and headed down the long steep hill together, picking up speed. Not a lot. But enough. Faster. A little bit faster.

"Hang tight," I warned Tamar. "When I say hit the deck throw yourself off the seat and stay down. There might be gunfire."

"What are you going to do?"

"We're getting out of here." It sounded optimistic. I put our chances at one in three and that was optimistic. But that was better than zero.

I looked in my rearview mirror. I'd have to be precise. I let the Lincoln Continental creep closer and then I slammed the truck into reverse and stomped the gas pedal. There were ugly grinding sounds coming from the clutch, but the gear caught solid after we slid forward several yards and fishtailed a bit, the back wheels spinning wild and throwing gravel until the treads caught. I was backing up fast. Not a lot of room between me and Ardak but I didn't need a football field. With his momentum carrying him towards me, we crunched beautifully. I was slammed back into my seat on impact. I kept my foot pressed on the gas pedal, not a little impressed that, after the collision, we pushed the Lincoln back a yard or two. Good old Chevy truck. Then I shoved the gear into low and pulled forward with the sound of rending, screeching metal, double clutched, slammed on the gas, and we were flying fast as we could down the steep road.

A quick check in my rearview informed me Ardak's Lincoln was stopped in the middle of the road. A stream of brown water poured from the radiator and clouds of steam rose into the night air. That heavy trailer hitch had done its job perfectly. The rest was up to me.

I rocketed past Carino, passing on his right instead of his left. Caught a glimpse of Jimmy's pale face and his mouth wide-open in shock. As drivers we're conditioned to cars passing on our left on a single lane roadway. It's normal. With me slamming through on Carino's right, half my wheelbase off the gravel road and thumping over dirt, he was caught by surprise. I turned sharply to sideswipe him. He did the natural thing. He swerved left to avoid me; driver's instinct when a lunatic comes barreling past you on a narrow, dangerous roadway. I turned left with him, and the front end of the truck smashed his front right fender. With luck I'd burst his tire, but he was quick and as soon as we made contact, he hit the brakes and fishtailed and broke free. It was a neat maneuver. Maybe someday he'd teach it to me, assuming we ever became friends, and I didn't kill us all by driving like a maniac.

Tamar was shouting but I wasn't paying attention to her. We were flying downhill at a modest clip. Carino had collected himself and was back coming fast. I heard a crack. The back window in the truck cab starred. Goddamn Jimmy. He was a good shot, though. Hitting a car, any car, with a handgun in the midst of a chase is damn hard to do.

They make it look easy in the movies, but the movies make everything look easy. Maybe that's why people like them so much.

"Get down," I shouted at Tamar. She flung herself off the seat and lay curled on the floor.

There was a dip in the road at the bottom of the hill. I gripped the steering wheel. Ah, hell. Forgot about that. We slammed into it, scattering gravel. Carino came after, gravel and sparks showering out from under his car like a demon rising from the Pit. Ardak's Lincoln Continental was racing after us, too, but I didn't think he'd get far with that blown radiator. Give it enough time and his water-starved engine would clap out. Of course, he had the radio trigger and if he thought I was actually going to escape, he'd hit the kill button. If anything, he'd let me pull ahead so he wouldn't be caught in the explosion. I had no idea what conversation or interaction was happening between Wanda and Ardak —maybe there was a tussle over the walkie talkie. I had my own problems. Ardak was out of the running. Or would be soon. My present concern was Carino.

Jimmy's .38 cracked twice more. Lead slugs punched the back of the truck. He was going for a tire. I relaxed. Maybe Jimmy watched too many movies as well. It was one thing to hit an entire truck in front of you. Quite another to single out and hit a tire in the dark with a .38, or any handgun, really. Unless Jimmy got lucky. Sometimes people get lucky. Jimmy might be one of them. I wasn't going to give him the chance to find out.

We were on straight and level road—gravel goat path overgrown on the edges with tall milkweeds was more like it. One side was bordered by an irrigation ditch two feet deep and half as wide. If I hit that at any speed, it would tear the bottom out of this truck. The other side was not much better. A haphazard stone fence lined the road and beyond it, the stinking onion field. It wasn't much of a stone fence, but it looked substantial enough. Those were my borders. I had to execute my bootlegger's turn between them, and I chose to turn towards the fence, since it would catch the truck if I wasn't able to keep it on a true 180-degree turn.

The truck's speed touched forty, fifty. Carino's headlights were coming fast. Wind whistled through the broken back window. Jimmy's gun cracked but I didn't hear any lead hit the truck. I doused my head-lights. Carino would see my taillights when I braked and he might think I was stopping. Or he might think I was going to try to pull off some-thing no sane person would ever try at night without headlights. I hoped he'd think the former. The only thing I had going for me was the element of surprise. No one would think a person was dumb enough to try what I was going to try.

"Watch me, Carino," I muttered.

The whole thing went smoother than expected. All that training in my misspent youth paid off. I stood on the handbrake and spun the wheel hard feeling the back end of the truck slide sickeningly. Tamar screamed. I fought the urge to overcorrect and keep the truck centered. I let the back end whip around. The wheels shuddered, kicking up shovel-fuls of rock and dirt that showered the stone fence like summer's hail.

But we were through, and I released the brake and the back wheels tore at the road and spun and gripped and there was the smell of burning rubber, but I'd done it; we were facing the opposite direction. I hit the gas and went up through the gears headed straight for Carino in a game of chicken. He saw me coming at him. I'd cut it close. He didn't have time to stop and I switched my lights on bright, blinding him, while blaring the horn at the same time.

It had the effect I wanted. Blinded and deafened, Carino whipped his steering wheel hard to the right. The safer move would have been to go towards the wall, but I was coming head on and his driver's instinct took over. He jerked the wheel right, as anyone would do to avoid a head-on collision. It's how we're taught when we learn to drive and it becomes ingrained. Second nature. Carino was a professional killer, but he wasn't a professional driver, so he spun the wheel to the right and went into the ditch.

I'm not saying I planned all this down to the last maneuver. I wish. I hadn't known what the situation would be after I punched Ardak's radiator, assuming that trick even worked. I was doing all this on autopi-lot. Tamar and I were going to be killed anyway, so I'd chosen to fight back with the only weapon I had: the truck.

Carino's car powered into the deep ditch with so much force the back wheels lifted clear off the road. He didn't hit it straight on, but the front end crumpled, and I saw a tire fly off into the blackness and hit the ground rolling at an angle. Jimmy launched headfirst through the windshield. He rolled down the hood and was crushed between the car's front bumper and the ditch when the back wheels came down and then the whole night sky lit up in a towering fireball.

The shockwave from the TNT inside the Lincoln blew out my windshield and that's when I lost all control and we barreled through the stone wall and then an old barbed-wire fence with the sound of shrieking metal and breaking glass and came to a sudden lurching stop, the truck canted crazily to one side.

We were in the middle of the onion field and a steeling cloud of dust. Blood was on my face and in my eyes. I'd hit the steering wheel with my forehead. Bits of metal and glass and large twisted pieces of flaming wreckage from the Lincoln rained from the night sky. It hit the tilled ground and bounced and rolled, starting little fires throughout patches of dry grass. I smelled gasoline.

"Tamar."

I couldn't wrench open my door. It was jammed shut. I slid across the seat and forced open the passenger door so I could see to Tamar. She was out cold but breathing.

I shook her. "Come on, Tamar. Wake up. We've got to go."

I slapped her face trying to bring her around. I didn't see any wounds, but she'd had it rough down there on the floorboards.

I started to pull her out. "Come on, kid, don't die on me."

Her eyes fluttered open. "I smell gas."

I did, too. That's why I wanted to get clear before a trickle found the hot engine.

"We've got to get out of here," I told Tamar. I stanched blood from my forehead on my blouse. "Grab my hand. We'll head for the garage. It has a phone. We can call for help."

We helped each other crawl and stumble clear of the wrecked vehicle. Tamar was limping, her weight heavy on my supporting arm. We had to make our way over the planted rows of onions which made the going more difficult. That trickle of gas finally found the red-hot engine and the truck went up behind us. I threw Tamar to the ground and went down with her, feeling the hot wash of air rolling over our bodies from the fire.

"Are you okay?" I asked her.

"I lost the gun you gave me."

"Forget it." So much for Chekhov's gun.

Tamar's stricken face reflected the red light from the fire. All her art, everything she wanted to covet and to remember Dolores by, was engulfed in an inferno.

"Come on," I said, "we've got to go. What's wrong?"

"It's my knee. I think it's broken or something."

I helped her to her feet, but she couldn't stand, and I had to take most of her weight in my arms. We stumbled for the garage with shifting light from the truck fire illuminating the ground and the onion rows.

When we reached the garage, I propped Tamar against the wall and tried the door.

Locked. I used a stone to break the window. I reached through sharp glass and unlocked the door. It was pitch black inside. It smelled of rancid oil and tobacco smoke. My fumbling fingers found a light switch.

Home sweet home. I recognized the card table and wooden bench. The phone was in the main bay.

"Sit down." I helped Tamar into one of the folding chairs. Her bloodless face was ghostly. She clutched her leg, wincing.

"I can't walk anymore," she said.

"Don't move. I'm going to call for help."

"Can I have some water?"

"Sure. I'll be right back."

I was filling a glass in the restroom when I heard Carino shouting outside.

"Come out," he said. "I've got Jimmy's gun."

I threw the glass of water in the sink and hit the light switch plunging us into darkness. "Get down, Tamar," I hissed across the room.

She did, half-crying from the pain shooting through her leg.

"Come out, Parrish," Carino said.

I felt around and my hand picked up a pair of Channellocks beside the acetylene torch. Not the best weapon, but they were heavy. "Where's Jimmy?" I asked him.

"You killed him. Ardak and Wanda, too."

I didn't think I'd killed Jimmy, or the others, but it wasn't time to argue semantics.

"I've called the police already. They're on their way."

"No you didn't," Carino said. "I saw you through the back window when I cut the phone line."

My stomach dropped. "I don't believe you."

"Try it."

Staying in a crouch, I crab-walked across the bay floor and reached for the phone on the wall. Dead line. *Bastard.*

"You're not going anywhere," Carino said. "Now come on out."

"Where's Staaken?"

"After that little episode you pulled? He's probably in the next county by now. He wouldn't have even made it to the testing sample site."

"Let's talk about this." My mind was racing.

"We're not talking. You're doing. Come to me at the count of three or I set fire to the garage. Then I shoot whoever comes through that door."

"Let the girl go first."

"Tamar? She's with you?"

"Yes."

Brief silence. "I don't want her."

We both knew who he wanted.

"She can't walk. Her knee's broken, I think."

"Drag her out."

"I can't do that. I'm hurt myself."

"If I come inside I'm killing you both."

I moved slightly. My shoulder bumped the maroon acetylene tank and I lost my balance. It clinked against another tank. I felt around in the blackness for the flint striker. I'd seen Jimmy place it on the wooden bench beside a metal toolbox, but I must have knocked it on the floor when I bumped the cylinder. There wasn't much light streaming through the window. Starlight, a nip of moon. I was on my hands and knees, groping around in the dark. In more ways than one.

"What do you think I'm going to do?" I shouted back. "You have the gun."

"Come out."

"The door's open, for Christ's sake. Tamar's hurt bad. She's lost a lot of blood and I'm worried about her." My hand closed on something. I sought Tamar's eyes across the room and held my finger to my lips.

I had the striker. I didn't know which of the two valves on the acetylene cylinder to turn first. One was oxygen and the other acetylene. One valve was painted green. That had to be oxygen. I twisted it open. It hissed like a snake.

Carino kicked the door open. It slammed against the wall. He wasn't framed in the doorway. Smart.

"We're by the card table," I said. "You can switch on the light. I want the girl to go free and then we can talk."

His hand reached for the light switch. I turned on the acetylene gas.

When the lights blazed, Carino stepped around the door jamb, gun in hand and held low. He knew the sudden light in the darkness would destroy my night vision, blinding me momentarily to give him the killing edge.

I snapped the striker and lit the torch as soon as I saw his fingers touch the light switch. He came through the door, I shot to my feet, and shoved a 4000-degree blue-white hissing flame in his face. He jerked back with a terrible scream, flailing wildly, trying to fight off the thing burning straight through him. The gun flew out of his hand. I only had the torch on his face a few seconds, but I'd got his eyes and a good chunk of his cheek. It was enough. He fell backward onto the floor, clutching his face and kicking his legs wildly and screaming a high-pitched guttural scream that cut the night. His body rolled and twisted and the heels of his shoes left black streaks on the concrete floor as his body bowed this way and that in terrible agony, like a snake with a broken spine. There was another scream accompanying his. It was Tamar, alarmed at what I'd done to another human being. Holding the torch I started towards Carino, determined to cut him to pieces with the flame.

I bent over him. He wasn't human. He was a thing.

"Say when," I told Carino.

"Pidge!" Tamar shrieked in horror.

That cleared my mind. I'd been in a dark and ugly place where I would do something unbelievably savage to save our lives. When you drop into a dark hole like that all the human light in your soul closes off. I didn't like the feeling. I didn't like being that way, trapped in some Attic tragedy. As if I was watching myself become something ugly and fierce, a thing warped and twisted beyond recognition. No longer human, no longer animal, but into the shadowed realm of demons.

Carino's cries of anguish faded into guttural, whining gasps. There was the awful smell of burned flesh that turned my stomach. He was alive. Maybe he would live. But he was fully encompassed by the unbelievable agony I'd given him. Tamar sobbed heavily, hands clapped to her mouth, eyes wide with terror.

I turned off the acetylene torch and dropped it on the concrete flooring.

"Are you okay?" I asked Tamar.

She nodded dumbly with unblinking eyes, like she'd never seen me before. I guess she hadn't.

I found Carino's .38 in the corner. I picked it up, checked the wheel. It had a couple good rounds left. I looked at the gun in my hand and smelled the seared flesh, hearing again the guttural screams and the ugly hiss of gas. I stumbled into the bathroom and was violently ill. I was tired and exhausted from the case and everyone involved, and I didn't like what it had brought out in me.

I stared at myself in the shaving mirror. Face caked with dried blood. Looking like hell.

I went back and sat at the card table and stared at nothing while Tamar continued to weep. Staaken was out there somewhere, but Tamar and I weren't going anywhere. We'd have to cross the open onion field exposing ourselves to attack and Tamar couldn't travel far on that knee anyway. If we had to fight, we'd make our stand here. We sat in the half-dark for I don't know how long while Carino made high-pitched bubbling cries of anguish until he finally fell silent. Far away I heard a siren, then more than one.

Lights swung back and forth through the dark, breaking up the night. Running men holding flashlights, the cherry red flashes of police cars. Voices, shouts. The squeal of brakes and more radios squawking. More flashlights walking in a line up to the garage in a group and a man stepping through the open doorway. Tall and dark and grim-faced. He glanced at Carino on the floor. Other people entered the room. Someone led Tamar away.

The man came and stood near me. He lowered his automatic pistol, his face unreadable.

"Pixie," Aiden said.

I raised my head. I was tired and I wanted to go home and sleep for a year. He took the .38 revolver from my hand.

"Took you long enough," I said.

NINETEEN

TWO DAYS LATER I WAS in Sacramento. I had an afternoon appointment with Mrs. DeMoines. I'd submitted my notes on the case along with my resignation. She wanted to discuss that, but as far as I was concerned there wasn't much to talk about.

She called me into her office with the big bright window behind her semicircular desk. She stood over an aluminum tea trolley, pouring. She wore a navy-blue dress with white pique cuffs, collar, and belt. Her eyes were light gray and her hair worn in a crown braid. Touch of lipstick.

"Milk, one sugar, do I have that right?" she asked.

"Yes, ma'am."

I followed her to a set of chairs around the serving table.

"We'll sit here," she said. "This isn't going to be official."

We got settled. "How's your head?" she asked.

I reflexively touched the white bandage on my forehead. "I didn't need stitches. Head wounds bleed a lot. It looks worse than it is." The first time I'd seen it without the covering bandage it resembled the mark of Cain. That was true, in more ways than one.

"How is Tamar?"

"I've got her safely stowed away in a hotel. Her knee is bunged up, and she's on crutches for a bit, but she'll be fine."

"You told her about Pola?"

"She took it as well as could be expected. That's one tough girl. I think maybe she knew all along something was up. She told Juanita there were a lot of secrets in her family. I guess you can't grow up in that environment and not learn something about what's going on around you. She thinks of Dolores as her real mother and I see nothing wrong with that. But she's coming to terms with the idea Pola is her biological mother and I think she will be able to accept it for herself in time."

Mrs. DeMoines sipped her tea and lowered the cup in its saucer. "I read your case notes last night. Did you know those two men were with the Drug Enforcement Bureau?"

"Eddie and Aiden? I figured they had to be federal. I didn't know they were using me to go through the pipeline and open it up for them. They wanted to nail Ardak with the heroin. They didn't know, or didn't care, about the art. That was inconsequential to them."

"They found Staaken, however. Krille."

"Yes. He ghosted soon as he saw the Lincoln Continental blow up. I would have, too. But they already had the area cordoned off and picked him up this side of Junction City. He tried to shoot it out with them and was killed in an alley. He killed two policemen. Eddie is the one who killed him."

"Not a pleasant thought. That man running loose and getting away with the heroin, too. At least they stopped that."

"I suppose." There are always loose ends in a big case. Untidy questions. Having everything wrapped up in a neat bow is never a reality in our profession. "They got the big fish, but a lot of guys who were going to help Ardak put the stuff on the streets got clear."

"That was the impression I had, too," Mrs. DeMoines said. "Maybe one day they'll surface again, but let's hope they won't be our problem. So, Pixie. What's next?"

I didn't think she was asking about my future, but what was next for the case. I hadn't cleared it completely. I'd need her help for that.

"I want to bring this to a close once and for all."

Agatha DeMoines pressed her lips firmly together in thought. "Of course, you do. We all do. How are you going to accomplish that?"

I looked at the untouched tea in my cup. I put it on the serving table, sat back, and looked at her.

"I'm going to lie," I said.

Mrs. DeMoines watched me with her wide blue-gray eyes. She said nothing and the silence hung fire.

I shrugged, tired. "I was hired to find Tamar. That's what I did. Mr. Shavin and Pola Goddard don't have to know the truth. Telling them Tamar is really Wanda's child helps no one. Far as I know Tamar *is* Shavin's daughter. You know how impossible it is to prove absolute paternity. Those cases always wind up in court. You never know which way they'll turn."

"What about Juanita Drexford?"

I looked away and then back. "I was hired to find Tamar. Not Juanita."

"But Juanita Waverly, née Drexford, is Pola Goddard's real daughter through Landers Shavin. Isn't she?"

I pushed back. "We don't know for certain. We don't know if what Wanda told me is true. That woman told so many lies over the years I'm not sure she kept them all straight. Maybe she had Hollack falsify the paternity test. Maybe not. Hollack destroyed those records before he was arrested last night. It's not our purview anyway. I was hired to find a girl named Tamar Bandesi. That's what I did. That's all I did. Everything else is incidental."

"Yes, but do *you* believe Juanita is Pola Goddard's daughter?"

I fell stone quiet. Then: "Juanita has a full and happy life. I had Nate Lasker do some discreet digging for me. I talked to him yesterday when I was writing up the case notes. He said she doesn't need the money. She's happy and content with her life and husband. What good does it do to tell her everything she thought about her life was a lie? How does that help her in any way? Pola Goddard sent me a check for a $10,000 bonus for bringing the case to a successful resolution. I forwarded it to Juanita. Maybe it will come in handy for her future. Baby's college fund, or whatever. That's the way I see things, anyway."

Mrs. DeMoines stirred her tea quietly. She tapped the spoon three times. "I'm not saying I disagree," she said diplomatically, "but I've always had a view on how we should proceed with any work that came our way. Wouldn't you agree? I mean, in principle?"

"In principle. . .yes. But I don't think the truth helps anyone out this time. I maintain we may never know the real truth. Even if it does go to court." I shook my head. "You've been in enough courtrooms to know that doesn't mean truth will out. More often than not it's whatever is convenient, and who has the deeper pockets." I disassembled. "It's your agency, Mrs. DeMoines. You can do as you wish. I won't dispute anything you say. But I won't be party to it. Nor will I hang around to be served a subpoena."

The elderly woman smiled. "I don't think it should come to that, my dear." She placed her cup and saucer on the low table. She picked up my report and signed the last page and dated it, then tossed the pen and the report back on the table.

"There, now it's official, as far as our agency is concerned. You know, Pixie, I've always strived to pursue the truth in Valkyrie." She raised her eyes to the Gérôme painting on the wall. *Truth Coming out of Her Well to Shame Mankind*. "I felt it was the one constant in the world, even when we couldn't see it, or didn't want to believe it. I suppose in my final act as Director I can bend the rules a little. Or, in this particular instance, into a horseshoe."

She brought her gaze back down to mine. "I agree with both your sentiment and your judgment. We may never know the truth, if there is such a thing this time, and muddying waters and upending innocent lives doesn't benefit the people involved. I don't like making this decision on an ethical basis, but I'd be lying if I didn't think it was the correct one. Anyway, we were hired to find Tamar Bandesi. We did that." She pointed at the case report. "This thing is a sleeping dragon. Let it sleep. Forever, if need be."

"Thank you."

She held my eyes. "Let's talk about your resignation."

"There's nothing to talk about, Mrs. DeMoines. I'm sorry, but I'm leaving Valkyrie."

"Are you upset I passed the mantle to Artie instead of yourself?"

I stifled a laugh. "Not at all. I'm relieved. I never wanted the position; despite the gossip I kept hearing. I was too busy with the case to give it a lot of deep thought. Artie will shine as the new head of Valkyrie Investigations. He's the perfect choice. I'm happy for him. Really."

I'd told him as much yesterday when I came into the building to turn in my full case notes and final report. The place was abuzz. A lot of operatives thought it was the correct business decision. Not that they had anything personal against me, but Artie had solid contacts with the banks which could help Valkyrie with its money troubles, along with ideas of modernizing and expanding its reach into the European continent. Valkyrie would never take down Pinkertons, but it could give Arcadia Investigations a run for their money.

"There's always a place for you here, Pixie," Artie had pressed upon me that morning. "I wish you would stay. I'll double your retainer. Anything. Just ask."

I thanked him, but I told him my mind was made up, and that was that.

"What are your plans for the future?" Mrs. DeMoines asked, drawing me back to the present. "I hope I'm not prying. I'm merely questioning as a friend."

"Someone asked me that recently. I don't know, honestly. Maybe I'll go back to college and finish my degree. I might start my own agency and work cold cases. I have the experience." I grinned wolfishly. "Maybe I'll poach a few off Valkyrie."

Mrs. DeMoines laughed easily. "You might at that." She stood up and I followed. She took my hands in hers and pressed them together. "You are part of the Valkyrie family and always will be, Pixie. But whatever you decide is all right with me." She was talking about the Bandesi problem again. "If you think not telling Mr. Shavin the truth about his daughter is the right thing to do then who am I to gainsay that? As I said, I'll make it my last official decision as head of the agency. Only you and I ever need know the truth." She smiled conspiratorially. "Whatever the truth is."

She led me to the door. "Don't be a stranger, dear. Should you ever need anything I do hope you will call on us."

"I will, Mrs. DeMoines. Thank you, for a great four years."

I rode the elevator down to the ground floor. My car was parked down the street. I found a pay phone and dialed Pola Goddard. "We're coming over," I said. "We'll be around directly. That is if the traffic isn't too bad."

"We will be waiting," she breathed with excitement. "Landers is so happy. I haven't seen him like this in years. May I speak with Tamar?"

"She's not with me at present. We'll be there soon as we can."

"I can't wait," Pola said. "I know I have a lot to make up for. Both Landers and I do. I hope we can do right by Tamar from now on and in memory of Dolores. I'm sure we will."

"I'm sure you will, too. See you soon." I hung up.

Aiden was waiting beside my car. I slowed.

"Another debriefing?"

He smiled and shook his head. "Only saying goodbye, and thanks for your help."

"You know, you could have told me who you and Eddie worked for. It wouldn't have changed anything."

"True," he said, "but we wanted you to carry as much deniability as possible if you got caught. It was for your protection."

"How is Eddie?"

"He's getting around. He sends his regards."

"Arcadia isn't going to like you using them for cover. They've got a lot of pride."

"But they're not going to find out, are they?"

"Not from me. By the way, I lost that stupid gun of yours."

Aiden shrugged. "I'll write it down as a tax loss on the government's expenses." The sun was in his face. "It doesn't have to be goodbye between us."

"I'm not normally in the habit of going out with men who lie to me." I met his smile and stepped close and put my hands on his shoulders and kissed him softly on the lips. "I'll make an exception this one time."

"Where are you going now?" He touched my face with the back of his hand. The warmth of his skin on mine felt nice.

"I'm taking Tamar home. Then I'm taking some time for myself. Call me next week and I'll let you take me to dinner and a show. That is if you want to."

"I'd like that very much," Aiden said. "You're a lot of woman, Pixie."

We kissed again. It felt good being in his arms.

Driving to Los Angeles, Tamar and I talked about her future. We'd been doing that a lot in the days since the garage. She had a slew of questions, and a host of doubts.

"I just. . .I don't know if it's right," she said. "After all this time that's passed. They never did much for me when they had the chance. I have a lot of suppressed anger towards them. Especially Pola. Now I'm supposed to believe they love me unconditionally and want to shower me with gifts."

"Everything that happens from now on is your decision," I told her. I had the top down. It was a fine June day. The sun was bright, and the wind tossed my hair.

"You're going into this with your eyes wide open, Tamar. No one can tell you what to do. You're standing between two different worlds, but no matter which world you pick, or which world you decide to make for yourself, it remains your choice. Not everyone has that luxury. Not every *woman* has that luxury. You do. Grab it, Tamar. Grab it and run with it. Run like hell with it for every woman out there."

"But I don't love my father, or my mother. If they really are my mother and father. I guess they are. I suppose I always knew something was wrong. One day I found that letter behind Landers's picture and would read it over and over. It was like holding the biggest secret in the world between my hands. But it's a lot to take in when you know it's real. I grew up surrounded by lies, Pidge. I was buried in lies and deception from everyone around me. I was complicit in that, too. I don't love them. I don't know if I ever did. Maybe I never will. If that's true, then where am I?"

"Perhaps you won't love them," I said. "That's something no one can decide for you, either. But if you ask me, I think they want to make amends. I think the things that happened recently have opened their eyes a bit. We can hope, anyway."

I turned the car off the road into a drive-in restaurant.

"Why are we stopping?" Tamar asked.

"I need to make a phone call. Something I've put off far too long.

Here comes the car hop. Order what you want. There are a couple of dollars and change in my purse. I'll be back."

I walked across the sunbaked lot to a rank of phone booths. I closed myself in one and placed a call to Soledad and shoved in the correct amount of change. A minute later the operator connected me with the number.

"Hello?"

"Hi, Pop," I said into the receiver.

"Pidge," my father said. I could hear the excited smile behind his familiar, gravelly voice. "How are you? I haven't heard from you in months. Are you all right?"

"I'm fine," I said. "Lost my job, though. Actually, I quit."

"Oh, Pidge."

I laughed. "It's all right. I'll tell you all about it soon as I finish up this last detail. I'm driving to Soledad when that's done."

"This is your home, Pidge," my father said. There came a pause. "Are you doing all right, otherwise?"

"Yes," I said. "I'm doing wonderfully."

I watched Tamar through the glass of the booth. She was seated in my car sipping a Coca-Cola through a white paper straw. She had the whole world before her. It was bright and scary, and she was going to have to decide a lot of things on her own. But she would do it. She was strong and smart and determined, and she could do it. Like another girl I knew back when.

I put my mouth close to the receiver. "I'm all right, Pop. I wanted to let you know how much I love you. That's all."

"Pidge. . .I love you, too." I'd caught him off guard. Myself, too, a bit.

"Don't feel bad because I lost my job. I'm thinking of starting my own agency. Maybe I'll call it Phoenix. It's time I begin a new phase of my life anyway. I'll start by coming home. I'm coming home, Pop. I'm finally coming home."

THE END

ABOUT THE AUTHOR

Kenneth Mark Hoover is the author of the Haxan series of weird westerns, and a professional writer who has sold over sixty short stories and several novels including *Haxan, Quaternity, and Litha: A Love Story*. He is a member of the Science Fiction Writers of America and the Western Writers of America. His short fiction appeared in *Ellery Queen's Mystery Magazine, Beneath Ceaseless Skies, Strange Horizons*, and many others. You can read more at his blog kennethmarkhoover.me, his website kennethhoover.com, or follow on Twitter @kmarkhoover. Mr. Hoover divides his time between New Mexico and Texas. He writes full-time.

www.ingramcontent.com/pod-product-compliance
Lightning Source LLC
Chambersburg PA
CBHW020638260626
47157CB00008B/2800